New Bos
Iona Rose

New Boss, Old Enemy

Copyright © 2020 Iona Rose

The right of Iona Rose to be identified as the Author of the Work has been asserted by her in accordance with the copyright, designs and patent act 1988.

All rights reserved. No part of this publication may be reproduced, stored in a retrieval system, or transmitted, in any form or by any means without the prior written permission of the publisher, nor be otherwise circulated in any form of binding or cover other than that which it is published and without a similar condition being imposed on the subsequent purchaser.

All characters in this publication are fictitious, any resemblance to real persons, living or dead, is purely coincidental.

Publisher: Some Books

978-1-913990-08-4

Author's Note

Hey there!

Thank you for choosing my book. I sure hope that you love it. I'd hate to part ways once you're done though. So how about we stay in touch?

My newsletter is a great way to discover more about me and my books. Where you'll find frequent exclusive give-aways, sneak previews of new releases and be first to see new cover reveals.

And as a HUGE thank you for joining, you'll receive a FREE book on me!

With love,

Iona

Get Your FREE Book Here[1]:
https://dl.bookfunnel.com/v9yit8b3f7

Chapter One

Ashton

I rub my hand over the back of my neck, massaging out the hard spot of stress, as I stare at my computer screen. My personal assistant quit three days ago because her boyfriend walked out on her. Hell, she was so damn cut up about it she couldn't even work out her notice period. It annoyed me to no end, but what can you do. Women! You can't live with them, and you can't live without them.

Someone knocks on the door of my office.

"Come in," I call.

Sandra, one of the general secretaries, steps in with a large stack of papers in her hand.

I groan internally at the sight of the pile of papers. What now?

"I've got the resumes from some of the applicants for the personal assistant position Mr. Miller," she says, getting straight to the point. "I've weeded out the total no goes and these are the ones I think are worth considering. If you can look through them and give final approval, I can get them over to HR and have them organize interviews straight away."

3

I'm tempted to tell her to just send the lot over to HR and have them deal with it, but I don't. I don't need another obvious mismatch. Plus, I'm a bit of a control freak, but I built this company myself from the ground up, so I'm used to doing everything myself. Now it's a multi-million-dollar concern, but old habits stick. "Thanks, Sandra." I jerk my head towards one corner of my desk. "Put them down there, and I will get back to you after I've gone through them."

She does as she's told, flashes me a quick smile, and scuttles back out of my office.

If I can go through these quickly, HR might be able to set the interviews up for the end of this week, and if everything works out well, I might have a new personal assistant starting with me on Monday.

I pick up the top resume from the pile and glance through it. Julie Anderson. Good qualifications, plenty of experience. Nothing that waves a red flag. I start my keep pile with her. The next three I scour over are no good. Two of them have children and the third, while having no obvious baggage, doesn't have the kind of experience I need. I don't know if she could keep up with the pace of this position. The next two are both good candidates. Millie Brown has worked in various high paced environments and Angus Heron has over five years of experience in a very similar industry to mine. At the moment, Angus is looking like the front runner. A man would never fall apart because his girl walked out on him.

I keep going through the stack sorting them into the two piles. Angus still looks like the winner. Then I open the last file and stare in disbelief at the name on it.

Elena Woods.

My heart starts hammering in my chest. It can't be the same person. Surely not. That would be the most bizarre coincidence imaginable. I lean back in my chair and suddenly the past rushes back, vivid and in full color.

Elena was standing in front of me, her small, white face defiant.

"All that money and you bought *those* pants?" I taunted.

The rest of my gang laughed as I strutted away, proud as a peacock. Outside, I was smiling— inside I was devastated.

Elena Woods and I went to the same high school, but we were from completely different worlds. Her family is old money, so rich her father knew the President of the United States of America. My family was the opposite. We were dirt poor. My dad left us when I was just two years old, and he never came back even to see me. My mom worked three jobs just to keep a roof over our heads, and the only reason I got to attend the Franklin School, a private school full of Elenas, was because I got a scholarship through a program for gifted students.

My mom made sure my clothes were always clean and well pressed, but they were hand me downs, sourced from charity shops, or as the years went by, from the well-meaning mother of an older student, which shamed me immensely. I was the poor kid, the charity case, and I knew I would never fit in with my peers on their level. I made myself the dare devil rebel, always misbehaving. It made me popular, and I soon forgot I had nothing in common with any of my friends.

I wore my hand-me-downs so aggressively, sewing skeletons and skulls on them and ripping them to shreds that I started a fashion all of my own. Soon, all the kids were ripping their jeans the way I had them while sewing on skulls and crossbones onto their clothes. I was king of my world, until Elena's family moved to town, and she came to Franklin School.

The first moment I saw her, I knew I had to have her. She was the most beautiful thing I'd ever seen in my life, with green eyes and long blonde hair flowing down her back like liquid sunshine. But she was also the daughter of an extremely rich banker and a supermodel. She was rich, spoilt, and not someone to be messed with.

A girl like Elena would never date a poor kid like me. Ever.

Date? Hell, she didn't even notice I existed. My slicked back hair, my skulls, ripped clothes and my tattoos, didn't impress her one bit. I don't think she even knew my name. I decided to ignore her, but the more I tried to suppress my feelings the more violent they became. Knowing I could never have her made me want her more and more. It became an obsession. Who knows? If she didn't live in a massive mansion surrounded by high brick walls, protected behind big, black gates I might have ended up under her bedroom window every night. That's how crazy about her I became.

I was infatuated and infatuated bad.

To ease the hurt of my unrequited obsession, my childish mind found a different way to get her attention. I started to mock Elena. I just wanted a reaction. And it worked too. She for sure knew my name after a couple of comments I made about her that cracked up the whole class. But then she be-gan to give me hateful looks that made my gut burn. I had ruined it. It escalated from there, and before I knew it, I was full-on bullying her.

I'm ashamed to admit it, but I became an insufferable asshole.

I wanted to stop, I hated myself even while I was doing it, but I couldn't. I was a bunch of raging hormones and reject-ed pride. If I hadn't been so caught up with feelings I didn't know how to handle, I would have made her notice me by making her laugh. Instead, I made her cry.

I remember one time, I was walking along the corridor with some of my friends and Elena was coming the other way with some of her friends. She hadn't noticed me yet, and she was laughing with her friends.

I started to mimic her laugh and my friends laughed, egging me on.

She looked at me with surprise as I snorted, something she did when she was laughing hard. I curled my nose up like a pig's and snorted again, adding in an oink this time. My friends started to oink too. Even now, I can still remember the way she looked at me. Her eyes were full of hurt, but her jaw was clenched tightly. It still makes me feel ashamed of myself to this day.

"Why do you hate me so much?" she asked in a shaky voice. "I've never done anything to you."

Chapter Two

Ashton

And that was the problem. She'd never done anything to me because I was nothing to her.

I looked back into her eyes, and biting down the black shame I felt inside, I smiled evilly. "Because you're nothing. You're just a grunting pig."

This got another round of oinks from my friends.

Elena's face had crumpled and she'd run.

Like I said, I was an unforgivable asshole. A monster.

It's fair to say Franklin School taught me nothing about how to get girls to notice me, but it did teach me something valuable. It taught me that in this world, the rich get more than the poor. The rich get respect... power. They have their own secret little club that stands head and shoulders above the poor. And I knew before I left that school that one day, I would be one of them.

I worked my ass off through college and university, studying business, and the day I left Oxford with a first-class degree in business and management, I started my own business. Now I'm twenty-seven and the CEO of a very successful company and I'm a multi-millionaire in my own right.

Yet, the name Elena Woods reduces me to the poor teen I once was. I can't take my eyes off the photo on her application. There she is. All grown up. A gloriously beautiful blonde goddess. I should be way past my infatuation but here I am, heart racing and palms sweating. It's like I'm a teenager again. Only this time, it seems Elena is the one trying to get my attention now.

And she has it.

I stare at her photo. Her hair is wavy and long, her green eyes are sparkling, her skin is flawless. I imagine what it would feel like to run my finger over her full lips. To kiss them, and then to have her kiss her way down my body. Or wrap that sexy mouth around my cock, making my body hers. I imagine plunging into her pussy, fucking her until she's begging me for more.

My cock throbs and hardens

Jesus! I shake the thought away. The CEO of the company sitting behind his desk with a raging hard on is never a good look.

But damn.

Even just looking at her picture, brings my obsession back to the fore. Hell, who am I trying to kid? It never really went away. When we left school, we went our separate ways, going to different colleges, but she was never far from my thoughts. I dated girls – of course, I did – but none of them were Elena. I carried such a big torch for her, all the other girls felt like second best. No matter what they did or how hard they tried.

Elena had always been perfection to me. She still is.

And... now she just landed right back in my life and reignited a hundred old thoughts, a hundred lost feelings. I know deep inside that this is my chance to do two things. First, to show her I'm not that same jerk who made her life hell in high school. Second, to show her that now we're both in the same world, maybe, just maybe, I'd be worth her time.

I wonder if she would have applied for this job if she knew I was the one she would be working for. She couldn't have known. I changed my name when I left school. I decided I wanted nothing from my father. He had abandoned me to my own devices and I wanted to show my mother how much I appreciated the sacrifices she'd made for me. I changed my surname from Winston to Miller.

If Elena had seen the name Ashton Winston instead of Ashton Miller, would she still have sent me her resume? The answer to that is easy: 100 percent... no.

I tear my eyes away from her photograph and look over the rest of her resume. It's pretty impressive. She went to the University of Warwick and her experience is impressive too. She's worked as a personal assistant to a CEO in a tech start up for the last two years, which means I can put her resume on the keep pile without having to defend the choice.

I debate throwing some of the other resumes off the pile to increase the chances of Elena being chosen for the job, but a handful of applications going to HR, they won't be happy. They like choice, plus they're expecting a lot of applicants – this job comes with a multitude of benefits – and if they only see four or five applicants to choose from, they'll be looking to widen their scope.

There are other ways to make sure Elena gets this job, and I plan to do whatever it takes to make sure it happens. She's getting this job if it is the last thing I do.

This is my second chance to get the girl of my dreams.

Chapter Three

Elena

I sit in the waiting area in the entrance lobby of Wave, a multimedia solutions company, wringing my hands while trying to not be obvious that I'm a nervous wreck. I'm the only person in the waiting area, but I know that doesn't mean anything. There's no way there aren't hundreds of other applicants for the personal assistant job I'm here to interview for.

I look around me subtly, taking in the ultra-modern monochrome décor and glass where walls should be. I can see people moving around the corridors all around the waiting area. In the corner of the waiting area, a receptionist is sitting behind a large desk with an earpiece. She takes call after call, directing the callers to the right lines without missing a beat. I would hate her job. Even if there's no client sitting here, with all these glass walls, she must be conscious of the fact she can be seen from almost every direction, so any client walking around the building might be able to see her.

Still, I need a job so badly maybe I can put up with such a goldfish bowl environment. Hopefully, the position I've applied for is not going to have me situated at the front like her.

But if I have to, I can cope with the glass. It's really a small price to pay if I get this job. Because my God, do I need it.

This is my third interview and while I was prepared for the last two with dedicated research as soon as I was called for the interview, I still didn't get either of the jobs. This time, I didn't have a chance to do much research. I got the call to come for the interview just hours ago and there was no negotiation as to the dates.

The woman was extremely inflexible. "This job has to be filled as soon as possible and if you are not interested, then I have other candidates to call," she informed me coldly.

All I know is the company offers multimedia solutions to other businesses and they have a steady growth. Oh, and the CEO's name, Ashton Miller, which is nothing, seeing I have applied to be his assistant. It bothered me a bit that his first name is Ashton, because the last Ashton I knew was a real asshole who made my life a living hell, but I'm not going to let the fact he shares a first name with the boy who left a bad taste in my mouth stop me from a plum job like this.

All I really know about him is that he started the company from pretty much nothing and built it into an empire. And he's a millionaire. I don't think HR is going to be all that impressed with the extent of my knowledge.

I force myself to concentrate on the positives instead of the negatives. I might not know the company inside out, but I do know the job inside out. I was the personal assistant to the CEO at my last job for two years. So I know a thing or two about keeping everything organized and running smoothly. I'm going to concentrate on talking about that in my interview.

It's still going to be hard because Wave is one of those companies everyone in tech wants to work for. It's fast paced, growing steadily, and the benefits that come with the job are amazing. There is going to be a lot of stiff competition for this job. I'm just hoping the short notice works in my favor. It's a small straw to clutch, but right now, it's the only one I've got, so I'm taking it and clinging onto it with both hands.

"Ms. Woods?" the secretary in the corner says with an overly bright smile plastered on her face.

"Yes," I reply with a nervous smile.

"You can go through to your interview now. It's in conference room D. Down the hall in front of you, right to the end. You can't miss it."

"Thank you."

I start walking down the hallway she pointed to, and I'm relieved to see solid walls along here. The thought of having an interview in full view of the whole office really didn't fill me with joy. As I walk, reminding myself to walk tall, which isn't easy when you're just over five feet tall, I wipe my sweaty palms down my skirt, pretending to smooth out the material.

I reach the end of the hallway and come to a door marked conference room D. I take a deep breath, exhale it out slowly, then I knock on the door.

"Come in," a man's voice calls through the door.

I put my game face on. I don't want to go in there acting like this is my last option before I lose my house, which isn't far from being true, but the last thing I want is for the interviewer to smell the desperation inside me. I have to act like

I am made for the position and give off an air of confidence, even if I don't really feel it.

I push the door open, slipping on my best corporate smile as I do it. The room is huge and is dominated by a long glass table that could comfortably seat twenty people. Only three people are in the room though. A woman and two men. They are all dressed in suits, as am I, and I start to feel a little more at home. This is my world. It has been since I left school and yes, there will be other candidates for this position, but that doesn't mean I'm not the best match for the job. It seems my *fake it until you make it* attitude is really starting to pay off. Already I can see myself working here. I can see myself fitting right in.

The three people stand up as I step into the room as I move towards the table and extend my hand.

The woman reaches out and shakes my hand first. "Sally Atkins, assistant HR manager," she says with a clipped smile.

"Elena Woods," I smile back.

I repeat the process with the man in the middle who is David Malone, the HR manager, and Aaron Grey, an assistant HR.

"Take a seat, Elena. By the way, we're all on a first name basis here," David says.

The three of them sit together on one side of the table and I sit down opposite David, so I am central to the three of them. I'm outnumbered, but I swallow down my nerves and square my shoulders. There is a glass of water in front of my seat and I pick it up and take a sip. My mouth is dry as a desert.

"Your resume is impressive," David begins.

"Thank you," I reply.

David gives me a slight nod and continues, "So you have a degree in business studies from abroad," he's reading from my resume.

"Yes, I was sent to study in England. It was a good, enriching experience."

He looks up. "And you have plenty of experience of working as a personal assistant in this industry, but the start-up you worked for most recently went bust, didn't it?"

I nod.

"Why do you think that was?"

I decide again to go with honesty. If I try and sugar coat my answer, it could make it look like I don't see what's right in front of me. "Well, the CEO was rather short sighted. At first, he loved the company, and he was excited to expand their offerings, but as the market got tougher, that excitement just sort of fizzled out of him. It's my belief that he got scared and rather than developing any new ideas, he coasted it out on the dying one until it was no longer viable."

"Right," Aaron says as he makes a note on his pad.

I'm not sure if that's the answer he was looking for, but he asked for my opinion and he got it. If this job needs someone quiet who won't speak up, then it's definitely not the position for me.

"So why Wave?" Sally asks.

"I took a chance on a start up in my last job and this time, I'm looking for a position within a company that is a leader in the industry."

Sally and David look a little bored. Maybe that answer wasn't as genius as I thought it was. What can I say to pull this back a little? My brain scrambled to make it better. I could try a little humor. "And let's be real here. The benefits are pretty good," I quip with a smile.

None of them return my smile.

I cringe internally and take another sip of water, trying to ignore the panic welling up inside of me. Get it together, Elena I tell myself.

"Why do you think you'll be a good fit here, Elena?" Sally asks.

This is my moment. I launch into a long speech about my past experience and how I can use it in this role. They still don't look impressed and it started to be pretty clear I'm not getting this job, but I plough on, trying to land on the one bit of experience that sets me apart from the other candidates.

When I finish, Sally smiles.

I'm not fooled by the smile. She's going for the kill and I know it. "That's very impressive Elena and I'm not doubting for a second that you'll be very good at this job. But your answer didn't really answer the question you were asked. I don't want to know why you think you can do the job. What I want to know is why you, Elena Woods, think you will work well within the existing infrastructure at Wave."

My throat is dry and scratchy. All four of us know I'm not getting this job, but I'm not a quitter. Never have been, never will be. But people talk. I'm not giving up until the fat lady sings. I take a deep breath.

"Take your time, Elena. We're not trying to catch you out, we're just trying to establish who will be the best fit for our team," Aaron says gently.

I flash him a grateful smile. "I'm good at my job," I say. "And I'm adaptable, so I can fit into the way any company works. I have no intention of causing any sort of drama. I like to keep myself focused on the job."

"Thank you, Elena," David says. "Moving on. Where do you see yourself in five years' time?"

At least that's something I can respond to in the way I hope they're looking for."I see myself here, David," I say, sounding more confident than I feel.

"I'm just going to cut to the chase here," Sally says. "And please don't think I'm being rude, but I get the impression you have sent out multiple resumes in the hope that one sticks somewhere. You clearly haven't done any research on the company or how we work. And that's a concern for me."

Full marks to her for accurately seizing the situation.

I clear my throat. "I'll be honest. I have applied to more than one company, but that doesn't mean I'm not damned good at what I do, and it for sure doesn't mean that I can't do this job. It wasn't a case of sending out resumes everywhere and hoping one sticks. It's a case of finding companies I like and would want to work for and keeping my options open."

"So if we were to give you this job, how could we be sure that six months down the line, you might not get another offer and leave us in the lurch?" Sally probes.

"Can you ever be one hundred percent sure that won't happen with any employee?" I reply. "I am a good bet to stick around. You can see from my resume that I took a little time in the beginning of my career to find the area I enjoy working in. And once I did, I stuck with it. I have no intention of leaving within a couple of months. As I said earlier, I see myself working here in five years' time."

The three of them look at each other again. They're not even bothering to make notes anymore, and I know in my heart that I've blown this interview. The worst part is knowing I would do a damned good job if I am given the chance.

"Thank you for coming in today and at such short notice, Ms. Woods," David finishes.

I know for sure now I've blown it. We're back to Ms. Woods. And he hasn't even asked me if I have any questions for him. That's a bad sign. I debate asking a question, but what's the point? Even if I came up with a question so insightful it blew them all away, it's almost certainly too late to change their minds about giving me the job.

"You'll hear from me by the end of the day if your application is successful," Aaron adds, standing up.

I nod my thanks and stand with him, then shake his hand politely. As I turn to leave, the door opens, and a man walks in. I stare at the man and try not to show the disbelief and shock inside me. It cannot be. No way. Not him. He's all grown up, but I can never ever forget those gorgeous, cruel eyes.

Ashton Winston.

Chapter Four

Elena

Ashton was always handsome and that hasn't changed one bit. If anything, he's only gotten more delicious. He takes a few more steps and towers over me. I imagine he must be at least six feet two or three. His dark brown hair is cut in a casual, almost messy style that looks as if he just rolled out of bed, or has been in an open-top sports car. His brown eyes are as beautiful as they ever were, but there is absolutely no recognition in them.

He smiles, showing me two rows of perfect Hollywood teeth. "Would you mind sitting back down for a moment please Ms. Woods?" His eyes sparkle.

I sit down heavily, glad to be off my shaky legs. Seeing Ashton has totally thrown me. I had no idea he worked here. If I would have known, then I most likely wouldn't have applied for a job here and I'm actually relieved now, since I won't be getting this job.

Ashton is still as gorgeous as ever, but one thing about his appearance has changed. He's no longer the poor kid in the hand-me-downs. The suit he's wearing is clearly expensive and he has an air of authority about him in this room.

The three HR managers are all silent now, waiting for Ashton to speak. And that's when it all clicks into place. Ashton changed his name. Ashton Winston became Ashton Miller. My school bully is now the millionaire CEO of Wave.

Fuck. Why is he in here? Has he come to have one last dig at me? To make me cry like he used to in school one last time? Surely not. Even if he recognizes me, which is unlikely at best, he's not going to do that at his own company. Maybe he couldn't resist the chance to gloat after my appalling interview? Did he put the interviewers up to being such hard asses just to embarrass me? But I realize that one is a stretch of my imagination. I'm just being paranoid. I've had tougher interviews than this one before.

"Is there a problem, Ashton?" David asks. He sounds cautious and looks as thrown as I feel.

Ashton smiles and takes a seat at the head of the conference table. He sits with the relaxed movements of someone who owns everyone and everything in the room. "Not at all," he says. "I just have a few questions for Ms. Woods."

"Ok," David says, trying to act as casual as Ashton but failing miserably. His slightly flushed face gives him away.

The way the three interviewers exchange looks again, tells me this isn't normal procedure. It's surprising them as much as it is me. Great. So Ashton does recognize me, and he's here to humiliate me again, just like he did that day in the cafeteria at Franklin School on what was pretty much the worst day of my life.

From pretty much the first time I saw Ashton I had a major crush on him, but it was obvious to me it would never happen. We were from different worlds. People thought

I was a spoilt, stuck up rich brat, but in fact, I was just an incredibly shy girl. I covered my crippling shyness by being aloof. Ashton, on the other hand, the most popular boy in school, a rebel and a show-off extrovert, with his own gang of rabid followers who looked up to him as if he was a god. Boys like that didn't date quiet mice like me. They didn't even know we existed. I had to make do with watching him from afar while pretending like I hadn't noticed how hot he was.

He didn't know I existed and I pretended like I didn't know he existed. That should have worked, right? It did – until it didn't. On that fateful day in the cafeteria when it all changed. I was sitting with Lottie, who had quickly become my best friend at Franklin School, and a couple of other girls, when Ashton and his group of followers sat down at the table behind us.

I couldn't help but listen as they talked. They were talking about a big math assignment we had. Ashton boasted that he was almost done with his, and it would easily be ready for Friday. I knew it had to be in on Wednesday. I don't know how or why, but my desire not to let him get in trouble overcame my natural shyness. Even though my stomach was in knots and my palms were sweaty, I turned around and called his name.

He whirled his god-like head and looked at me.

He was so beautiful I almost fainted. "The assignment has to be in on Wednesday," I croaked out.

Instead of thanking me for saving him from being late with the assignment like I had expected him to, he rolled his eyes at me. "Ah, the teacher's sheep dog wants to corral all the sheep into the pen. News flash. I'm not a sheep. I'm a wolf," he growled.

His friends laughed.

I felt myself blush. I then tried to explain which of course, only made the situation worse. "I didn't mean anything by it. I don't care one way or the other really, just that you said you were almost done, and I didn't want you to lose marks by being late with it. That's all." I turned back to him then. I was shaking. The only time I had stepped out of my comfort zone and I had failed so spectacularly.

My friends told me to just ignore him, reassuring me I had tried to help and if he didn't want my help then screw him. I was hurt and sad, but I thought that would be the end of it. I had spoken to my dream boy and he'd cruelly taunted me. Surely, that was enough pain for one day. But I was wrong again. That wasn't the end of it. It was far from the end of it.

"You know what that was about, don't you?" Ashton said loudly from behind me. "Teacher's sheep dog is terrified someone will upset her precious Mr. Duncan."

Mr. Duncan was our math teacher. And it seemed I was his pet in this little game.

"Yeah, teacher's pet has to make sure everyone follows the rules," one of Ashton's friends agreed with a sycophantic laugh.

"Give the girl a break," Ashton said.

My heart skipped a beat. Had he realized I was trying to help him? Was he going to defend me?

"It's not that. Woods is probably getting wood from Dusty Duncan."

I thought I would just die on the spot when not only his group burst into laughter, but the kids at the other tables around us began to giggle and snicker. I realized then, that he knew I existed, he even knew my name, but for some reason he disliked me and he had just found a way to cement my humiliation. He had managed to seed the lie that I had a crush on my math teacher, who for the record was ancient, wore a tweed jacket with elbow patches, and sometimes smelled like he hadn't bathed for days.

My friends tried to convince me to ignore him, even going so far as to say he was only acting like that because he liked me and he wanted to get my attention. Well, I knew that was just bullshit. If he liked me, he wouldn't have humiliated me like that. It became clear to anyone with eyes he already had my attention. He didn't have to be an asshole too.

The rumor that I had a thing for Mr. Duncan spread quickly through the school, and I spent the rest of my time there being thought of as the girl with a crush on a crusty old man who was old enough to be my grandfather. It was hell. But that wasn't even the worst part of it. The worst part of it was that was only the beginning. After that day, every time I saw Ashton he came up with some new way to humiliate me.

My crush slowly turned to hate and I avoided Ashton as much as I could. It was hard though. He might have been mean and a bully, but he was clever, and he was in a lot of the same classes as I was. I just felt glad when school was over as we went to different colleges and never saw each other again.

Until now.

It's like history repeating itself. Of course, Ashton should appear at one of my most humiliating moments. He's probably going to start a rumor that I have a thing for David Malone or something.

I am still staring at Ashton. I can't help it. As much as I hate him, I can't help reacting to the strong, animal-like attraction of the man. I find myself pressing my thighs together to try and stop the tingling feeling in my clit. Pressing my thighs together only intensifies the feeling, and I relax my muscles a little, trying not to gasp.

"Ms. Woods," Ashton says, pulling me right back into the moment. "I'm Ashton Miller, CEO of Wave. If you get the job, you'll be working closely with me, so I'd just like to weigh in if that's okay with you?"

His warm and charming smile tells me he doesn't remember me. I nod mutely. I can answer his questions, then get the hell out of here and never see him again. I can do this. I can.

"At what point did you realize the last company you worked for was going to go under?" he asks.

"About eight or nine months before it did," I reply, my voice strangely steady even though I was dying inside.

"Interesting," he says. "Did you make your opinion known to your CEO?"

"I gave him the facts. More than once. He chose to disregard them. That's probably the point I should have left, but despite his reluctance to take any of the advice given to him, I didn't want to bail when the company needed me the most."

"You start on Monday, eight am. Don't be late," Ashton announces.

I open my mouth and then close it again—sure I've mis-understood.

"Mr. Miller, we still have other candidates to see, and..." David trails off.

"And what?" Ashton says.

David gives me an apologetic look. "And there are other candidates we're considering from earlier interviews."

He says *other* but I still hear what he means. He means *better*.

"The personal assistant's job isn't that hard," Ashton explains smoothly. "It needs someone organized and flexible and with experience in the tech sector. Every applicant who has got this far in the process has that in abundance. What I'm looking for is loyalty. Ms. Woods has shown she was loyal to her old firm and I see no reason to think she wouldn't show the same loyalty to my firm."

"Got it. I'll get on that right away," David says.

"Thank you," Ashton says crisply. "Elena, do you have any questions for me?"

I sat and watched the exchange between Ashton and David while I tried to process the incredible scene unfolding in front of me. I don't want to work for a guy who used to bully me. Definitely not the way he came in here and took over the whole process. He is still that same asshole who likes to belittle people and humiliate them, but I can't afford to turn this job down. I can't take a risk on something else coming up. Especially not something with the salary and benefits I can get here. "No, I don't have any questions," I reply slowly.

Ashton gets to his feet and comes towards me with his hand outstretched.

I get up quickly and shake his hand. I feel sparks flying up my arm where our hands touch and Ashton holds onto my hand for just a fraction of a second too long. He felt it too. And that makes me confident he has no idea who I am. That's good. I can do this.

"Great. See you Monday, Elena. I'm looking forward to working with you," Ashton says. He flashes me a final smile and leaves the room.

I stand in a daze for a second, not really sure what I'm meant to say to Sally and Aaron, but knowing I can't just leave without saying goodbye to them. "Umm, thanks for your time," I say awkwardly.

"Welcome to the company, Elena," Aaron says, looking as shell shocked as I feel. He stands up and shakes my hand.

Sally follows suit with a similar sentiment to Aaron.

I finally leave the room, not sure if I'm on a high or a low. I've either just made the best career decision of my life, or the worst, and only time will tell which one it turns out to be.

Chapter Five

Ashton

I knew from the second I saw Elena's resume that she would be getting the job. I just hoped she would nail the interview and the panel would choose her without me having to get involved. It became apparent quickly that wasn't going to happen.

I have never sat in on an interview, but there's a camera and a microphone set up in the interview room so I could watch the interviews if I wanted to. I have never availed myself to the privilege until today. When I saw Elena completely botching the interview, I knew I had to step in.

I think Sally was right. It did sound like Elena had sent out a batch of resumes and just hoped someone would give her a job rather than choosing to apply for this job because she wants to work for Wave. Normally, I would have reacted to this, exactly the same way as the panel did; cut the interview short and mark her as a no chance. But this is Elena.

All the normal precautions and rules are not applicable.

But I would have hired her even if she couldn't do the job. I know she can do this job. Her resume speaks for itself. She'd always been clever, always organized. I'm just glad she gave me something I could use. And it's particularly good that it's something HR will believe. They all know how much I value loyalty and Elena gave me the perfect answer to hire her, based on her loyalty to her last company.

I wanted to hang around after the interview and talk to her, but I knew that would seem even more suspicious. The last thing I want is anyone in HR putting two and two together and accusing me of only giving Elena this job because we went to high school together. Neither of us did anything in the interview to imply that we knew each other, and that's good. It's my company and I can do whatever I want, but I have strict hiring policies in place for a reason and I have always prided myself on leading by example and I don't want that to change now.

But I have to see Elena again, before she leaves today. She gave no indication she knew me at the interview, but I acted the same even though I would have recognized her a mile away, with a bag over her head. I frown. Is it possible she really didn't recognize me? I thought about it. I had come a long way from that gangly, rough rebel wearing ripped clothes and behaving like a prick.

Even so, I'd made Elena's life hell. She couldn't possibly have forgotten that. I can't be that lucky. But if she remembered me, wouldn't she have walked out the moment she recognized me. Or she really is desperate for a job.

Instead of going back to my office, I walk towards the waiting area next to the elevators, pretending to talk on my phone. I know Elena will have to come by this way. She shouldn't be long.

I hear footsteps coming from the hallway, and pause as though I'm listening to the call I'm meant to be on, when really, I'm listening for her footsteps. As she appears, I turn around and my breath catches in my throat. I actually feel my heart fucking skip a beat. How interesting that she still has such an effect on me after all of these years, but I never really did get over her. "Yeah," I say into my phone. "Catch you later." I pretend to disconnect the call and put the phone away. I smile at Elena as she draws level with me.

She smiles back. It's a cautious smile, but that could just be because I'm going to be her new boss.

"Looks like we're both on our way out," I say and walk to the elevator with her.

She gives me another cautious smile, but she doesn't say anything.

I reach out and press the call button for the elevator. "Do you have much of a commute to get here?" I ask.

Elena shakes her head. "No. A ten-minute drive, fifteen minutes at most."

"No excuses for being late then." I laugh.

Elena laughs with me, but I get the distinct impression she's forcing the laugh. She seems much less confident now than she did in the interview room. Surely, it should be the other way around if anything. "Relax, I wasn't being serious," I say, giving her my most charming smile.

She smiles back and she looks a little less tense.

The elevator pings announcing its arrival and the doors open. There's no one else in the elevator car and we step in. We both reach for the button at the same time, and for a very short second, our fingers touch each other. I feel a shockwave of desire flood me.

Fuck!

I freeze and Elena pulls her hand away like I've burned her. I don't know if it's because she's so tense, or if it's because she feels the chemistry between us too. Maybe it's both.

She laughs awkwardly and gestures for me to press the button.

I do and the doors slowly close. We start moving down. We're completely alone. The air around us sizzles with electricity. I want to say something, but I can't think of a single thing to say to Elena.

I can't keep my eyes off her either. I force myself to look away from her, but within seconds, my gaze flies back to her as if she is a magnet pulling me toward her. My cock starts to hang heavy and hot. I want nothing more than to push her up against the wall and fucking ravish her. I want to claim her mouth, push my tongue into it. I want to shove her skirt up around her hips, lift her up and fuck the life out of her. I imagine her legs wrapped around my waist, her hands groping over my body as I pound into her.

Inside this damn elevator that I have taken a million times before.

She looks up and catches me staring at her. Her face has taken on a slight sheen of sweat and she looks pale. She flashes me an uncertain smile before she quickly looks away from me again. There is a haunted expression on her face as she glances at her watch then at the elevator doors.

"Are you late for something? I hope you don't have another job interview lined up," I tease gently.

She shakes her head quickly. "I don't." Her voice is shaky. She tucks her hands behind her back and looks down at the ground, then at the red numbers counting down on the floor marker.

This time when I sneak a look at her, she doesn't look back. I can see her shoulders hitching as she snatches in fast little breaths. Too fast. And that's when I know for sure that she knows exactly who I am. She knows it's me— and she's scared of me.

This isn't good. This isn't good at all. I don't want her to be afraid of me. I want to tell her that I was crazy about her. That I was a stupid kid who just wanted her to notice me.

I don't know how to ease the tension in the elevator car. Anything I say in this confined space is only going to make things worse. I want to run my hand over her cheek, caress it gently and show her how tender I can be now, and how I want to make love to her. But I know what a big mistake that would be. I clench my hands into fists. I'll try and talk to her once we're in the lobby. She'll probably be less tense with other people around.

The doors open and Jess, a member of the tech team, is standing outside.

"Mr. Miller? I was just heading up to your office with that report you wanted," she says.

"See you," Elena calls and practically runs from the elevator car.

"Thanks Jess, just leave it on my desk," I say, stepping around her.

"Ok," she says, clearly a little surprised by how I'm acting. She knows how important that report is and how I would normally be all over it instantly.

I scan the lobby and realize I'm already too late. There's no sign of her anywhere. Hell, she must have flown like a bat out of hell.

I don't fancy going back to my office. I feel too restless. My blood is pounding hard in my temples. I make my way across the lobby and step outside. The sidewalk is full of people. I pull out my phone and stand with my back against the wall.

I look through my contacts until I find the name I'm looking for. Billy Sanchez. Billy is my best friend and we go way back. All the way back to Franklin School, and if anyone will know how to fix this thing with Elena, it's Billy because he was there through all of the teasing. No, it wasn't teasing. That's letting myself off too lightly. It was bullying, pure and simple. And whatever my reasons for doing it were, it was wrong. I knew back then and I really know it now after seeing Elena's reaction to being alone with me so many years later.

I press call and wait.

Billy picks up pretty quickly. "What's up, man?"

"You're not going to believe who I've just given a job to," I say.

"The Dalai Lama? Ariana Grande? Oprah?"

"Elena Woods."

"Who?"

I say nothing and let the name sink in.

"Ohhhh," Billy whispers. "Did she take it?"

"Yup."

"Shit man, she must be desperate for a job. You were a fucking demon to her."

"Yeah, thanks for reminding me."

"What do you want from me? Kid gloves?" he asks.

He's right. Of course, he's right. "It was a long time ago, Billy. I've changed."

Billy's tone mellows. "I know that. And you know that. Does Elena know that? Why did she apply for a job anyway?"

"I don't think she realized it was me. She knew me as Ashton Winston. I went into the room where she was being interviewed, and she acted like she was meeting me for the first time. I figured she didn't recognize me. But then I rode down in the elevator with her... and she was afraid of me."

"Fucking hell, man what did you say to her?"

"Nothing," I say quickly. "But she does remember me."

"Maybe it's not such a good idea having her working for you," Billy points out.

"I've already given her the job now. I can't just take it back. And I don't want to. I still have the hots for her big time and I feel like maybe I'm getting a second chance with her."

"Yeah right, because you coming on to her in the office isn't going to scare her at all, is it?" Billy says sarcastically.

"I'm not planning on locking her in my office and demanding she do a striptease or anything, although that would be a damn sight more interesting than what I normally do with my PA s."

Billy laughs. "I bet."

I sigh. "I want her to get to know me. To see I'm a different person now. We have chemistry. I'm sure of that. I just need to make her see it too."

"Maybe you could start by apologizing to her. And then keeping your dirty fantasies at bay until she gets used to the idea of you not being a total ass."

"You think I should apologize to her straight away?"

"Yeah, I do," he insists. "If you pretend not to recognize her, then it's only going to get more awkward. And you definitely owe that girl an apology."

"You're right. Then at least it's out there. And if she chooses to leave after that, I'll know I tried if nothing else."

"Exactly. Now I have to run. We can't all just swan in and out of work when we feel like it."

I laugh. "Because the whole world stops turning if you step out of your office for a second."

"You know it." Billy laughs.

I put my phone back into my pocket and go back to my office, but all I can think of is the haunted look in Elena's beautiful eyes.

Chapter Six

Elena

I lay awake in bed alternating between staring at the ceiling and checking the clock. It's now three AM and I've started doing that thing where I work out how many hours of sleep I'm going to get if I fall asleep right now. At the minute, I'm down three hours and there's still no sign of me dropping off any time soon. It's not even like I'm not tired. I am. I just can't seem to switch my brain off.

I'm always a little restless like this when I have to get up early for work on a Monday after a weekend off, and I knew tonight would be extra bad because I've been out of work for a few months and gotten used to just getting up when I wake up. What I wasn't banking on was Ashton turning back up in my life and setting my head spinning with thoughts and memories of him.

I can't get him out of my head, and the picture of him as I saw him on Friday and the picture of him as a merciless school boy mix together in my head causing a strange juxtaposition that leaves me feeling on edge and dizzy.

I know he looks different now, but that doesn't mean he has changed. All that's changed is his clothes, his surname, and most likely his zip code. How strange. We've had a reversal of fortunes. My dad lost all his money and Ashton looks like he's now loaded. If the past is anything to go by, money and power can only be a bad thing for someone like Ashton. I pause. I should give him the benefit of the doubt. Maybe he has changed inside too. The trouble with that theory is I don't really believe it.

I believe people change as they mature, sure I do. But I think those changes are usually quite small. I'm not sure I believe a person can change who they fundamentally are, and the way Ashton spoke to David in my interview didn't do much to make me think he's not the same old douchebag he always was.

I don't think he remembered me though. If he did, I'm sure he couldn't have resisted making a couple of digs at my expense, and there's no way he would have hired me. He hated me. He once described me as nothing. I also think if he has changed, it would make him feel awkward having a constant reminder of his nasty childhood hanging around.

I should just take the job, keep my head down, and get on with my work. If by chance, he ever does remember who I am... I can feign ignorance and just act like I don't know who he is. The thing is, I'm no longer the quiet little wall flower I once was, and I honestly don't know if I can keep my mouth shut about it all. I certainly won't be taking any shit from him like I used to.

Or maybe I should just call the HR department in the morning and tell them I've changed my mind about the job. It's not like they wouldn't be relieved. But even as I think it, I know I won't actually do it. The pile of bills in the hallway tells me I can't do that. This is the last of the bills I can pay out of my meagre savings and there's no guarantee another job will come along in time. Especially, not if word gets out that I've messed Wave about like this.

Oh God, why did it have to be his company that offered me a job? Why couldn't it have been literally any other one?

I can't even imagine what it's going to be like working for Ashton. Not good would be my guess. I never thought I would end up in a position where I gave him any power over me. This is what scares me the most. He will have power over me. He'll be my boss. This will be direct. I'll be his personal assistant, working closely with him every day.

My palms start to sweat and my heart races as I think about what that actually means for me. The worst part about it all was the way he kept looking at me in the elevator. He wasn't looking at me like he wanted to upset me. No, that I could have handled. Instead, he was looking at me like maybe he wanted to fuck the living daylights out of me. And actually, that isn't the worst part about it. The worst part about it is that I wanted him to do that to me. As much as that bastard made my life a living hell, I still haven't managed to shake off the crush I had on him.

It makes me feel weak, pathetic even, that after taking so much crap from him, I still can't help melting when I look into his eyes. I still can't stop imagining what his lips would feel like on mine, what his hands would make me do roaming over my body. Even now, in the middle of the night when I'm trying desperately to just fall asleep, I can feel my body tingling when I think of him. My clit throbs and my pussy is wet and it takes every bit of willpower I have not to move my hand lower, not to start to touch myself and think of Ashton.

But I won't go there. Not again.

Every time I succumb to the craving, I feel terrible afterwards.

My mind flashes back to the past. To that first time I did it. It was in our last year. I'd stayed back after school to run track. After my training, I'd gone to the locker room to shower and change. I was alone, or at least I thought I was, so I took a long hot shower, then stepped out of the shower without a towel, or anything to wrap around myself. As I walked across the room to my clothes, I felt eyes on me.

I whirled around and for a second, I was frozen.

My eyes were locked on Ashton's. He was in the locker room watching me. I didn't see hatred or disdain. I saw uncompromising lust. I remember feeling a spark of excitement in my body mixed with terror. Why was he here? What was he going to do to me?

He didn't come any closer nor did he flee when he knew I'd spotted him. He just stood there, his eyes drinking me in. And to my perpetual shame, I did nothing. I didn't attempt to cover myself. I didn't scream for a teacher. Instead, I stood stock still, flaunting my body, letting him see what he was missing. What he would never have. My eyes grazed over his body and locked on the hard-on he was making no effort to hide from me. He wanted me. Even if he would never admit it, his body had told me the truth of the matter.

Finally, when my heart was racing so hard I thought I would collapse on the spot, Ashton turned and left the room without a word. I finally broke through my paralysis and went back to my clothes. But I didn't put them on. At least not straight away. Instead, I sat down on the bench that ran around the outside of the room beneath the clothes pegs and I opened my legs. I rubbed my fingers over my clit until I couldn't stand it anymore. I slipped two fingers inside of myself and I brought myself to orgasm. The whole time, I thought of Ashton, of the expression in his eyes. I pretended he was crouched in front of me, that those were his finger jamming into me.

As soon as I came, I felt a mixture of disgust and lust.

I was still turned on at the thought of what had happened, but I felt so ashamed of myself. How could I let myself feel that way about the boy who humiliated me time and time again? How could I be so turned on at the thought of his eyes on me, the idea of his hands on me? I got dressed quickly and ran from the school. When I got home, I showered again. I spent hours that night lying awake. First masturbating, then berating myself for being such a fool.

I had gone to school the next day full of dread, just waiting to hear the rumors spreading, to hear the other students talking about what Ashton had seen the day before. But no one was talking about it. And they never did. Whatever passed between us in that moment to my knowledge never got discussed with anyone. I certainly never told anyone, and the fact no one mentioned it to me told me Ashton hadn't either.

I'd like to say the bullying ended there, but it didn't. If anything, it went up a notch, but every time Ashton threw an insult at me after that, it felt charged with sexual energy, and somehow, it never really bothered me much after that.

How could I be offended by what he said when I knew deep down he wanted me bad, real bad. He could say I was disgusting all he wanted to. He could oink at me all he wanted to. But I knew the truth now. He had been as aroused by me as I had been by him in the girl's locker room.

I had the one thing he wanted and the one thing he would never have.

And now I was about to get back into the lion's den with him. I'm all grown up and he may not remember me, but I do know the chemistry that bubbled up between us in the locker room all of those years ago is still there. It's going to sit between us, the elephant in the room, and it's going to make for one hell of an awkward atmosphere. It could be worse though. At least I know who he is, and I know that no matter what feelings he stirs up in me, no matter how wet he makes me, I can never, ever go there with him.

I look at the clock again. It's almost five and I have my alarm set for six. It's a waste of time lying here underneath the sweaty mess of sheets, so I push myself free from the sheets and get out of bed. I'm not going to be able to sleep now, and even if I do, an hour is neither here nor there. I'm just going to have to drink coffee all day and make sure I use plenty of concealer underneath my eyes.

Because as much as I hate Ashton, and as much as I would never go there with him, I can't help but want to see that look of lust in his eyes again, when he looks at me. I can't help but want him to want me. Maybe it's a power thing. Maybe it's finally my turn to hold all of the power and use it to humiliate Ashton, even if just in my own mind.

I tell myself that's what it is because it's safer that way. It's much safer than letting myself admit the truth. I want to impress him. I want him to like me.

Chapter seven

Elena

I arrive at Wave just before eight and ride up in the elevator, alone thankfully, As soon as I get to the reception area I duck into the bathroom to quickly check myself in the mirror. I'm wearing a black shift dress and a black jacket with nude sensible heels. A safe outfit, one I feel comfortable and professional in. My hair is blown out into loose blonde waves and my make-up is minimal – just enough to cover up my sleepless night and add a bit of gloss to my lips. I run my fingers through my hair and take a deep breath. I look the part and I know it.

I step back out of the bathroom and I realize I have no idea where to go from here. I don't know if I'll even have an office, let alone where it might be. I falter for a moment, then I tell myself to forget about Ashton and treat today like how I would my first day at any job. I nod to myself and step up to the reception desk where a pretty redhead is sitting typing.

"Hi," I say as she looks up at me with a smile. "I'm Elena Woods. I'm starting work here today as Mr. Miller's personal assistant. I'm not really sure where I'm supposed to be."

"Pleased to meet you, Elena," she says. "I'm Becky. Welcome to the company."

I thank her.

She goes on, "Mr. Miller isn't in yet, but he's due any second. Why don't you take a seat over there and wait for him to get in?"

I thank her again, and go and sit down in the waiting area. It's the same waiting area where I waited for my interview and I'm actually even more nervous this time around. I take long, slow breaths, trying to steady my nerves.

I give myself a talking to as I wait. Either Ashton knows who I am or he doesn't. Either he's still an asshole or he isn't. Neither of those things change what I'm here to do. Do the job to the best of my ability and earn my wages. I can do that. And if somewhere along the way, I prove to Ashton that I'm not some worthless piece of trash he can bully, then that's just a bonus. I am starting to feel confident again. I know I can do this job with my eyes closed.

Ashton appears at a couple of minutes after eight and all of my new found confidence drains away. He steps out of the elevator and walks towards me. He's wearing a different suit from the one he was wearing when I came for my interview, but it looks just as expensive and he looks every bit as hot as he ever did.

"Good morning Becky," he says as he passes her desk.

"Good morning Mr. Miller," she replies. "Would you like your usual coffee?"

"Please," he nods. "And whatever Elena is having. Elena?"

I freeze for a moment, tongue tied. Whatever I say will be wrong. He'll mock my choice of drink, or my accent, or my clothes, and Becky will laugh then I'll be right back at school. Except this isn't school and if he does any of those things, chances are, Becky won't laugh. She'll be disgusted at him. I force myself to smile. "Black with one sugar please," I say.

Becky gets up and goes to fix the coffee.

Ashton nods at me. "Good. You're on time."

Which is more than I can say for him, but of course I don't say that. Instead, I just nod.

"Right, let's get you settled in," he says. "Follow me."

I get up, my legs slightly shaky and follow Ashton along a hallway. A different one from the one I went down for my interview. There's a thick, springy blue carpet beneath my feet and a lot more glass along this area. Each office is glass fronted. Most of them are empty, but a few already have workers in them.

"That's Bruce, he works in accounts," Ashton says as we pass one of the offices. "And that's Jess in there. She's one of our best techs. She's the brains behind our latest organization app."

That makes me feel a little better. At least, he's not misogynistic. It was just me he hated, not all women. We're almost at the end of the hallway now, which widens out to a large open plan area filled with cubicles and people on phones.

"This is the secretary pool," Ashton says, nodding towards the group of workers.

I nod and we carry on into the hallway that narrows down again. The end of the hallway is dominated by a huge glass fronted corner office with amazing views of the city. It has a large mahogany desk with black leather seats, including a couch and armchairs arranged around a low coffee table.

"That's my office," Ashton says, nodding into the huge one. He then points to a smaller one beside it. "And that will be yours. Charlie, our handyman, will be along later to put your name and job title up, and Stewart from IT should already be on his way up to get your computer and phone line up and running."

"Ok," I say, trying to hold on to all of the information I'm being given. Right now, I'm just glad the partition wall between my office and Ashton's isn't made of glass.

"Come on into my office and we'll go over everything while Stewart is getting set up and then you can get started," he says. He pulls the office door open and stands back holding it, gesturing at me to enter first.

I smile my thanks and step into his office.

Chapter Eight

Elena

"Take a seat," he says.

I move towards his desk and sit down taking another deep breath. He puts his briefcase down and takes his jacket off then he comes to sit opposite me behind his desk.

Before he can get started, there's a light tap on the door.

Ashton waves his hand in a come in gesture.

Becky steps into the office with our coffees. She informs Ashton that Stewart has arrived in my office and leaves.

I curl my fingers around the hot mug.

"It's a pretty standard set up," Ashton says, taking a sip from his mug. "You'll be in charge of running my diary and whatever other daily tasks that crop up. You've done this before, so I won't insult your intelligence by going over every detail of what that entails, but if you do have any questions, just stop me at any point." He turns the monitor on his desk around to show me the screen. "This is our computerized diary system. It's another one of Jess's babies so if you hit any snags, she's your gal, but I've never known any of her features not to work." He clicks around in the system, showing me how it all works.

It looks straightforward enough and I'm confident I can pull off using it.

Ashton opens his top drawer and hands me a red leather bound diary. "Call me old fashioned, but I like a paper copy of everything in this schedule too. It doesn't matter how much something is backed up, if our systems go down, I need to know where I should be and when."

"That makes sense," I say. It's the first time I've spoken to him and I'm pleased my voice comes out sounding normal. I take a sip of coffee so Ashton can't see the look of relief on my face.

"I'll have one of the secretaries give you a tour of the building later on today, so you can start finding your feet," Ashton says.

I nod.

He smiles. "You're very quiet," he points out. "But I'm assuming that won't last. I'm not one of those bosses who wants everyone to bow down to me and be afraid to state their opinion. I like strong people who will stand up to me when they need to, and I like people with ideas who will come and talk to me and pitch things to me. Will that be a problem for you?"

"Not at all Mr. Miller." It feels strange calling Ashton Mr. anything, but especially Miller, a name I still don't really associate with him.

"It's Ashton," he corrects.

"Ok," I agree.

"Do you have any questions?"

How do you not remember me after you spent so much of your time making my life hell? "No," I say. "I'm sure I'll pick it up as I go along and if I think of anything, I'll let you know."

"Sounds good," he says.

I can't wait to get out of this office. Although I think I'm holding my own, and I'm pretty sure I'm not giving away how nervous I am— inside, I am actually a bag of nerves, just waiting for the penny to drop. For Ashton to remember who I am and fire me or dredge up the past again.

I start to stand up, but Ashton motions me back into my seat.

I sit back down, already hating the fact that I have to do as he says now.

"Wait Elena," he says. "Before you go, there's something else I want to talk to you about." He takes a drink of his coffee, puts the mug back down and gets to his feet.

I wait patiently while he goes and stands at the window, and looks out over the city. It is such a long pause I'm starting to think I'd misunderstood and I was meant to leave his office when he speaks

"I know you remember me. I wasn't sure at first, but you do, don't you?"

I want to say no. To be able to act casual and then be surprised when he tells me who he is, but I'm not confident I can pull it off. If I let him think I'm lying about remembering him, he's going to know for sure how much his treatment of me bothered me, and how it still plays on my mind, even after all of these years. "I remember you," I say coolly. "I didn't say anything because I wasn't sure you would remember me."

He turns back to face me. He doesn't come back to his seat. Instead, he perches on the extra wide windowsill as he studies my face. "I do. And I want you to know I'm not proud of the way I treated you back then."

I shrug. "It was a long time ago. We were just kids."

"I know. But I was old enough to know better. I'm sorry, Elena. Really I am. I was an asshole. I want you to know you have nothing to fear from me, ok?"

"It's fine," I say coolly. "Let's be honest, maybe if I had noticed you existed before you started having to act like an ass, none of it would have happened." I give him a clipped smile as I say it. I notice some of the spark goes out of his eyes and his shoulders slump slightly. It's exactly the effect I was going for. I wanted him to think he hadn't been important to me growing up, that I had barely known he existed. But now that I've done it, it doesn't make me feel good like I thought it would. In fact, it makes me feel awful. I remind myself of how many times Ashton made me feel awful. Of how many lunch breaks I spent locked in the bathroom crying. It should help, but it doesn't.

"Is there anything else or should I get started?" I ask crisply, trying to push through the awkwardness.

"That's everything," he says, recovering himself. He gets up from the windowsill and smiles at me as he makes his way back to his seat. "Remember I'm only next door if you have any questions. Welcome to Wave, Elena."

"Thanks," I say as I stand up. I practically run from the room, conscious of Ashton's eyes on me the whole time.

Chapter Nine

Elena

I'm shaking when I get into my office. I want nothing more than to turn around, leave this place and never come back. I'd settle for being able to close the door, sit down, and compose myself with a few breathing exercises. I can't do either. I can't just walk away from this job because I like not being homeless. And I can't take a moment to centre myself because of all the damned glass. Anyone coming along the hallway outside of my office would see me.

I hate this glass set up already.

I close the door quietly, although it seems a little pointless really. I take a proper look around the office. I have a smaller version of Ashton's desk, a comfy looking leather computer chair and two more chairs opposite the computer chair. There's also some filing cabinets and a small coffee table in the corner with two arm chairs. The office is a little bigger than my old one and if it wasn't for the glass, I'd be more than happy with it.

I step towards my desk. As I do, a head pops up from behind it and I gasp. The head laughs, a good-natured laugh that I can't help but join in with.

"I'm Stewart from IT," the head says. "I'm sorry I scared you. I thought you knew I was in here."

I did. Ashton told me Stewart was in here, I just forget in my panicked state. Suddenly I'm grateful for the glass. If I had a solid wall, I likely would have been hyperventilating with my back pressed against the door when I met Stewart. "I'm Elena," I say with a smile. "Ashton mentioned you were getting me all set up but when I didn't see you in here, I thought you were done."

"Almost," Stewart smiles. "Go and grab a coffee or something while you wait if you want. The kitchen is just along there." He points to my left with a thumb

I realize now, the hallway didn't actually end with Ashton's office. It turns ever so slightly. I nod. Coffee sounds like a good idea, and it's not like I can do any work without a computer or a phone. "Would you like one?" I ask.

"I'd love one. Cream, no sugar, please," Stewart says.

I move over to the arm chairs to leave my bag and jacket on one of them then step back out of the office. I go in the direction Stewart pointed me in. The hallway doesn't go much further. I find four rooms. A small cleaning supply closet, a male and female bathroom then a large kitchen that seems to double as a break room, judging by the tables and chairs in it.

I go into the kitchen and see a pot of coffee. I touch the pot, glad to discover the coffee is hot. I open up a cupboard, the one directly above the coffee pot, and smile when I see I guessed correctly. I pour and fix two coffees.

Now I'm out from underneath Ashton's gaze and I have had a moment to center myself, I feel much better. I don't feel so mean about what I said to him now. I finally stood up for myself and I shouldn't have to feel guilty for it. It's not even like I can say I'm even. Ashton has done a lot more to me than I ever could do to him.

I head back to my office shaking off thoughts of Ashton.

Stewart is no longer under my desk. He's sitting in my office chair, doing something on my computer. He smiles when I step back in. "It shouldn't be much longer. I'm just installing a few programs and then you're good to go," he says as I hand him his coffee.

He takes a sip. "Thanks."

I sit down in one of the chairs opposite Stewart and sip my own coffee. "So what's it like working here?" I ask.

"It's hell," Stewart says. "Everyone is awful and Mr. Miller is the worst boss I've ever had. Always yelling and cursing."

I feel my heart skip a beat and I stare at him incredulously.

Stewart breaks into a grin that turns into a laugh. "Relax, Elena. I'm joking. Everyone's lovely and Ashton is a great guy to work for as long as you're doing what you're supposed to be doing."

"Oh. Yes, of course," I say, a relieved laugh slipping out of me. As if Stewart would have told me any of this if it were true.

By the time the first of the programs has been installed, Stewart and I have finished our coffee, been back to the kitchen, washed the cups and put them away. We've talked about what universities we went to, and I know Stewart is a Baseball fan who has just split up with a long-term girlfriend and has a two year old son named Mason. He knows that I'm single and not looking for a relationship.

I decide I like Stewart and if everyone here is as friendly as he is, I'll soon be settled in. We're laughing about the kind opportunities out there for people our age who do want to date when my door opens.

I turn and see Ashton. I notice he doesn't knock, but it's not like I can exactly tell him off about that.

"Stewart. Are we almost there?"

"Another hour or so," Stewart replies.

I wait for Stewart to change, to stop the laughter that's still on his face, to jump to attention, but he doesn't. Instead, he actually pulls Ashton into the conversation, "We were just talking about how much of a disaster dating can be," Stewart says. "And how it's pretty slim pickings out there."

"Maybe it is if you have no natural charm." Ashton grins.

"If by charm you mean money, I'd have to agree. How about a pay rise?" Stewart shoots back.

Ashton laughs. "I don't see it happening Stew. I don't need any more competition."

I start to relax a little. Ashton isn't a monster. His employees don't fear him. Maybe people can change. Or maybe Stewart just doesn't get to see the nasty side of Ashton. I went to school with so many people who thought Ashton was hilarious and charming and that I was just being over sensitive to his humor.

There's a lull in the conversation and I turn to Ashton, determined not to let my nerves affect my job. "Did you need something?"

"Oh, this one is going to keep you on the straight and narrow." Stewart laughs. "No casual conversation when there's work to be done."

"Yeah," Ashton says, looking me in the eye. His eyes are dark and suddenly full of lust. He holds my gaze. "It seems she's really going to be riding me hard." He looks away.

Stewart laughs along, seemingly oblivious to the look Ashton gave me, and to the way my body bursts out in goose-bumps as a shiver of desire passes through me. I feel heat in my cheeks and I know I'm blushing slightly. "I'm sorry. I just..." I start.

Ashton waves away my apology.

"Relax. I know what you meant," he smiles.

"You're going to have to get used to the strange humor in this place," Stewart points out. "We're all constantly ragging on each other, but it's all in good fun."

I've been on the end of Ashton's teasing before and I don't think I'm ready to be on the receiving end of it again, but I force myself to laugh along with Stewart. "I'm sure I'll get used to it."

"Yeah, you'll be giving as good as you get by the end of the week," he says.

"Damned right I will. I'm not here to be everyone's punchline." I laugh.

I'm sure I see Ashton wince and the mood in the room shifts ever so slightly.

Again, Stewart remains oblivious to the tension. "That's a shame. I was looking forward to making you blush at least twice a day," Stewart smiles. The computer makes a pinging

sound and Stewart switches his attention to the monitor and
starts typing in a few commands.

Chapter Ten

Elena

"Elena," Ashton says.

I look over at him, bracing myself for my body's reaction. It doesn't disappoint. My clit tingles as I look at Ashton.

"I thought while Stewart was still busy, you might like to meet the secretaries and have a quick tour of the office."

"Yes of course," I say, getting to my feet. I turn back to Stewart. "It was nice meeting you."

"You too, Elena," he calls cheerfully. "I'll likely still be here when you get back unless the tour includes a few tourist hotspots in the city."

I smile and follow Ashton out of my office.

He walks a step ahead of me, giving me a great view of his muscular back and his ass. I have to look away quickly when I find myself fantasizing about grabbing his ass, digging my nails into his flesh and pressing his body up against mine.

"So you get along well with Stewart," Ashton says glancing back at me over his shoulder.

It's like he knew I'd been checking him out. I smile and nod. "Yeah. He seems like a nice guy."

"Hmm... he's been with me for a few years now."

We step into the wide part of the hallway filled with cubicles.

Ashton steps closer to the cubicles. "Good morning, Ladies."

The women at the cubicles greet Ashton.

He gestures towards me. "This is Elena, my new personal assistant. I expect you all to help her settle in," he says. He turns to me and starts pointing at the women in turn. "These are my personal secretaries. Sandra. Beatrice. Melanie. And Karen."

Each of the women smile and nod at me as their name is announced.

Karen even gives me a little wave.

I return their smiles.

"Sandra, how do you feel about maybe giving Elena a tour of the offices," Ashton says.

Sandra glances at her watch. "I have a call with a client in five, but if it can wait an hour, I'd be happy to," she smiles.

"I can do it," Beatrice says.

"Great, thanks," Ashton says. He smiles at me. "I'll leave you in Beatrice's capable hands."

Beatrice, a dark haired, olive skinned beauty, stands up and comes towards me. She shakes my hand enthusiastically, smiling at me. "It's nice to meet you."

"You too," I reply, noticing that her smile doesn't quite meet her dark brown eyes.

"I'll be in my office," Ashton says. He turns and starts to walk away.

"Let's go." Beatrice smiles at me. "I take it you've found the break room and the bathroom next to your office?"

I nod.

She nods back. "Good." She strides quickly along the hallway. Her long legs mean she takes long strides and I have to almost jog to keep up with her. She points to either side of herself as she walks. "This here is accounting," she says. "And this is our tech team. These are just their offices. The magic happens in the computer labs. You'll see them soon enough."

A woman is coming towards us.

Beatrice smiles at her. "Elena, this is Jess. She's the head of the software development team. Jess, this is Elena, Mr. Miller's new personal assistant."

Jess and I greet each other.

"Jess is the one to go to if you have any problems with any of the software," Beatrice says, repeating what Ashton already told me. "Since she developed most of it." She doesn't give me time to respond before she addresses Jess.

"So clear your schedule, Jess, because there's bound to be a lot of calls," she says with a fake sounding laugh.

Jess raises an eyebrow. "I hope you're not implying my software is riddled with holes," she says.

"No. God no, of course not," Beatrice gushes.

So as I suspected, she's implying I'm stupid.

"I'm just saying Elena might struggle to find her way around it with her being new to it and all that," Beatrice adds.

I really don't like where this is going. "Ashton showed me the basics and I think I've got it." I smile at Jess.

Beatrice stiffens slightly when I use Ashton's first name.

Jess grins at me. "You'll be fine. Just because Beatrice here doesn't know a spreadsheet from a diary page doesn't mean you don't, right?" Jess laughs.

Beatrice laughs along, but it's clearly forced. "What can I say? Some of us spent our college days having a life," she says.

"And some of us didn't need a university to tell us how to do our jobs at all," Jess says. She shoots me a grin. "No offense."

"None taken. So... you're self-taught?"

"Most developers are," Jess says. She winks. "Or at least the good ones are."

"Yes, well, we best be moving along," Beatrice says.

Jess gives a mock salute and ducks into her office.

I find myself trotting along beside Beatrice again. I debate asking her why she seems to think I'm too stupid to learn a new program, but I bite my tongue, remembering Stewart's warning that everyone here teases each other. She's probably just teasing me.

We cross the lobby and go down a different hallway.

"This is the marketing team," Beatrice says, pointing to her right. "And on the left is the main conference room. That's conference room A. It's usually just referred to as the conference room where the others get their full names. Make sure you remember where this one is, as Mr. Miller takes a lot of client meetings in here and you'll likely be expected to sit in on the meetings and take minutes."

I nod, making sure to remember where this conference room is.

Beatrice turns and heads back out of the hallway. She leads me down another one. "That's conference rooms B and

C. They're smaller ones that the developers use and they're often used for staff department meetings. And through here are the main computer rooms." She opens a door and steps inside.

I follow her into a large room that's jam packed with computers. At the end of the room, hulking black machinery with an array of flashing lights sits behind a glass partition.

Beatrice sees me looking at them. "Those are the servers. They're manned twenty -four seven and they're closed off to keep the temperature in the room constant. There's all sorts of security on them so I won't be showing you them in any great detail. The rest of the room is where new apps and pro-grams are developed and algorithms are coded and tweaked."

The room is busy and the noise level is high, but no one in the room seems put off by the noise. They're all working away and I don't really want to disturb them.

Beatrice seems to have the same idea because she backs out of the room. She leads me back into the lobby and points down the hallway where I had my interview. "Along there is HR on the right and IT on the left. And conference room D where you had your interview." She starts to head back down the hallway leading to my office. "Your interview didn't go so well huh?" she says.

I raise an eyebrow.

"What?" she says.

"I just find it a bit strange that HR was gossiping to you about interviews," I say.

"Oh relax." She smiles, another smile that doesn't reach her eyes. "The interviews are all recorded and I typed up the transcripts."

"Right," I say. "Of course."

"Yours was kind of bad," she says as a statement not a question.

I chose to answer it anyway, "It can't have been that bad. I got the job, didn't I?" I say with the same fake smile as she gives me.

"Hmm," she says like she isn't sure how that happened.

You and me both Beatrice. You and me both, I think to myself.

Chapter Eleven

Elena

I think my first day is going well so far. The only slight hiccup has been Beatrice, who I can't fathom. I can't decide whether she's taken a dislike to me, or whether she's just trying to fit in with the office banter and isn't all that good at it. I don't let it worry me. It's not like I'm going to be working closely with her, and everyone else I've met has been nothing but nice to me.

I've familiarized myself with the diary system and it all seems straightforward enough. I've sent a few emails I was asked to send and made a few calls to set up meetings for Ashton for next week. I even sat in on a short meeting and took minutes. I have to get those typed up this afternoon and on Ashton's desk by the end of the day, and I have a report to type up too.

The job is nothing I can't handle, although I know the pace is going to pick up quickly once I get my first day over with. I'm just grabbing a sandwich with Jess in the kitchen and I really like her. She's intelligent and funny and we have a lot in common.

"So how you are finding everything?" she asks.

"Good," I reply. "I've been doing the personal assistant job for years, so I'll soon find my feet with that."

"And the people? How are you fitting in?"

"I've met a ton of people. I have a list of names in my head and a list of faces, but I'm not sure they all match up yet." I smile.

"Within a week or two, you'll feel like you've known everyone your whole life." she smiles at me. "Everyone will understand if you don't instantly remember their names."

"I hope so," I say. "I don't think Beatrice likes me much, but luckily, I have her name down, so at least I can't offend her by forgetting her name." I didn't really mean to say that. I don't want Jess to think I'm paranoid, or worse, a gossip. She smiles and I relax a little.

She doesn't seem to be bothered by what I've said. "Beatrice is a little standoffish at first. It's nothing personal. It's just the way she is. Once you get to know her, she'll warm up a little," Jess says. "I think she's just a little shy and she tries to overcompensate for it and it makes her come across as a little brusque at times."

That makes sense I suppose. There's no reason for Beatrice not to like me. I haven't known her long enough to have offended her in any real way.

Jess stands up and stretches and her back clicks audibly.

I try not to wince.

She laughs. "That's my party trick," she says. "And speaking of parties, I have a meeting so I have to dash." She puts her trash in the bin and flashes me another smile as she leaves the room.

I debate going back to my office, but I've only been on my lunch for fifteen minutes and I don't want to get a reputation as an ass kisser. I nibble on my sandwich and sip from a bottle of water. My thoughts go back to Ashton.

He's been nothing but nice to me, complimenting me on my work and making it clear he's available if I have any questions or anything. I can't help but be suspicious though. Part of me wants to just move on from my suspicions, but part of me is clinging onto them so if anything happens, I'm not completely blindsided by it. I just can't bring myself to trust him. I'm sure he's playing some sort of game with me where he lulls me into a false sense of security and then goes back to his old ways, undermining me and humiliating me.

If I keep thinking like that though, I'm never going to settle in here fully. I sigh as I dig in my pocket and pull my phone out. I scroll idly through Twitter for a while, and then move on to Instagram, but I'm not really paying any attention. I'm just thinking about Ashton and whether taking this job was really a good idea.

I sigh again and scroll through my contacts until I find Lottie's name. She'll be the voice of reason, the one who tells me to get out of here. I press call and wait for her to pick up.

"How's your first day going?" Lottie asks instead of hello when she takes my call.

"Good," I answer. "But weird."

"Weird how?"

"The CEO who I'm the assistant to. It's Ashton Winston from school. Remember him? Only he's calling himself Ashton Miller these days," I say.

"I remember him," Lottie confirms. "It's been forever since I last saw anyone from school except for you of course. How's he doing?"

"Well, good obviously. He's a multimillionaire."

"Coooooool."

"Lottie, do you remember how he used to bully me?"

"Sure I do, but I'm not sure he was really a bully. He teased you for attention and you overreacted and made it worse for yourself."

"Thanks for the support," I mutter.

Lottie laughs. "Oh come on Elena. I know it felt bad at the time, but it was years ago. We can laugh about it now surely? You were so touchy about it because you were into him. Other kids said way worse stuff and you laughed with them."

"I guess." I think about it. Is that true? Did I make it out to be worse than it really was?

"Wait, is he still doing it?" Lottie asks.

"No. That's the thing. He's been nothing but super nice to me. He even apologized for the way he used to act. Unless it's an act right? Like some sort of game."

"Or maybe... just maybe... he just grew up like we all did," Lottie says gently.

"Maybe. The thing is Lottie, he's smoking hot. Hell, he's hotter than he's ever been. How can I find him attractive after everything he put me through? It's weird, right?"

"The heart wants what the heart wants," Lottie trills.

"Yeah, it's not my heart that wants him," I shoot back with a giggle.

"Go for it."

"He's my boss," I whisper.

"So what? I'd do my boss if he looked as hot as you say Ashton turned out."

"You would?"

"Absolutely. I can always find another job, but hot men. Thin on the ground, girl. Thin on the ground."

"I've caught him looking at me in a way that suggests the attraction isn't one sided," I say. "And there's a definite chemistry between us."

"How are you making this sound like a problem?" Lottie asks.

"Well, I just... How am I supposed to believe that someone who hated me so much can suddenly feel differently about me?"

"Oh Elena, you still don't get it do you? I'm going to tell you the same thing I told you every day at school. Ashton doesn't hate you. He never did. He just wanted to get your attention."

"Whatever." I sigh. "I have to go."

"Ok. Don't let this whole overthinking thing you do cloud your mind and ruin a perfectly good job." She ends the call.

I don't feel any better. All Lottie has done is make me question everything once more. And then I wonder why she always accuses me of overthinking everything.

I stand up, put my trash in the bin and head back to my office. I'm a little surprised to see Beatrice sitting behind my desk as I approach.

She looks up guiltily as I step into the office. She covers the guilty look with a smile. "I was just sending a few emails while I waited for you," she says quickly.

"On my computer?"

"Just making sure it all works."

I smile tightly. "Okay. What can I do for you?"

She points to a stack of papers that she's placed on my desk. "Mr. Miller asked me to print these out and bring them to you to send to our top twenty clients. Their names and addresses are in the database. Do you need any help using it?"

"No, I'm good thanks. I'll get on it right away."

Beatrice gets up rather reluctantly from my chair. She flashes me a smug smile that I don't really know how to take before she leaves the office.

I sit back down and bring up the database.

By four o'clock I've sent out the letters, wrote up the minutes from the meeting and completed the report. I open up the diary app, just wanting to familiarize myself with Ashton's schedule for the next day, so I can keep on top of what's going on. My heart sinks when I see the app. All of the text is written in what I think might be German.

Fuck. What do I do now? I think for a moment and reach for my desk phone. I'll call Jess and ask her how to switch it back out to English. I pull my hand away from the phone. I can't help but remember the way Beatrice laughed on my tour and told Jess she'd be hearing from me a lot. I don't want to be the newbie who can't do anything for herself.

I think back to Beatrice sitting behind my desk looking guilty when I came back from my lunch break and I smile to myself. I know what this is. It's trick the newbie time. And I won't fall for it and run to Jess. I can figure this out myself. If I panic at the first trick, more will come. If I fathom this out and get it sorted myself, the novelty will wear off, and I'll be accepted as one of them.

I don't know a lot about coding, but I know enough to get into the backend of the system and I know enough to find what I'm looking for. The language tag. There's a whole load of gibberish that I don't understand – symbols and commands – and then I find it. The part I need to change is simple. Sitting between two quotation marks is the word German. I quickly delete it and change it to the word English. I cross my fingers, click save, and exit the backend of the program.

A triumphant yes escapes my lips when I see everything has reverted back to English. I go back to my original task and familiarize myself with Ashton's day tomorrow. He has an early meeting and then another one later on in the afternoon. I make a few notes on my notepad of what he'll need for the two meetings, so I can make sure everything is ready for him when it should be.

Finally, at five, I shut down the computer and slip out of my office. I steel myself for the moment I'll come face to face with Ashton and I tap on the glass door.

He smiles and waves me in.

"I'm all done unless you need anything else," I say.

"Nope, all good," he replies. He holds up the report I brought him earlier. "This is really good Elena, thanks."

I feel myself blush at his praise. I'm going to wear a little more make-up tomorrow. I can't have Ashton seeing me blush every time he says something nice to me.

"How was your first day?"

"Good," I confirm. "I think I'm finding my feet."

He smiles. "Give it until the end of the week and you'll feel like you've been here all of your life."

I nod and return his smile. "So goodnight then," I say.

"See you tomorrow."

I go back to my own office and gather my things. I'm just about to leave when Beatrice appears in my doorway. I smile and wave her in.

"I just wanted to make sure everything's ok," she says.

"Everything's fine. Thanks for taking the time to check in on me."

"And you have Mr. Miller's schedule for tomorrow?" she asks.

I know exactly what game she's playing. She wants to know if I've encountered her handy work yet. I smile and nod.

"The diary program is working, ok?" she presses.

I could just keep nodding along, but I decide to put her out of her misery. "It is now," I say. "The coding was a little off. The text turned to German, but it's all fixed now."

"Oh. You must have hit the wrong button or something." She grins. "Did you call Jess to fix it?"

"It's not a button I could accidentally press. You have to go into the backend and manually change the code. Someone must have been in here and done that," I say pointedly. "Hazing the new girl and all that. But no, I didn't call Jess. It was a simple enough fix, so I just did it myself."

"You know coding?" she demands. She looks pretty pissed off that her hazing didn't have the desired effect. Either Jess is right about her and we'll be laughing about this soon enough, or Beatrice really has taken a dislike to me.

"I know lots of things, Beatrice. Things you would never imagine I would know," I say cryptically.

She makes that hmm sound again and then she turns to leave my office. "Well see you tomorrow then, Elena."

"You sure will."

She walks away.

I laugh quietly. Maybe working here won't be so bad after all. Because whether this is harmless hazing or Beatrice trying to sabotage me, my school days with Ashton have done one thing. They've prepared me to stand up for myself and not let anyone get one over on me.

Chapter Twelve

Ashton

Elena has been working here for a week now and I think she's really starting to enjoy it. She's good at the job, always turning her work in on time and to a high standard, and she has even started pre-empting what I might need and getting it done before I have to ask her which is always a good sign in a personal assistant. She's fitting in well around the office and everyone seems to like her. Most importantly, she seems to be getting less nervous around me, and I think she might finally be accepting my apology and seeing that I've changed. Or maybe that's just wishful thinking and she's just being courteous to me because I'm her boss. Either way, it feels like a step in the right direction.

As if me thinking about her summons her, I look up and Elena appears in my office doorway. She's wearing a black trouser suit and a yellow blouse. I can't help but imagine myself ripping the buttons off her blouse and throwing it to the ground, pushing her trousers down and ripping her panties off her. I push the image away and motion for Elena to come in to my office.

"You have the report I need?" I ask.

It's clear she doesn't; her hands are empty. But I wasn't joking when I said I needed the report by the end of the day and it's already pushing on for three. I just want to give her a gentle reminder that I still need it without having to come down too hard on her.

"No," she says. "That's actually what I wanted to talk to you about."

She's still standing up, barely inside of my office door and I motion for her to come and sit down. She does, but she looks nervous now. Her hands are twitching as they rest in her lap and I'm almost sure she's been crying.

"What's going on?" I ask.

"I honestly don't know," Elena replies. "The report was almost finished. I thought I'd saved it but I can't have done. I went to the bathroom and when I came back, my computer was shut down. I figured there'd been a power surge or something so I rebooted it. But the document was gone. I've been in touch with IT, but they can't find any trace of the document to recover it. I've spoken to the secretaries and none of their computers did anything strange."

"Are you saying you think your work was sabotaged?" I ask.

She shakes her head.

"No. I'm not accusing anyone of anything and I'm sorry if I gave you that impression. I'm just at a total loss to what happened. I just wanted to make you aware of the situation. I still have all of the notes I made and I can get the report re-done. I'll stay as late as I have to make it happen. I just ..."

She trails off. She looks down into her lap and I hate how sad she looks. I don't honestly think anyone at the company would intentionally sabotage her work, but at the same time, I believe her story. If she'd forgotten about the report, she would have come up with a better cover story than this if she wasn't willing to just hold her hands up and admit she screwed up.

"You just what?" I press her.

"I just hate that I'm going to miss the deadline," she says finally.

She looks up at me and there are definitely tears shining in her eyes. I stand up and make my way around the desk. I sit down on the edge of it, directly in front of Elena. I reach out and put what I hope is a comforting hand on her shoulder.

She gasps as I touch her, but it's not a fearful gasp. It's a gasp that tells me she feels the sparing of electricity between us exactly the same as I do. My hand tingles where it touches her. She looks up at me with wide, lustful eyes and I want nothing more than to kiss her, but I stop myself. It would be unprofessional, and if I have misread Elena's reaction, I could make her really terrified of me.

"You said you could recreate the report tonight right?" I say.

She nods, her eyes focused on mine.

"Then you haven't missed the deadline. I need the report for my eight am meeting tomorrow. As long as I have it by then, we're good," I say.

It's the truth. I have a potential new client who wanted a meeting at eight am on a Saturday. Yes, eight am on a damned Saturday. Normally I would have said no, but she's interested in placing a huge order for our software, and if it comes off, we'll smash our quarterly target. Elena relaxes a little at my words and I feel some of the tension leave her shoulder.

"Thank you," she says. She sniffs hard and then she smiles. "I'm sorry for coming in here like this. I just wanted to keep you updated."

"You did the right thing," I say.

I am aware that my hand is still on her shoulder, and although it started out as a means of comfort, it's been there too long for that now. She's not making any effort to wriggle out of my touch, and if it's making her uncomfortable, she's hiding it well, but I pull it away anyway. It seems to break the spell and Elena looks away from me quickly and gets up.

"I'd better go and get started then," she says, flustered.

"Elena wait," I say when she reaches the door.

She turns back to me and I smile at her. What I hope is a warm and friendly smile.

"I'll be working late myself tonight," I say.

This technically wasn't true a minute ago. I had no intention of staying back tonight. But now I know Elena will be here and I'm confident she feels the attraction between us, I decide on the spur of the moment to be around. Maybe she'll thaw even more if she has a chance to get to know me a little bit better.

"Why don't you stop by my office for a drink once the report is finished? It'll be a good way to celebrate a successful first week," I say.

"Ok," Elena says, a little warily. She smiles and I wonder if I imagined her wariness. "I'd like that."

I think it's fair to say we'll both like that. And if I'm reading this right, we'll both like what's coming after the drink.

Chapter Thirteen

Ashton

Staying late actually worked out well for me. I've managed to get through a load of those little tasks that I knew needed doing but kept putting off in favor of more important things. The office was mostly cleared out by around six. It is Friday night after all, and generally the only people working late on a Friday night are those who have dropped the ball through the week.

By seven, I figured Elena and I were alone in the building. I have had a delicious warm feeling inside of myself ever since, and I keep thinking about what might happen tonight. I'd really like to get up the courage to ask Elena on a real date, and I might even kiss her if she accepts my invitation. To be honest, I'm hoping for a lot more than a kiss. I want to take her in my arms and make her body feel amazing things. I want to show her that my mouth, once used to hurl insults at her, can make her feel amazing as well as humiliate her. I want to show her how much I have wanted her all of these years. But despite that, I am planning on taking things slowly.

I don't want to rush Elena into anything. When I claim her pussy, I don't want any nagging doubts in the back of my mind that she's only doing it because she's afraid of what might happen if she says no. I want to know for sure she wants me as much as I want her. I know I'm not imagining the chemistry between us, but that doesn't mean Elena is ready for more. I'll take things as slowly as she wants to. I've waited since school for a chance with this girl, so what's another couple of months? She will be worth the wait no matter how long it takes to get her to see that we'd be good together. I know that much for sure.

I hear footsteps in the hallway and I pull a sheet of paper full of numbers towards me. It's this month's profit and loss sheet. I have already studied the document in great detail and I'm pleased that it shows consistent growth, but I need something in front of me so it looks like I'm working on something; like I have a reason to still be here. It will look pretty creepy if Elena gets to my office door and I'm just sat here grinning out at her like a lunatic, and even if she's not creeped out, she might think I stayed back just to check up on her and I don't like that idea much more than the creepy one.

I listen to the footsteps approaching. The anticipation sends shivers down my spine and my cock is tingling with the thought of what might come next. I can't believe that in just a few short seconds, I'll be sharing a drink with the girl of my dreams. After all of these years I have been obsessed with her, it's finally going to happen.

A quiet knock comes on my door.

"Come in," I say.

I finally look up from the sheet of paper that is supposed to be commanding my attention. I flash Elena a charming smile. The smile slips instantly when I see it's not Elena who has come into my office. It's Beatrice, one of the secretaries. I had no idea she was still here. How would it have looked if she'd come to my office later and saw me sitting drinking with Elena?

"What's wrong?" I ask.

"Oh nothing Mr. Miller," she says.

She's twirling a strand of her hair around her finger which is distracting. I want to tell her to stop it, but I don't. I just want her out of here. If Elena comes in now, I can't very well give her a drink without offering Beatrice one, and I haven't sat here for almost four hours after finishing up just to have a third party join us.

"Let me rephrase that," I say, forcing a smile. "Why are you still here at nine o'clock on a Friday night?"

She's holding a couple of files, but I haven't asked her for anything that couldn't have waited until Monday and I'm a little confused about why she's here at all. She moves around my desk and sits down on it, positioning herself way too close to me. I try to move subtly but there's nowhere to go without pushing the chair out and I really don't want to offend her. She crosses her legs, her skirt riding up a little as she does it.

"Oops," she grins, tugging at the skirt but not really pulling it down any.

Beatrice has flirted with me since the day she started working here, but she's never gone this far before. I'm not sure why she's decided tonight is the night, but it's the night

I've been dreading. I'm not in the least bit attracted to Beatrice. I mean don't get me wrong, she's a very attractive woman. But she's no Elena. No one is.

I've never done anything to encourage her flirting. If anything, I have been more formal with her than the other secretaries because I've always been afraid of giving her the wrong idea. Now it looks like she's decided to take the wrong idea regardless. I'm going to have to turn her down and risk upsetting her.

I don't want to upset her; she's good at her job, and she's a nice enough woman. But I really can't do this with her. And especially not tonight. Tonight is my shot at showing Elena I've changed. It's not going to bode well for that if she sees Beatrice running from my office in embarrassment.

"What are you doing here Beatrice?" I ask again, my tone a little more abrupt.

"You sound stressed out," she says. "Let me give you a shoulder rub. I'm very good at them."

"That won't be necessary," I say.

I'm too late. Beatrice is already getting back down off my desk. As she stands up, the files she's holding slip from her hands and drop to the ground. Papers flutter everywhere.

"Oops," Beatrice says again.

She gives me a smile that I can only describe as lecherous. If I gave her that look without any interest on her part, I'd likely be facing a lawsuit. At least her dropping the papers gives me a reason to move without it looking like I'm just trying to put some distance between us. I push my chair back, ready to bend down and retrieve the papers, but Beatrice beats me to it. The second my chair goes back she falls to her knees in the gap I've made.

And of course that's the moment I notice Elena standing at my door, her hand balled into a fist ready to knock. Her mouth drops open and I realize with horror that she can see Beatrice's feet. From where Elena is standing, there's no way this looks like anything other than Beatrice giving me a blow job.

Elena turns and quickly walks away, almost running. I jump to my feet. Beatrice looks up at me with a grin.

"Sit back down. I've got it," she says.

"Beatrice this behavior is inappropriate and you know it. I'm going to leave my office now, and when I return, I want those files reordered on my desk and you gone for the night and then we'll never speak of this moment again. Is that clear?"

"Perfectly," she says.

The flirty smile is gone and she's no longer purring her words at me. She blushes and starts reaching for the papers. I know I should stay and talk to her, try to make her feel a little less embarrassed, but my chief concern right now is Elena. I need her to understand that this wasn't what it looked like. I mean it would be weird me staying to comfort Beatrice. It's not like I've led her on or anything. Talking to her would likely only make her more embarrassed. I'm pretty sure I've made my point.

I walk out of my office and go to Elena's. She's back behind her desk, the report sitting on it in front of her. She has her jacket on and her handbag is over her shoulder. I knock on the door and she looks up and nods for me to come in.

"Here's the report," she says, standing up and handing me the report.

"Thanks," I say, taking it from her. "And thanks for staying late to get it done. Elena what you saw back there ..."

"Is none of my business," she interrupts.

"It wasn't what it looked like. I didn't even know Beatrice was here, and then she came in with some files. She dropped them and she got down on her knees to pick the papers up before I could react."

"Ok," Elena says.

Her tone tells me that she doesn't believe me.

"I'm serious Elena," I tell her, desperate for her to understand. "I would never ..."

"Like I said it's none of my business. You really don't have to explain yourself to me. And if you're worried that I'll tell anyone what I saw, I can assure you that I won't," Elena says.

She looks embarrassed. Her cheeks are flushed and she's flustered, tripping over her words.

"There would be nothing to tell because nothing was happening," I say again.

"Ok," she repeats.

She still doesn't sound convinced, but the more I bang on about this, the bigger it becomes. I know it looks like I'm protesting too much and that's the last thing I want. I decide to let it go. Maybe after a drink or two, I'll tell Elena how Beatrice tried to seduce me and we can laugh about it.

"So are you ready for that drink then?" I smile.

"Actually I need to take a rain check on that if you don't mind," Elena says. "I'm tired and I have a headache coming on. Have a good weekend Ashton."

She moves towards her office door and as much as I want to beg her to stay, I know it's pointless. After what she thinks she's just seen, there's no way she's going to agree to come and have a drink with me, and if I press it, I'll just look like a creep.

"You too," I say. "And I hope your headache goes away quickly."

Chances are it'll go away instantly, you know, being that it's not actually real. She flashes me a nervous smile and scurries out of the office.

I stand in place for a moment, anger surging through me. I slam my fist down on Elena's desk. Fucking Beatrice. I can't believe she's ruined this for me.

Chapter Fourteen

Elena

I practically ran from Ashton on Friday night. I can't believe how close I came to letting my guard down with him. I agreed to a drink with him, knowing fine well more than just a drink was on the cards. I was actually starting to believe that maybe he really had changed. And then I went to his office and found Beatrice on her knees giving him a blow job.

He denied it – of course he did – but his excuse for it was lame. If she'd dropped some files, wouldn't she have waited until he moved away to actually pick them up? If she wasn't giving him a blow job when I appeared, it's only because I interrupted them before she got started.

No wonder she hates me. The mess with my diary software obviously wasn't any sort of hazing. Beatrice was jealous of me. She must have seen the way Ashton looks at me and not liked it and so she decided to sabotage me and make Ashton question my suitability for the job.

Although Friday night was embarrassing, I'm glad I saw what I did. It told me why Beatrice is so standoffish with me, and it told me that Ashton hasn't changed a bit. Maybe Lottie was right and he never really hated me. He doesn't act like he hates me. But he's still an asshole. He obviously thought he could have his way with Beatrice and then have her gone before I got to his office when he would have started trying to charm his way into my panties.

The worst part about all of this is that I'm actually jealous of Beatrice. How fucked up is that? I'm jealous that she's got something going on with Ashton, someone who I should never even consider touching with a ten foot barge pole after what he did to me. And yet here I am. As naïve as ever, willing to believe Ashton could change and willing to maybe see where things could go with us.

That's well and truly out of the window now. I have plenty of experience of craving Ashton from afar while hating myself for feeling that way. I guess I'll just have to go back to that.

I tell myself this at least once an hour, but it's hard. Ashton has been nothing but nice to me, and he's the boss. He doesn't have to go out of his way to make me feel welcome. This makes it damned hard to keep hold of the old resentment and hate him. But the more I let go of the old resentments, the more I notice Ashton's eyes on me. The more I feel the chemistry between us. And the harder it gets to focus only on my job and not on him and how fucking good he manages to look all the damned time. Even when he's stressed out he's hot with it. He doesn't get dark circles under his eyes, or stress lines around his mouth. No that would be too much to ask. Instead, he gets a brooding look about him, an intensity that only makes me more turned on when I look at him.

I just wish I could get past this whole mess one way or the other. I need to either stop finding Ashton so fucking attractive or find a way to let go completely and learn to trust him, at least to the extent that I can stop thinking him liking me is all just a game designed to humiliate me when I least expect it.

The phone on my desk rings startling me out of my thoughts. I pick up the receiver, glad of the momentary interruption to my thoughts.

"Elena Woods, personal assistant to Ashton Miller. How can I help you?" I say.

"Elena it's me," Ashton's voice comes down the line.

It's so close I imagine I can feel the warmth of his breath tickling my ear lobe. I shudder with pleasure as I imagine it. So much for an interruption to my thoughts about Ashton. I catch myself and quickly recover my senses.

"Where are you?" I ask, checking my watch. "The shareholders are already in the conference room."

Panic grips me. Have I dropped the ball and double booked Ashton?

"I'm on my way back to the office now," he replies. "The traffic is heavy. There's been an accident and they've had to set up a diversion."

I relax. There's no way I can get the blame for that.

"Anyway," Ashton goes on. "The reports I asked you for are sitting on my desk. Can you take them along to the shareholders meeting and just explain I'm on my way, but if they want to familiarise themselves with the figures, now's the time?"

"Consider it done," I say.

"Thanks Elena," Ashton says and then he hangs up.

I listen to the dial tone in my ear for a second, and then I leap into action. I rush through to Ashton's office and grab the reports. They're the only files on Ashton's desk so I don't waste time thumbing through them.

I head to the main conference room. I feel a little nervous, but facing the room of shareholders can't be as bad as my interview, and it can't be anywhere near as bad as coming face to face with Ashton for the first time since school. I take a deep breath when I reach the door and step in.

"Good afternoon everyone," I say with a smile. "I'm Elena Woods, Mr. Miller's personal assistant."

I don't know why I revert to Mr. Miller instead of Ashton. It just feels right and so I roll with it. All of their eyes are on me now, but it's not a hostile look. In fact, most of them are smiling at me.

"Mr. Miller is caught in traffic. There's been an accident and as you can all imagine the diversions are causing some problems. He's on his way and he's assured me he won't be long. In the meantime, he's asked me to give you these reports to start going over."

I hold the files up and then place them on the table next to the shareholder on the end. He picks the file up and begins leafing through it.

"Does anyone need any refreshments or anything while I'm here?"

"No thank you," one of the shareholders, a woman wearing a purple dress that I really like replies. "Beatrice has been taking good care of us."

I bet she has, I think to myself. I dismiss the thought and flash them all another smile.

"Fantastic. Please don't hesitate to let me or Beatrice know if you need anything."

I leave the room and head back to my office. My phone is ringing as I approach it, and by the time I've dealt with the call, the shareholder's meeting is the furthest thing from my mind.

I go about my day, filing, calling clients, writing reports and responding to emails from clients and developers. I also get a good few spam emails which I quite enjoy being able to delete without opening.

A couple of hours later, my phone rings again. Again it's Ashton, and this time, he asks me to come to his office. I agree and get up and head for his office. I raise my hand to knock but he beckons me in before I can. He looks kind of pissed off. His eyes have that dark intensity about them; the one I can't look away from.

I can't understand why he seems to be pissed off though. He seemed confident the shareholders would be happy with this month's performance, and why wouldn't they be? I printed off the financial reports for him and they show good figures. It must be about something else. I guess I'm about to find out what it is.

I open the door and step inside. Ashton waves me closer, pointing to the chair in front of his desk.

"Is everything ok?" I ask as I sit down.

"Not really," Ashton says. "Elena, which reports did you print off?"

Oh God he's pissed off with me not the shareholders. I didn't see that one coming. What have I done that could have upset him? I try my best to think of something I've overlooked but I can't think of anything. I must have missed one of the reports I was meant to print out for the meeting or something.

"The monthly one and the quarterly one like you asked me to," I say. "I definitely printed both of them. I trebled checked."

"Right," Ashton nods. "From what year?"

"This year," I say. I feel my heart sink. "Did I get it wrong? Was it meant to be last year's so you could all compare them?"

"No. It was meant to be this year's reports," Ashton says.

Now I'm confused. It sounds like I've printed off the correct reports, but if that's the case, then why does he look so stressed out. He points to the file in front of him.

"This is the file you gave to the shareholders right?"

I nod and he nods back.

"Elena these reports are from two years ago. I walked into chaos in that meeting. The shareholders thought we were losing money. I finally convinced them it was the wrong report and no real harm was done, but you've got to be more careful."

"I was careful," I say instantly. "I know I printed off the correct reports."

"Then you picked up the wrong file," Ashton says. "Didn't you think to check it before you took it to the shareholders?"

I feel myself blushing.

"No," I admit. "The meeting was running late and I didn't want to waste precious moments looking back over something I had done myself and knew to be right. That file was literally the only one on your desk."

"So you're saying I got the wrong file out?" Ashton says with a raised eyebrow.

"No, not at all," I reply quickly. "I'm saying I don't understand how this happened. I know I printed off the correct document. You can come and see my print history to prove that. And this file was the only one on your desk. That's all I'm saying."

Ashton sighs and rubs his hands over his face. He looks at me after a couple of seconds, his eyes unreadable.

"I hate to say this Elena," he says. My heart sinks further. He doesn't believe me. He's going to fire me. "But I think someone is purposely sabotaging you."

That takes a moment to sink in. Who would want to do that? Funnily enough, it's something Ashton would have pulled back in school. But he's not going to risk sabotaging his own company to make me look bad. If this was him, the mistake would have been flagged up before the reports got taken into that meeting. But who else could it be?

My mind goes to one place. I don't say it out loud. I don't want to falsely accuse anyone, but there's only one person who has been less than nice to me, and I've already caught her tampering with my computer. Beatrice.

"Do you really think someone would do that?" I ask, choosing my words carefully.

"Honestly Elena, I would have said it was ludicrous before today. But it certainly seems that way. I left the file on my desk this morning, and for it to be wrong by the time of the meeting suggests someone switched it. For now, I'm going to assume the best of my staff and think it was a genuine accident, but I will definitely be looking into this."

"Thank you," I say.

I open my mouth to say something else, but I close it, thinking better of it.

"What is it?" Ashton says noticing my reluctance to speak up.

I shake my head.

"It's nothing. It doesn't matter," I say.

"If you have your suspicions, I'd like to know. They will remain confidential," he says.

"Oh no, it's not that," I say. It's only half a lie. I do have my suspicions – Beatrice – but that's not what I wanted to say. I'm certainly not going to point any fingers without solid proof. I'm going to have to say what I really wanted to say now though, or Ashton will never believe I wasn't about to accuse someone. "I just ... I don't mean to sound ungrateful because I am happy you believe me. But why? Why are you taking my word for something when everyone else has worked here longer?"

"I've seen your work experience. I figure you don't get a career like that if you're prone to screwing up and lying about it. Plus, you always did have integrity," he smiles.

I risk returning his smile and for a second, the atmosphere in the room changes. It becomes charged and I imagine myself getting up out of the chair and going to him. I see myself straddling him, kissing him, my hands in his hair. I can feel myself blushing again, but I don't look away from him. His gaze holds mine as surely as if we were magnets, drawn to each other. I swallow hard, unsure where this is going, but wanting to find out.

I don't get to find out. Someone is knocking on Ashton's door and the moment is broken. He looks up to see who is knocking and waves them in. I look down at the ground, my cheeks burning with embarrassment and frustration. I look up as footsteps approach.

"I'm sorry. I didn't realize you were busy," a voice says.

Of course it's Beatrice. It just had to be.

"Really? Can you not see through glass Beatrice?" Ashton says coolly and its Beatrice's turn to blush.

"I just meant that this is important and I thought you would want to know right away," she stammers out.

"Fine," Ashton says. He looks at me. "Thanks Elena."

I realize I'm being dismissed and I stand up quickly and leave the office, nodding to Ashton as I go. I hurry back to my own office. Once more, I wish I had a wall rather than glass. It takes everything I have to sit down and force myself to look composed. I am anything but composed inside. I am a raw and aching mess and I have a feeling that only Ashton can make that mess feel any better.

Chapter Fifteen

Elena

The office is deadly silent as I walk across the lobby. It's after eight and everyone has gone home for the night. Everyone except Ashton and I that is. He asked me to work late tonight as an important client was coming in for a meeting and he wanted me to take the minutes for it. He didn't come out and say it, but I know he was worried about the meeting. I got the impression he thought the client was going to cancel some of our services. He couldn't have been more wrong. The client was full of praise for Wave and in fact, he had come in to discuss an expansion of his company and talk about the solutions we could offer for his new venue. His main concern was data security in the new venue and although a lot of the conversation went over my head, Ashton was able to propose a package he loved and he signed up for it on the spot. It's catapulted our monthly sales and we're now way ahead of our sales target.

I've just been to walk the client to the lift and now I'm heading back to my office to type up the minutes of the meeting. As I make my way down the hallway, I can't help but notice how strange it is to pass the secretaries area and see it empty. The building is so quiet, but rather than feeling eerie, it feels calming. Maybe it's because Beatrice's negative energy isn't here. She's not going to be happy when she learns Ashton and I were alone in the building for a few minutes. The thought makes me smile and I catch myself. It's not a competition. It's not like I even care about Ashton and who his attention is focused on. Except I do. I really, really do.

I reach the end of the hallway and movement in Ashton's office catches my eye. He's standing up – him getting out of his chair must have been what caught my attention - he meets my eye and smiles and beckons me into his office. I go inside. He grins at me. He's taken his tie off and opened out his shirt collar. He looks so hot it takes everything I have to not throw myself at him.

"That was a better result than I ever could have hoped for," Ashton says. "I'd like to offer you a glass of champagne to celebrate but I only have scotch. Would you care for some?"

"I shouldn't," I say. I nod to the notepad in my hand. "I have to get the minutes typed up and ..."

"Do it tomorrow Elena," Ashton interrupts. "I don't expect you to work late to type those up. Have a drink. Live a little."

He smiles and I feel my clit tingle. I nod and Ashton's smile widens. He goes to his drinks cabinet and pours us both a generous measure of scotch. He hands one of the glasses to me and raises his.

"To making new deals," he smiles. "And new starts."

He looks a little sheepish and the humble look on his face only makes me want him more. God what am I going to be like after this drink if I'm like this now.

"Cheers," I smile.

We both take a sip of our drinks. I feel the heat from the scotch travel down my insides and sit warming my stomach. I move over to the couch and sit down. Ashton sits on the other end of it. My heart is racing.

"You know, I really think this is our year," he says thoughtfully. "We've landed some big clients and this extension is only a small part of it. And Jess has some new software in the making. I think this might be the year that puts us on the map."

I relax a little. This is safe ground. Ground I can talk about without butterflies in my stomach.

"I think it's fair to say Wave is already on the map," I smile.

"Oh sure locally," Ashton says. "But I'm talking about globally here."

I smile and raise my glass.

"To global domination," I say.

Ashton clinks his glass against mine and drinks. He grins at me.

"I know you're mocking me, but I'm still going to drink to that because I like the way it sounds," he says.

I laugh softly.

"It does sound pretty good doesn't it?"

"Yeah. Imagine the business trips. No more Travel Lodge in Birmingham. It would be the Four Seasons in Paris, the Plaza in New York, maybe even seven star luxury in Dubai."

"Now that's worth drinking to," I say.

We clink our glasses together and again and I take a drink. I force myself to swallow the scotch normally, but my inside are churning and it's nothing to do with the heat from the drink. I can't help but wonder if Ashton is including me in those trips? I don't even care that they're imaginary. A pipe dream. I want in. And as much as I hate to admit it, it's not about the fine dining, the elegant rooms and the cosmopolitan lifestyle. It's about him. I want to be alone with him in a nice hotel. God this scotch is going to my head.

Suddenly I know I have to get out of here. If anything happens between Ashton and I, I'm afraid there will be no going back. And as much as I find him irresistible, I'm not ready for that. I'm not ready for any of this. I drain the last of my drink and stand up.

"Well if you don't need me for anything, I think I'll make tracks. Thanks for the drink," I say.

"Anytime," Ashton smiles. He downs the last of his scotch. "I'll walk down with you. I rather like the idea of ending today on a high."

I feel a stirring inside of myself. I know he's talking about the deal, but for just a moment I wonder if maybe he's talking about something else. I tell myself to get a grip. Even if he is, I've just told myself I'm not ready to forgive and forget and that means nothing can happen between us.

"I'll just go and grab my stuff," I say.

I go back to my own office and leave my notebook on my desk ready for tomorrow morning and then I grab my handbag and phone. I turn the lights off and leave the office. I realize I've left my jacket behind but I can get it tomorrow. It's not like I'm going to be outside for long. I only have to walk from the front door of the building to the car park.

"Ready?" Ashton smiles, stepping out of his own office.

I nod and we start to walk towards the lifts.

"Any plans for tonight?" Ashton asks.

"Nothing exciting. Dinner and then bed most likely," I say. "You?"

"Same," he says. "But I might push the boat out and watch a movie in bed."

I feel a tingling between my legs as I imagine Ashton in bed. We reach the lifts and he reaches out and presses the call button. I imagine his fingers on me pressing my buttons, making me come at his touch.

"Let me guess. The Notebook?" I say.

"I was thinking more like The Avengers," he grins.

I laugh softly. The lift comes and we step inside, Ashton gesturing for me to go first. I press the button for the ground floor and we start going down. Ashton is standing beside me, ever so slightly behind me, and I can feel his eyes on me. My cheeks burn, but it's not embarrassment this time, it's desire.

I can't wait to get out of here. My heart is racing and my pussy is dripping wet. It's like my own body is betraying me. Suddenly, the lift lurches. I stumble and Ashton catches me. There's a screeching sound of metal on metal and the lift car comes to a dead stop.

"What happened?" I ask.

"No idea," Ashton says.

I reach out and press the button marked G again but nothing happens. My heart is racing again, but this time, desire has nothing to do with it. I can feel panic clawing at me.

I hate small spaces and lifts aren't a favorite thing of mine at the best of times. I've always had a fear of being trapped in one, and now it's happening. Oh dear God it's happening. I'm going to freak out, pass out or throw up or something. I have to get out of here. I have to get out of here right now. Except I can't. We're not going anywhere and my futile attempt to pry the doors open does nothing except break one of my nails.

My breath is coming in short gasps and I feel dizzy. I can feel my chest tightening and there's a sharp pain in my stomach. I can hear my pulse in my head and my body is hot suddenly, sweat springing out all over me and a strange tingly warmth is spreading out over me. It's not a nice tingling, it's a horrible one, one that tells me I am seconds from passing out.

I'm going to die in here I think to myself. I know that's irrational, but once the thought takes hold, it's hard to shake it off. I can't breathe and I am getting more dizzy by the second. I press one hand against my chest, trying to get my heart to stop convulsing. I reach out with the other hand and press my palm against the wall of the lift. The coolness on my hand helps a little but not enough. I put my head down and try to breathe slowly. I can't. I'm not getting enough air. I revert to panicky gasping.

I am vaguely aware of Ashton talking on his phone, but I don't hear what he's saying. His presence barely even registers with me. I just have to concentrate on breathing. Oh my God, what if I'm having a heart attack? If I am, then I am as good as dead. The thought brings forth another fluttering palpitation. I imagine my brain starved of oxygen and I close my eyes, trying to force myself to calm down.

The more I try to calm down, the worse my panic becomes. I feel a warm hand on my shoulder. It's too warm, burning me. Another hot rush of sweat rushes out of me and I suck in a strangled feeling breath.

"Elena? Elena listen to me," Ashton says.

His voice penetrates the fog in my brain and I look up at him.

"It's going to be ok," he says calmly. "The repair man is on his way. It won't be long and then we'll be out of here."

"I can't breathe," I manage to gasp. "I can't get any air."

"Yes you can. You're having a panic attack. Nothing more. You're safe Elena. I won't let anything happen to you I swear. Now I need you to do as I say. Take a nice long breath in through your nose. Count to five as you do it."

I do it but it doesn't help.

"Now out through your mouth. Count to five again."

I do it, tasting the copper of adrenaline coating my tongue.

"Again," Ashton says.

I repeat the process and after a couple of deep breaths, I start to feel better. My heart is beating normally now and I feel like I can breathe again. I'm still a little dizzy though and when I take my hand off the wall, it feels as though the ground shifts beneath me. I stumble forwards and Ashton reaches out and catches me, stopping me from falling.

On some level, I am aware of his arm around my waist, my body pressed against his, but in the moment, I'm just trying to shake off the left over vertigo. Ashton was right. I had a panic attack. I haven't had one of those for years and I definitely haven't missed them.

I take a few more deep breaths and the dizziness starts to pass. In a couple of minutes, I feel reasonably normal again, if a little shaky. The whole thing can't have lasted more than two or three minutes, but it felt like a lifetime when I was trapped in that bubble of panic.

"Better?" Ashton asks.

I nod slowly.

"Yes," I say. "Thank you. God I felt like I was dying or something."

"Have you had a panic attack before?" he asks.

"A long time ago," I say. "I haven't had one in years. But I've never been a big fan of small spaces and I haven't been trapped in a lift before, so yeah."

I'm babbling, trying to cover my embarrassment at Ashton seeing me at my most vulnerable. I realize with a start that his arm is still around my waist, although we're not pressed together anymore. Perhaps we never were.

I take a half step backwards and Ashton starts to move his arm away. I don't know what comes over me. Maybe it's a little bit of adrenaline left in my system. All I know is I don't want Ashton's arm to go away. I don't want to be anywhere but right here in his arms.

I look up at him and close the gap between us. I put my hand on his chest. He looks down at me, a look on his face that tells me he wants this as much as I do. I know he's not going to make the first move now though. Who would after what I've just been through?

I smile at him slowly and then I move my hand from his chest and rub it gently across his cheek. I crane my neck and move my hand around to the back of his head, pulling his face down to meet mine.

"Elena ..." he starts.

I don't let him finish. There are a hundred reasons why we shouldn't do this and I don't need to hear another one. I cut off his words by placing my lips firmly against his. I kiss him gently, barely a touch really. I pull back from his mouth and smile at him.

"Thank you," I say.

Chapter Sixteen

Elena

The indecision has gone from Ashton's face. All I can see now is pure lust. His eyes seem to have gotten darker and for a moment, he looks deep into my eyes. I feel my pussy clenching just looking at him.

He leans down and presses his lips to mine, and this time there's nothing gentle about our kiss. Our mouths come together in an almost desperate kiss, our bodies hungry for each other.

His arm is still around my waist and he puts his palm on my lower back, pulling me in towards him. I can feel his chest pressing against mine, the taut muscle unyielding. He pushes his other hand into my hair as his tongue finds mine. I feel like I have been unleashed, and my hands roam over Ashton's body, moving up and down his back and over his ass. All of the pent up desire, the need to feel Ashton's hands on me, is coming to the surface and I have to have him. I have to feel him inside me.

His hands skim down my body and he rubs them over my ass. He bunches his hands into fists, balling my skirt up in his hands. He pulls on it, dragging it up around my waist. He moves his lips from mine, kissing down my neck as he slips his hands into my panties, kneading my bare ass. I moan as my body responds to his touch. My clit is screaming for attention, and my pussy is so wet I can feel liquid soaking into my panties.

I tug Ashton's shirt out of his trousers, pushing my hands beneath it and running them over his bare skin. Electricity flies through my hands and up my arms, spurring me on, making me want him more.

I fumble his belt open and then his button and flies. He moves his hands from my ass. He keeps one hand on the small of my back and the other one comes around to the front of my body. He pushes his fingers into my panties and parts my lips, his fingers finding my clit. I gasp as a shock of pleasure floods me.

He kisses my mouth again, stifling the moan that escapes my lips as his fingers work their magic on my clit. He walks me backwards, slamming me against the wall. My breath catches in my throat as he ups the pace of his fingers on me. I pull my mouth away from his, needing to release the pent up moan that's playing over my lips. I moan his name loudly in a voice so different to my normal voice.

I go back to his trousers, pushing them down. I lift one of my legs, hooking it over Ashton's hip. He pulls his head away from my neck where his tongue was sending delicious floods of goose bumps through me. He looks at me with such longing that I almost come on the spot.

"Elena," he purrs. "God Elena."

He moves his fingers away from my clit. It's too soon. I need the release of an orgasm. I moan in frustration and he smiles at me and kisses the tip of my nose. His hands move over my ass and slip beneath it. He lifts me and I wrap my legs tightly around his waist.

He reaches down and pushes his boxer shorts down, freeing his huge cock. I can feel it pressed against me. I know he's as ready for this as I am. I put my head back, resting it on the wall behind me. Ashton reaches between our bodies and rubs his fingers through my lips, spreading my juices. He moans when he feels how wet I am. He grabs his cock and presses it against my pussy.

A loud clanging sound echoes through the lift as he's about to penetrate me.

"No," I whisper.

"Hold on Mr. Miller. I'll have you out of there in a couple of minutes," a muffled voice shouts.

I unwrap my legs from Ashton's waist and once my feet are back on the ground, he takes a step back from me. We hurry to get our clothes back into some sort of normal state. I can't believe the repair man is here, and I can't believe what I was about to allow to happen if he hadn't shown up when he did.

The moment between Ashton and I is well and truly over. We barely look at each other as I pull my skirt back down and run my fingers through my hair, trying to get it back into some sort of order. Ashton has already pulled his boxer shorts and trousers back up and now he's fastening the trousers.

He looks at me and smiles.

"Bad timing huh?" he says.

I nod, not trusting myself to speak. I wanted him. I wanted this. But now I'm relieved the repair man is here. That he arrived in time to stop me making a huge mistake. I feel cheap and dirty. I practically threw myself at Ashton, and I'm so ashamed of myself.

I try to tell myself we're both consenting adults. There was nothing dirty about what we did. We just got a little carried away that's all. It's hard to convince myself that's true when all I can see in my head now is Beatrice on her knees beneath Ashton's desk. I'm a fool. A fucking mug. Just the latest conquest of Ashton's.

The lifts doors finally pop open and I step forward.

"Careful there love," the repair man says. "The car is about a foot above the ground level."

"I'll go first and then help you out," Ashton says. "And then maybe we can talk about ..."

"It's fine," I say cutting him off.

I know what he wants to talk about. It's the last thing I want to talk about. I just want to forget it ever happened. As it stands, I can blame the panic I felt for letting my guard down. If I spend any more time with Ashton I don't think I'll be able to stop myself from finishing what we started, and then I'll have nothing and no one to blame but myself.

I move to front of the lift and reach my hand out to the repair man. He takes it and holds me steady as I hop down onto solid ground. I release his hand and thank him. I hear Ashton stepping down behind me. I want to just run from him, but I know I'll have to face him eventually. Tomorrow in fact. And it'll be easier to just get it over with now.

I wait a couple of steps away from Ashton as he talks to the repair man about when the lift will be fixed. The repair man assures him it won't take long and it will all be in working order again tomorrow. I make a mental note to take the stairs anyway.

"Thank you for calming me down," I say, glancing at Ashton when he moves to join me.

"Of course," he says. "Elena ..."

I cut him off quickly before he can go on. Anything we say about what we just did now is only going to make working together even more awkward. It's hard to be so focused on getting away from Ashton when he's left my clit begging for more. My body is tingling, urging me to go with him now and finish what we started, but I've already made the mistake of listening to my body once tonight, and now my head is firmly back in charge.

"Good night Ashton," I say.

For a second, a hurt look crosses his face, but he covers it quickly with a smile, leaving me wondering if I imagined the look.

"See you tomorrow," he says coolly and then he walks quickly across the lobby and out of the door, leaving me wondering what the bigger mistake was. Starting something or not finishing it.

I give him a minute, needing to make sure he's definitely gone. If he's hanging around the car park and he tries to kiss me, I know I won't have the resolve to stop him. I'm just going to have to keep my distance from him and hope he takes the hint and doesn't try anything with me.

The thought of us never finishing what we started bothers me a lot. I don't know what's happening to me. It's like Ashton is making me crazy. One moment I hate him for everything he's done to me in the past, and for being with Beatrice in the office when he was supposed to be waiting for me. But there's another part of me, a larger part, that feels anything but hate towards him. It's all a mess.

I debate calling Lottie as I walk to my car, but I already know what she'll say. That he's changed. That I've changed. That I've always had a thing for him and that I should just let go and give us a chance.

I want to do that. I really do. But I don't think I can.

Chapter Seventeen

Ashton

I went home last night feeling a strange mix of frustrated and elated. Elated that something finally happened between Elena and I and frustrated that we didn't get a chance to finish what we started. I was also a little disconcerted that she wouldn't talk to me afterwards. She would barely even look at me. But I know I didn't force anything on her. She was the one who instigated it, and I know that look in her eye when she kissed me wasn't fake. She wanted me.

Now I've had a little taste of what Elena and I could be together, now I've seen for sure that she wants me like I want her, I am more determined than ever to have her. I spent most of last night tossing and turning, thinking about Elena. I jerked off twice to thoughts of Elena, remembering the way her pussy felt beneath my fingers, warm and slick with lust. It didn't help. It didn't release the frustration inside of me. Only Elena can do that.

I have to find a way to make her open herself up to me, to tell me what stopped her from going all in. I'd like to believe she was flustered and embarrassed because of the repair man's terrible timing, but I feel like it's more than that.

When I told her I knew who she was and apologized for the way I treated her back in school, she played it casual, but I think there's more to it. I think she's still carrying a lot of that around with her, and I think that's what's getting in her way when it comes to letting me all the way in.

I'm not ready to give up on her yet though. Far from it. I'll find a way to make her see that everything I did to her was just a misguided way of getting her to notice me. And I'll show her that I've grown up now and have much better ways of getting a woman's attention. I'll woo the fuck out of her until she can see it for herself.

I head out to my car ready to go to the office. I am driving along the high street when a florist's shop catches my attention. I smile to myself and pull over to the curb outside of the shop. I get out of the car and go inside. A little bell rings overhead as I push the door open and a dark-haired woman holding a pair of pruning shears and wearing a green apron with tiny cherries on it appears through an arched doorway.

"Good morning," she smiles brightly. "Do you need any help?"

"Good morning," I reply, returning her smile. "I need something special. Something unique. Something as impressive as roses but without the cliché."

"I know just the thing," she says. She bends down and pulls out a brochure. She flicks through it. "I think our blue dendrobium will be perfect. They're an orchid and they're vibrant and colorful while being unique and special."

She finds the right place in the brochure and turns it so I can see the orchids. I smile and nod.

"Yes," I say. "Those are perfect. I know it's short notice, but is there any chance you can deliver them this morning?"

"I can, but it'll cost extra," she says, almost apologetically.

"If she's worth orchids, she's worth the delivery fee right?" I smile.

"Right," the florist agrees, relaxing a little when she sees I'm not going to complain and try to get something for nothing.

"Where are they going?" she asks.

I give her Wave's address and tell her they're for Elena Woods.

"And do you want the small bunch, the medium, the large or the extra-large?"

"The extra-large," I say without hesitation.

She tells me the price and I push my debit card into the reader. It's a lot of money for something that will be dead in a week to ten days, but it's a small price to pay to show Elena that last night meant more to me than just a fumble.

"Can you add a vase to that?" I ask.

I haven't put my pin number in yet so it shouldn't be too late.

"Carry on with the pin number sir. I'll throw the vase in for free," the florist smiles.

I thank her and finish up the transaction. She hands me a receipt and a little card with an equally little envelope.

"If you want to put a message on there, here's a pen," she says, handing me a pen from off the counter. "Or you can choose from one of our pre-printed cards if you would prefer."

I take the pen and think for a moment. I bend down and write out a message on the card. I smile to myself when I read it back.

"Some people have Paris. Some people have Rome. But you and I will always have the lift."

I add an A and a row of x's to the bottom of the message and put the card in the envelope. I am writing Elena's name on the card when the florist speaks again.

"She must be special," she says knowingly.

"She is," I say. "She's the most special girl I've ever met."

I don't know why I'm telling this stranger all of this, but it just kind of comes out.

"I've loved her since I was fourteen. But back then I was an idiot to say the least. I got her to notice me by humiliating her and yeah ... I guess bullying her. Now she's come back into my life and I want her to know I've changed. I just don't know what to say to convince her of that."

"Actions speak louder than words," she smiles. "It's a cliché but it's true. There's nothing you can say to convince her you've changed. You have to show her. Give her time and treat her the way you wish you always had."

"That's kind of what I've been doing, but I'm afraid it's not enough," I say.

"It's enough," she reassures me. "A genuine gesture is always enough."

"Thanks," I say, pushing my wallet into my pocket and heading for the exit to the store. I look back over my shoulder. "And not just for the flowers."

"Good luck," she smiles back at me.

I might just need it.

Chapter Eighteen

Ashton

I get to the office building and go directly to my own office. The ride up to our floor is quite an experience. I can't help but remember Elena wrapped in my arms, her legs around me, my fingers massaging her clit.

I want to go to Elena the moment I step out of the lift, but I decide to wait a while. I tell myself it's to let her get settled into her work without being flustered, but the truth is, I'm a coward. I want to hang back as long as I can so I still have at least a small hope that she's not going to shut this thing down before it even begins. I also kind of want her to get the flowers first. If I see them in the kitchen bin, then I have my answer. Plus, if she shuts me down, it'll seem weird and inappropriate her getting flowers from me. If they come first, then at least it won't look creepy.

I happen to be looking out of my office door when the delivery man passes with the bouquet. Of course I've spent half of the morning watching the hallway so I can see him arriving. I really need to focus more on my work, but Elena is all I seem to be able to think about these days.

The bouquet really is huge. It's already in the vase, beautifully arranged, and I make a mental note to leave the florist a glowing review. I get up and move to the front of my office, opening the door a crack. I hear Elena asking if the guy has the right office and him assuring her the flowers are for her. He leaves and I wait a few minutes, giving Elena a chance to open the card.

I take a deep breath and leave my office, heading towards the bathroom. I glance in at Elena. She's holding the card in her hands, looking down at it and she's smiling. That has to be a good thing. I go to the bathroom and wash my hands at the sink for something to do. I don't think she saw me go by, but just in case, I don't want it to be obvious that I was passing by to gauge her reaction to the flowers.

I leave the bathroom and head back to my office. I am debating going into Elena's now instead, but I see Jess coming along the hallway. She could be going to use the kitchen or the bathroom, but I can't risk her wanting to talk to me or Elena and interrupting us, so I go back to my original plan. I glance into Elena's office again. The bouquet is sitting on the edge of her desk and although she's focused on her computer now, she's still smiling.

"Have you got a minute Ashton?" Jess asks as I reach my office.

"Of course," I say, holding the door open for her. She sits down without waiting to be asked. "Is there a problem?"

"Maybe," she says.

"The new software?" I ask, cold dread filling me.

She shakes her head quickly.

"No, nothing like that. We're right on schedule with that. This is a little more delicate. I don't want to cause any trouble, but I don't know ... something's a little off and I think you need to know about it."

I sit down and nod for her to go on. I'm intrigued rather than worried now.

"I got an email from Elena this morning. It was kind of nasty, attacking my diary program and saying basically that it wasn't sophisticated enough and that the interface was clunky. I went storming along to her office to give her a piece of my mind, but when I went in, she smiled at me and just started chatting like everything was normal. It threw me enough that I calmed down a little. I asked her how she was finding the diary program and she started singing its praises, talking about the features and how easy it was to use. I didn't say anything about the email and I left her office more confused than when I got there."

"You think maybe she hit a snag or something and lashed out instead of asking for help?" I ask.

It doesn't sound like Elena, but for Jess to be here talking to me about this, the email had to be pretty harsh and I want to at least hear her out.

"That was my first thought," Jess says. "But it just didn't sit right with me. Elena and I have become friends and I couldn't see any reason why she would be so nasty to me. I decided to reread the email and see if maybe I was being a little touchy. I wasn't. It was harsh. But I noticed that the email wasn't sent from Elena's work email address. Now that makes sense – you send an email like that, you don't want to risk HR seeing it."

"Ok," I say, still not sure where she's going with this.

"The email address wasn't anything you would expect. Not a combination of Elena's name or anything. It was just a string of random numbers and letters. I figured maybe she'd set it up rather than using her own email address, but that made no sense. Why set up an anonymous email account if you're going to sign your name at the bottom? I did a little more digging and the email had been bounced through a hundred and one servers to keep the original IP address masked."

"Right," I say, still a little lost.

"Well doesn't it strike you as odd that someone would do that when they put their name on the email?" Jess says.

"I guess," I admit.

"Look this might be me jumping to conclusions, but I kind of think maybe someone is trying to make Elena look bad. That they sent that email in her name to make me mad at her."

"Or that's what she wanted you to think," I say, playing devil's advocate.

"But why?" Jess says. "Why would she even send an email like that?"

I consider this for a moment and I decide to confide in Jess.

"What I'm about to say doesn't leave this office."

Jess nods. I tell her about the switched reports and that I have my suspicions that someone is purposely trying to sabotage Elena. Jess raises an eyebrow.

"She really must have pissed someone off. But who? She seems to get on with everyone."

"I don't know. Is there any way you can trace that email?" I ask.

She shakes her head.

"Seriously Ashton. The FBI wouldn't be able to trace that thing."

"Ok," I say. "Thank you for bringing this to my attention. I'll look into it. I'm determined to get to the bottom of this. I hate to think anyone here would do something like this, but if they are, I need to know who and why."

"I'll let you know if I hear anything or get anymore emails," Jess says, standing up.

I nod and she leaves my office.

Chapter Nineteen

Ashton

One of two things is happening here. Either Elena is in way over her head here and is making mistakes and acting out like this to cover them, or someone genuinely is sabotaging her. I'm inclined to think it's the latter. But who?

David Malone was pretty pissed off that I hired her against his recommendations, but he was pissed off at me, not Elena. And besides, surely someone working in HR would be above this kind of school yard behavior. I just can't think who else might have something against Elena. I intend to find out though.

Whatever the answer to this is, it doesn't make any sense. It makes no sense that one of my own staff, people who I have worked with for years in a lot of cases would suddenly start doing this. But it makes even less sense that Elena is doing this herself. If she made a mistake with the diary program, it would have made more sense for her to go to Jess and ask for help fixing it than accuse her of designing a bad program. And she clearly didn't know what Jess was talking about. Or she's one hell of a liar to convince Jess she didn't.

There's one explanation for this. One I don't want to consider, but I think I've reached a point where I have to. There's always the possibility that Elena has made a few mistakes and she's so afraid that I'll scold her or worse that she's covering her tracks anyway she knows how.

I don't like how that sits with me. The thought of her being that afraid of me hurts me deep inside. And it doesn't feel quite right. Elena's a woman now. Surely she wouldn't be so afraid of me.

I think it's past time I went to her office and talked to her. And not just about last night. I sigh as I stand up and leave my office. I tap on Elena's door as a courtesy and go in. She looks up from her computer, her cheeks flushing slightly when she sees me.

"Thank you for the flowers. They're beautiful," she says.

"You're welcome. I figured they might help you get over your ordeal," I smile.

I go and sit down and I look at Elena for a moment. She looks back at me, searching my face for the answers to a question she hasn't asked me and I can't even begin to guess at.

"Elena I'm going to ask you something and I want you to be honest with me," I say. She nods her head for me to go. I take a calming breath and then I just say it. "Are you afraid of me?"

"No," she says. "Should I be?"

Is she flirting with me? I hope so, but I don't want to read this wrong.

"Of course not," I say.

"What makes you ask that?" she says.

I don't want to tell her everything Jess has just told me. It's not going to help her feel relaxed here if she thinks someone is out to get her and that the someone almost cost her friendship with Jess.

"Well, the way you practically ran away from me last night when we got out of the lift for one," I say.

"If I remember correctly, you were the one who ran from me," she points out.

"I didn't run from you Elena. I got the impression you didn't want to talk about what had happened and so I left you alone so you didn't think I was being pushy or anything."

"I didn't want to talk about. And I still don't to be honest," she says. "It was a mistake and we shouldn't have let it happen."

That kind of deflates me, but I turn the conversation back around to my original point.

"I know we have some history, and I'd like to leave that in the past. But you don't have to be afraid of me ok? I would never do anything to hurt you. So if you ever make a mistake at work or anything, please don't feel like you can't just admit it to me," I say.

"This is about the reports from the shareholder meeting isn't it?" she says.

I nod.

"I don't know what to tell you. I've already told you what little I know about it. And I'm not lying because I'm afraid to tell you the truth. If I had printed out the wrong reports, or grabbed the wrong file, I would hold my hands up to it. I swear it."

She seems so genuine, her voice earnest, her eyes begging me to believe her. And I do believe her. As much as I don't want to believe someone here is trying to make her look in-competent, I do believe that.

"I believe you Elena," I say, meaning it. "I just wanted to be absolutely sure before I take this any further."

"Look maybe it was just some sort of prank. Can't we just let this go? I promise to be extra careful from now on and double check everything," she says.

If it was just the mixed-up reports, I'd probably agree to that, but the email makes this a whole lot more serious. What if whoever sent that email starts sending them to other people in the company, people who won't dig into it like Jess did? I don't want to make Elena think this is going to turn into some big witch hunt though.

"I'm not going to make a big fuss about it, but I'm not ready to just let it go either. I'm going to be keeping a very close eye on the staff ok?"

She nods although she doesn't look happy about it. She yawns which she attempts to stifle. I can't help but smile.

"It seems I'm not the only one who didn't get much sleep last night," I say.

I regret saying it the moment I open my mouth, but Ele-na surprises me. She doesn't seem mad or even embarrassed by my comment. Instead she laughs softly and shakes her head.

"I've had more restful nights," she admits coyly.

This is my chance. She's given me an in that I didn't think would be coming after she insisted she didn't want to talk about last night. Maybe she doesn't regret it quite as much as she seems to want to.

"Will you have dinner with me tonight Elena?" I ask.

"I don't think that's a good idea," she says quickly.

Too quickly. It's like she wants to agree, but something is holding her back. I think she knows that if we're alone together tonight that she won't be able to stop herself from finishing what we started last night.

"Why not?" I challenge her.

"I just don't," she says.

"Is it me you don't trust Elena, or is it yourself?" I ask with a grin.

She doesn't return the grin. She just shakes her head. I've gone too far and I desperately back track.

"Look it's just dinner," I say. "We'll go to a nice restaurant and eat too much. We'll talk, maybe laugh a little and that's it. I promise you that I won't do anything you don't want me to do."

She still doesn't agree, but she doesn't say no either. She looks torn.

"We both feel this chemistry between us. I know we do," I say. She blushes slightly and again she neither confirms or denies what I'm saying. "I think we owe it to ourselves to have one date and see how we feel about that."

"One dinner," she concedes.

I want to punch the air in delight but I resist the urge. Instead I beam at Elena.

"Great," I say. "We'll go straight from here if that's ok?"

She nods her head and I stand up and head for the door.

"It's just one dinner Ashton," she says. "As friends. Nothing more. And nothing is going to happen between us."

I nod my agreement and leave the office with a wide beam. I heard her. I heard her loud and clear. But I've waited my whole life for this moment and I'm going to make the most of it. And all I can do is hope that she comes around and sees for herself that we'd be perfect together.

I promised her I wouldn't do anything she doesn't want me to do and I meant it. But if she makes the first move like she did last night, I certainly won't be stopping her.

I go back to my office and pick up the phone. I call through to the secretary's pool.

"Good afternoon, welcome to Wave. Beatrice speaking, how can I help?"

Great. Beatrice was the last person I wanted to take this call. But it's not like she'll know who's coming to dinner with me. And even if she does, I don't care. Maybe it's a good thing. Maybe she'll finally back off me a bit if she knows I'm dating Elena. Because I'm definitely treating this like a date, even if Elena isn't quite there yet.

"Hi Beatrice, it's Ashton," I start.

Before I can go on, she interrupts, asking me what I need. If she would just shut up and listen, she'd know what I need.

"I need you to book a table for two for six o'clock tonight," I say. "In that little Spanish place down the street."

"Of course, Mr. Miller. I'll get right on that," she says.

Her tone has changed. She sounds a little pissed off. The restaurant is hardly somewhere I would take a client and Beatrice clearly isn't happy that I'm going on a date. I really should talk to her about this, but how do I do that without it becoming massively awkward? She's never said outright that she's into me, she's just flirted with me and hinted at it. If I confront her, there's nothing to stop her playing dumb and turning this around, and before I know it, I'll have gone from the one being made to feel uncomfortable by her constant flirting with me, to being accused of sexual harassment or something.

"Thank you," I say and end the call.

Within fifteen minutes, Beatrice appears at my door. I beckon for her to come in, wishing she would just use the phone like a normal person.

"Your table is booked Mr. Miller," she says.

"Thanks," I say.

"So," she says, fiddling with her hair and smiling at me. "Who's the lucky lady?"

Oh god, please don't let her think it's her.

"That would be telling," I smile.

"Oh Mr. Mysterious," she laughs. "You really need to learn to gossip more."

She ducks back out of my office, still laughing and I find myself questioning things with her. Maybe I was wrong and she doesn't have a thing for me. She certainly didn't seem to there. Maybe she's just a natural flirt and I'm reading too much into the situation.

Sandra calls down to my office to let me know that my next meeting is in the conference room and the client is waiting for me and I push all thoughts of Beatrice and Elena and what I hope is going to be one of the best nights of my life to one side and concentrate on the task at hand.

Chapter Twenty

Elena

I still can't really believe I'm here. I surprised myself by agreeing to come to dinner with Ashton. It was one thing giving into temptation last night, but that was purely physical. This is more than that. This is me making an active choice to spend time with Ashton outside of work.

I should have probably said no, but I have to admit that I'm glad I didn't. The food here is lovely and we've had a lovely time. We've laughed a lot and I have found myself relaxing. I'm sure the shiraz has something to do with that, but it's not just that. It's Ashton. He's making me feel comfortable in his presence for the first time. He's been charming and attentive and I hate to admit it, but I really think I was wrong. It seems people can fundamentally change, because there's nothing of the mean little boy in this version of Ashton who sits before me tonight.

Our waiter arrives and collects our desert plates and I have to admit that I'm a little upset that our night will soon be over. The waiter returns to our table almost immediately.

"Would you like anything sir or should I fetch you your bill?" he asks.

Ashton raises an eyebrow in my direction.

"Would you like a coffee or a cocktail or anything?" Ashton asks.

"I'd love a latte," I smile. "If you're having something."

I add the last part on quickly. I don't want to have coffee alone if Ashton would rather call it a night. He smiles at me and then at the waiter.

"We'll take two lattes please," he says.

The waiter nods and scurries back away.

"You were right about one thing," I say. "I'm so stuffed. I need the coffee to help me feel human again."

"Oh God I know," Ashton groans. "I think I might complain. They need to make their food less delicious so we can stop eating sooner."

"Good plan," I laugh.

The waiter arrives with our lattes. We thank him and I take a sip of mine. It's just right. Hot but not too hot and lovely and thick and creamy.

"So tell me how you got here," I smile as Ashton sips his own coffee.

"I just walked down the block Elena. Jeez how much wine have you put away to forget that? You were with me remember?" he says with a twinkle in his eye.

I laugh and shake my head, leaning over the table to give him a playful shove. I feel the tingling in my hand as soon as it makes contact with Ashton and I leave my hand there a second too long. I pull it away quickly before I can let the feeling permeate my body and make me act on my desire to lean across the table and kiss him.

"Seriously, how did Wave come about?" I ask.

"I finished university and I had a couple of offers for jobs. As I was debating between them, it hit me that I didn't want either of them. I had spent my whole life answering to other people, and I figured it was time to get out there on my own. I turned both of the jobs down and I started my own firm."

"Just like that," I smile.

"Just like that," Ashton agrees. "It was easy to make the decision, but it wasn't easy getting off the ground. The first few months were tough. Hell the first few years were tough. But it was worth it."

"What made you choose a tech based business? I don't seem to remember you being into tech stuff," I say.

"It was the biggest growing sector at the time. And I got a little more into tech while I was at university," he replies. "It's funny because I never pictured you going into the personal assistant thing."

"What did you picture me doing?" I ask.

"I'm not sure. I just figured you were more of the creative type than the corporate type."

"Ah so you pictured me being the struggling artist," I smile.

He laughs.

"I hardly think you'd be struggling. Money was never an issue for you."

"That's a nice way of saying I was spoiled," I laugh. "Seriously though money wasn't an issue for my parents. And to be fair, I could have talked to my dad and done the artist thing. When I graduated, he wanted to buy me a house and set up a monthly allowance. I said no."

Ashton raises an eyebrow and I smile.

"I guess we were more alike than we knew. I wanted to follow my own path too. And I knew if I accepted my father's help, I would always be beholden to him. He wouldn't have thrown the money back in my face; that was never his style. But I would have always been conscious of it, and I think it would have affected my life in a bad way rather than a good way. I guess I wanted to prove I could make it on my own."

"It seems you're doing a good job of that," he says.

"I'm not so sure that's true," I say, the wine making my tongue a little looser than it would normally be. "I had some savings but after I lost my job, I was basically down to one month's money in the bank. If I hadn't found this job when I did, I could have lost my house."

The reality of that hits me and I shudder slightly and make a mental note to up the amount going into my savings each month. I can afford it now.

"And by now, you would have been too proud to go to your parents?" Ashton asks.

I nod.

"I would have done it before I let myself become home-less, but it would have hurt. The worst part about it is I know my parents wouldn't have tried to make me feel bad for it. They would have quietly made my bills go away and said no more about it. And that's worse somehow than having them say I told you so."

"It's the other way around for me," Ashton says. "I have all of this money and my mom's too proud to accept my help. She still lives in the same house I grew up in you know. She works two jobs to support herself. I bought her a house and she refused to accept it. We almost fell out altogether over it. Eventually, I gave in and sold the house. And the day I tried to give her money, she really lost it. I've given up trying now. If I push too hard, I'll lose her for good and I don't want that."

"There's nothing more complicated than family is there?" I say.

"Tell me about it," Ashton agrees. "At first when my mom wouldn't take my help, I didn't understand it, but I think now I do. It's not just about pride. Her house is tiny, but it's all hers. She earned it. And while the estate isn't the nicest estate, it's full of good, honest people, and my mom is part of a community who gets her."

"It must be frustrating though," I say.

"It is. But she's always been stubborn and I should have known this would be no different."

"That's probably how my father feels about me," I smile. "When he first saw my house, he tried to hide his shock, but it came about when he asked me where the second bathroom was and I had to tell him there was only one."

"One bathroom? Oh the horror," Ashton laughs.

"Right," I laugh back. "Honestly, his face was a picture. I didn't dare tell him it was only two bedrooms."

"God no, it could have pushed him right over the edge," Ashton smiles.

"Can I ask you something personal?" I say.

Ashton nods.

"Why did you change your name?"

"Are you asking if I'm ashamed of who I was?" Ashton asks.

I shrug, a little uncomfortable because in a way I guess I am. Ashton smiles and my discomfort melts away.

"I'm not ashamed of being poor as a child. I am ashamed of some of the things I did," he says. He looks pointedly at me as he says it and I feel my cheeks flushing. He goes on without pressing it, something I'm relieved about. I don't want this evening to be ruined by talking about bad memories. "I changed my name when Wave started to take off, because while I wasn't ashamed of where I came from, I knew how other people saw me back then. The poor kid who would never be anyone. And I didn't want the name to affect my business if anyone recognised it."

"Having money or not having money doesn't define who you are or what you're capable of," I say.

"Maybe not," Ashton shrugs. "But we both know that having money opens doors that people without money don't even see. And we both know that no one from a rich background would give their business to the poor kid when they could help to make a rich guy richer."

"You're bitter for someone who is a rich guy." I smile.

"Not bitter. Just realistic," he says.

I can't argue with him because in some ways he's right. Privilege is a real thing, and if you don't have it, then there's a chance you'll always be on the outside. Ashton is an exception, but to become one of the elite, he had to leave behind who he used to be. It's sad really.

"Now enough maudlin talk," Ashton grins. "I love my life now, and I'm under no illusions. I owe everything I became to my mom. She showed me that hard work makes the man."

"She sounds like quite a woman," I say. "It's a shame I never got to meet her."

"Maybe you will one day." Ashton smiles.

I feel a spark of warmth inside of me at that. He really must see this going somewhere. I still don't really know how I feel about that, but maybe it's time for me to let go of my past like Ashton let go of his, and not let my teenage years define me. Maybe it's time for me to change a little and stop holding grudges.

"Yeah maybe," I smile.

His face lights up and I feel my stomach lurch. I was right. He really did mean meeting his mom as his girlfriend not just as his personal assistant. The conversation moves along and we start sharing funny stories from our university days. We're both laughing hard enough that tears are streaming down our face when our waiter comes back to the table.

"Excuse me," he smiles. "I'm just seeing if you would like to order anything before our kitchen closes for the night."

"Closes for the night?" I repeat, shocked.

I glance at my watch and I'm even more shocked. It's close to ten thirty. It feels like we've only been here an hour at most. The night has really flown by.

"Wow where has the time gone?" Ashton says, echoing my sentiments. "Just the bill would be good please."

He smiles at me.

"So apparently I'm a bad influence keeping you out on a school night," he says.

I laugh along with him and the waiter brings our bill. Ashton leaves his money on the table and we get up. We head out of the restaurant, calling out our thanks as we go.

We start heading back towards the office where our cars are parked. I quickly work out that we're ok to drive. We shared a bottle of wine, and that must have been two or three hours ago.

"Have you had a good time Elena?" Ashton asks.

I nod and smile.

"I really have. It felt good to reminisce about university and we've had a good laugh. Did you have a good time?"

"The best," he says quickly.

"It's funny isn't it?" I muse. "How well we get on considering how much you hated me at school."

"What?" Ashton says. "Elena I never hated you. I see why you might have gotten that impression, but honestly, it's not true."

"So why where you so intent on making my life hell?" I ask.

I don't want to ruin the mood of the evening, but if I want to be able to let go of the past, I need closure. And hearing Ashton finally tell me why he was always so awful to me might just give me the closure I need.

Chapter Twenty-one

Ashton

Tonight has gone really well. Even better than I could have hoped it would. Elena and I have laughed and joked and chatted, and it's always a good sign when you lose track of the time completely. There were no awkward pauses, our conversation just flowed naturally. It felt like we were really clicking together, and I don't think I was the only one who felt that. Elena visibly relaxed with me as the night went on. But now she's dropped a major bombshell and asked the question that could make or break the evening completely. And I have a feeling that how I answer the question might make or break how we move forward from here. It feels like a real pivotal moment and for a second, I'm filled with terror that I get this wrong.

In some ways I'm glad she asked why I made her life hell. I want to explain it to her, to make her see that I never saw her as an object of ridicule, that I always saw her as leagues above me. But in another way, I wish she hadn't brought it up now after such a magical night. I'm not sure I'm ready to be able to explain it properly. But I don't think I'll ever be ready for that, and I know deep down that if I want Elena to start to trust me, then I have to be honest with her. I have to give her the explanation she's always deserved. I might fuck it up, but if I don't at least try to explain it to her, it's always going to loom between us and it's always going to keep us from being all in together.

"I never meant to make your life hell," I start. "I know I did, but I didn't see it at the time. At least not until it was too late, and by then, I didn't know how to stop it."

I know that sounds lame, but essentially, it's the truth of the matter. I pause, giving Elena a chance to tell me to go to hell, or to say she understands. To say anything really. But she doesn't say anything. She's waiting for me to go on. And so I do. I'm going to tell her everything and just hope it's enough.

"On your first day at Franklin School, you were wearing your hair in two plaits. You always did. You had yellow ribbons tied in them. I noticed those ribbons the second you walked into the classroom. And a second later, I noticed your eyes, your nervous smile. And I was smitten."

I pause and smile at Elena. She smiles back, a nervous looking smile that reminds me of the smile she wore that day.

"You were smitten with me?" she says quietly. I nod. "My friends always told me you didn't hate me, that you liked me. But I never saw it. I couldn't understand how someone who liked me could be so cruel to me."

That stings, but it's the truth and she has a right to say it.

"I knew by the end of that day that you were completely out of my league. Not just because you were gorgeous and already popular, but because we were from different worlds. You came from money. I didn't. I knew you would never notice me. I told myself it didn't matter, that I could live with that. But as the days went by, I found myself craving your attention. I was the class clown, and you laughed along with the rest of the class when I played up. I figured that was my way in. Do you remember that day in the cafeteria? The day I called you a teacher's pet?"

"You mean the day you started a rumor that I was into a man old enough to be my father?" Elena says.

I nod sheepishly.

"It was the first time you ever spoke to me. And you used that opportunity to make me look stupid. I guess I just wanted to repay the favor."

"I didn't try to make you look stupid," Elena says. "I ... I liked you Ashton. But you were funny and popular and guys like that didn't notice the quiet academic kid. You were talking about your assignment being almost done, but then you got the wrong day for the deadline, and I thought that was my chance. That maybe you would notice me if I helped you out."

"So let me get this straight," I say. "We both liked each other, but we were both so convinced that it would never happen between us that neither of us ever just came out and said it?"

"Pretty much. But I didn't then go on to torment you for the next three years," Elena says.

"I know," I reply. "That moment in the cafeteria, I knew I could have gone two ways after that. I could have apologized to you, or I could have continued to use you for cheap laughs. I wanted to apologise. I really did. But I knew if I did, I would fade back into obscurity and you would just forget I ever existed once more. I figured if I kept making people laugh at your expense, that at least I would be on your radar in some ways."

I sigh and shake my head.

"Now I'm saying this out loud, it sounds so twisted, so pathetic. But to teenage me, it made perfect sense."

"Did you really think making me feel bad every day would ever make me want to date you?" Elena asks.

I shake my head.

"No. But I figured that would never happen no matter what I did. Not unless my mom suddenly won the lottery. Maybe not even then. And I thought your hatred and disdain was better than nothing."

"I can't believe you assumed I would be so shallow," Elena says quietly. "You judged me so completely before you even knew anything about me."

"No," I say quickly. "That's the thing Elena. I wasn't judging you. I didn't blame you for not wanting anything to do with the poor kid. That's how I became the class clown you know. On my first day at Franklin School, I looked around at all of these rich kids, and I knew I would never be anything but an outsider unless I could get their attention for something other than the uniform that was a little bit too small, the shoes that were a little bit scuffed on the toes. I made them laugh and they liked me. It took me a long time to see it, but none of those kids were judging me. I was the one doing that. I judged myself, found myself lacking, and projected all of that onto everyone around me."

"It must have been hard feeling like the odd one out," Elena relents.

"It was," I say. "But that doesn't excuse my behavior. There's nothing I can say to condone the way I treated you. All I can do is tell you that from the bottom of my heart I'm sorry. And that I wish every day I had a time machine so I could go back and do it all differently."

We enter the office car park as I say it. Our cars are the only ones left in there. I head towards my car with Elena still in tow. That's a good sign surely. She hasn't bolted straight to the sanctuary of her own car.

"If you could go back, would you ask me out?" Elena asks me.

"God no," I laugh. "It's a time machine not a confidence machine. I never would have dared even speak to you, let alone ask you out. I just wouldn't have made your life hell. And we would have gone off to college and then university, you still not knowing my name, and me still obsessed with you."

"The irony of that is I would have still known your name. I would have just assumed you didn't know mine," Elena says.

Chapter Twenty-two

Ashton

We reach my car. I go to get my keys out, but Elena makes no move to go to the passenger door. Instead, she rests her ass against the bonnet of my car and stands looking at me. The moonlight makes her hair shine, her eyes sparkle. I want to take her right here on the bonnet of my car, but I know better than to come on too strong now. Instead, I stand a couple of paces back from her. I look her in the eye.

"Elena, I know it's a big ask and it is way more than I deserve, but do you think you can ever forgive me?" I ask.

She doesn't respond immediately and the question hangs in the air between us, a tangible barrier. We're only a couple of feet apart, but it's like school all over again. I feel like we're worlds apart, that I can never reach out and touch her even though she's so close to me.

She studies my face for a moment, her eyes piercing and intense. I wish I could just disappear. I wish I hadn't asked her the question. It's obvious she's going to say no, and then all of my hopes of making her see I'm a different person now will evaporate and I'll be left with nothing but emptiness and regret.

"I want to," she says.

It's not a yes, but it's not a no, and it's way more than I was hoping for. I was so sure she was going to say no, to laugh in my face and demand to know how she thought it would be that easy.

"I really do want to. I always had a crush on you Ashton, and that's never really gone away. But I don't know if I can trust you," she adds. "I'll be honest. I've seen a different side to you and a big part of me thinks you've changed. But there's a small part of me that's just waiting for your true colors to come out. For you to laugh at me for being naïve enough to believe you are different now. Do you understand that?"

I try to find the right words. The magic combination of sounds that will convince Elena I have changed. That I'm not that horrible boy anymore. I can't find them. Instead, the florist's words come back to me. Actions speak louder than words. It's no use me telling Elena I've changed and she can trust me. I have to show her that's the case.

"I do understand it," I say finally. "And I know I can't just wave a magic wand and make you forgive me. But I promise that I'll be right here showing you every day that I'm not the same person anymore for as long as you want me to be. For every day you're willing to try to forgive me, I'll be right here giving you a reason to. How does that sound?"

"Good," she smiles. But then her smile fades and she shakes her head. "But I can't let you do that. What if I can never quite let go of all of the old resentments and you've wasted so much time on me?"

"Time spent with you could never be time wasted Elena," I say. "Please, just give me a chance. Give us a chance. And if you decide you can't forgive me, then just say the world and I'll walk away, no hard feelings."

She studies me again and then she nods her head once.

"Ok," she says.

"Ok you're willing to give us a shot?" I press her.

She nods again and this time, her face breaks into a full on smile. She pushes herself up off the bonnet of my car. She comes to me, but she doesn't tilt her face up, doesn't go for a kiss. Instead, she wraps her arms around my waist and presses herself against my chest. I wrap my arms around her shoulders and hold her, smelling the coconut scent of her hair and the sweeter scent just beneath it.

We stand that way for a long time, and then finally, Elena steps back from me, pulling herself out of arms. I feel cold where her warmth leaves me. She smiles at me again.

"We should probably head home," she says.

I nod and dig my car keys out of my pocket. Elena starts to walk away from me.

"Where are you going?" I say.

She glances back.

"You thought I was going to sleep with you tonight?" she asks.

"No," I say. "We'll take this as slowly as you want to. But I thought I would be dropping you off. You've had a fair bit to drink."

"I had half a bottle of wine. The same as you," she says.

"And three cocktails," I remind her.

"Shit. I forgot about those," she says. She starts to come back. "A ride home would be great if you really don't mind."

"Of course, I don't mind," I tell her.

We get into the car and Elena gives me her address. I head out that way. At first we drive in silence, but then Elena turns to me.

"You and Beatrice. Is that over?" she asks.

"Huh? There is no me and Beatrice. There never was," I say.

"Ashton, I saw her on her knees underneath your desk," Elena says.

Oh great. This again.

"I know you did. And if you'd have given me a chance to explain, you would know that it really wasn't what it must have looked like from where you were standing."

I glance at her and she nods for me to go on.

"I did think Beatrice had a bit of a crush on me. She's always been flirty. And to be honest, I thought at the time she was coming onto me. She sat on the edge of my desk and she was flirting with me, and then she said I looked tense and offered me a shoulder rub. I was tense because she was too damned close. Anyway, she had some files in her hand and when she stood up, she dropped them. She scrambled to pick them up and that's what you saw."

"You think she wanted more though?" Elena asks.

"I did at the time," I say. "But now I'm not so sure."

"Why?" Elena asks.

"I called through for Sandra to make our restaurant reservation for tonight, but Beatrice took the call. She came to see me to tell me the reservation was made and she didn't seem subdued or pissed off or anything. In fact, she teased me when I wouldn't tell her who I was coming here with, saying I should gossip more. I'm starting to think she's just a natural flirt and I read too much into it. It doesn't really matter either way because I wouldn't go there with Beatrice."

"Because she works for you? So do I," Elena points out.

"No. No because she works for me," I say. I look away from the road long enough to catch Elena's eye. "Because she's not you."

Elena swallows audibly and the atmosphere in the car changes just like that. It's gone from what felt like two friends chatting to a charged feeling that hangs in the air. It's like a promise of what's to come and I can feel my cock hardening at the look in Elena's eye. It takes everything I have to look back at the road, but even as I do, all I can see in front of me is Elena's eyes, the way her pupils dilated as she looked at me. The way they displayed her lust so clearly.

God I want her so badly. I meant what I said – I'll take this as slowly as she wants to – but it's going to be hard. The hardest thing I've ever done. I already feel like I'm losing control.

We drive the rest of the way to Elena's place in silence. I try to think of something to say, but I can't think of anything that won't risk ruining the mood between us and I don't want that. Still, it's not an uncomfortable silence. It's a silence filled with the promise of something delicious to come.

I know Elena feels the electricity in the air every bit as much as I do. She shuffles in her seat and I'd like to think it's because she's turned on and the seat rubbing against her pussy is driving her as wild as my trousers confining my cock is driving me.

"It's this one coming up on your right," Elena says, breaking the silence and nodding towards a modest but neat looking two bedroomed house that's coming up.

I pull up outside of the wooden gate and cut the engine. I look over the small front garden. There's a neatly mown lawn and a border filled with flowers and tiny shrubs. I turn back to Elena as she unbuckles her seat belt and smiles at me.

"Thank you for a lovely night Ashton," she says. "I really did have a good time. And thank you for being honest with me."

I nod at her.

"Good night Elena," I say with a smile.

She turns from me and puts her hand on the door handle, ready to get out of the car, and I know I can't let her go without kissing her. Surely a kiss isn't moving too fast. I reach out and grab her wrist and she turns back to me.

I lean closer to her. For half a second, she resists me and I think she's going to shut me down. I can see the indecision in her eyes, but then they clear and her hand falls away from the door handle and her fingers trails over my neck and into my hair as she leans in and our lips meet.

I brush my lips gently over hers. My cock is going wild, screaming to be freed from its prison of clothes. Heat floods my body and makes me crazy. My mind races, showing me all the things I want to do to Elena, all of the things I want her to do to me. I don't know how I manage to pull back from her, how I manage to tear my lips away from hers. I only know that it's the right thing to do. I don't want to come on too strong now and undo the bit of progress I think I've made with Elena tonight.

"Good night," I say again with a smile, my face a half inch from Elena's.

She makes no move to leave the car. She doesn't even try to pull further back from me. Her hand is still in my hair. My hand is still on her shoulder. She smiles at me. A smile full of sex and orgasms and I hear myself moaning. My moan is cut short when Elena pulls my head back down to hers and our lips meet again, her mouth swallowing my moan.

She brings her other hand up and runs it down my chest, sending shivers through my body. I move my hand from her shoulder, wrapping it around her and pulling her closer to me. My whole body tingles, and I feel ecstasy flooding through my veins.

I push my tongue into her mouth, tasting wine and chocolate. Her tongue comes to meet mine and they massage each other, both of us desperate to taste the other, to claim each other's mouths as our own. I want to taste every part of Elena. To claim every part of her body with my tongue, my fingers, my cock. I want to make her mine in every way conceivable.

My heart is racing and my breath is coming in short, ragged pants. It's taking everything I have not to push my hand beneath Elena's skirt and feel the sweet wetness I know I would feel between her legs. She has no such qualms. Her hand moves from my chest, getting lower. She rubs it over my stomach and then the back of her hand brushes against my swollen cock. I gasp in a breath and moan into her mouth again.

She moves her hand away from me and for a horrible moment, I think I've scared her off, but her hand comes back as quickly as it left. It's not on my cock though. She pulls my shirt out of my trousers and pushes her hand up inside of it, running her nails over the bare skin of my stomach.

My cock pulses, urging me to get some release. Heat floods me. I have never wanted anyone like I want her. I pull back from our kiss and look into her eyes for a second.

"God Elena, you drive me crazy," I say, my voice husky with lust for her.

She smiles, a half-smile that sends another pulse of desire through me. Her lips glisten, damp from our kiss. She leaves her hand inside of my shirt, rubbing her fingers over my nipples and making me suck in a sharp breath. Her other hand comes out of my hair and moves over my cheek. She runs her fingers over my lips and I suck them into my mouth.

I massage them with my tongue, licking and sucking on them. The whole time, she looks me in the eye, her lips parted slightly and her chest heaving. Just when I think I can't take the way she's looking at me like she wants to devour me for another second, she pulls her fingers away from my lips. She rests her hand on my shoulder, teasing at the sensitive skin of my neck with her fingertips and then she leans in and mashes her lips against mine again.

I lose myself completely in her kiss, in her. I have to have this woman. I have to make her mine, whatever it takes. My whole body is on fire. I feel like a giant nerve ending, one that is being teased and teased to within an inch of its life.

If this is what she can do to me with just a kiss, I can only imagine what she's going to do me if she ever lets us go any further.

Chapter Twenty-three

Elena

My whole body is on fire as Ashton kisses me. His kiss is deep and tender, the sort of kiss that makes me imagine not only having sex with him, but also building a life with him. It's not the sort of kiss you share with someone if you only want to fuck them and then move on. But it still awakens my nerve endings, makes my body tingle. It makes me want to take Ashton inside, take him upstairs to my bedroom and fuck the living daylights out of him if I'm being totally honest with myself.

Something still holds me back though. I know we've had a great time tonight, and Ashton has been nothing but charming, but I'm still not ready to throw myself at him physically, and consequently, throw myself at his mercy mentally. I'm hugely attracted to him, there's no denying this. And the more I get to know him, the more I realize it's not just physical. But it doesn't mean I'm ready to let my guard down and let myself be vulnerable with him. Not yet. I hope to get to that point, I really do, but I'm not quite there yet. It's going to take more than one good date to undo years of pain and despite everything, there's still a small part of me

146

that's waiting for the other shoe to drop; waiting for the old Ashton to come out, to make comments about my looks, my figure. To laugh at me and make me feel small.

Despite myself and my reservations, I still can't stop the way Ashton's touch, his kiss, makes me feel deep inside of myself. He makes me feel alive, sexually powerful — attractive. It's dangerous to let myself acknowledge this, to leave myself open to being hurt, but it feels so damned good that I just can't help myself. I feel like I am powerless to resist Ashton, and I think in part, it's because a large part of me really doesn't want to resist him anymore.

My pussy is dripping wet, aching for him to touch me down there, to fill me up and make me his. My clit is screaming at me, my body crying out for release. I try to ignore the feeling, focusing instead on the kiss we're sharing. Ashton's tongue massages mine, tasting me, delving deeper, becoming one with me, and my body is done listening to my head.

I reach up and push my hands into Ashton's hair, deepening our kiss, making it more passionate. I move my hands down his body, needing to touch every part of him, clawing at him in my desperation for him. I have to have him. I have to have some release. But no, I can't do that. Not yet. I try to tell myself it'll make it all the more special when we do fuck, but it's not working. What I know and what I feel are two completely separate things at this point.

As I kiss Ashton deeply, he wraps his arms around my waist and tugs me closer towards him. I know what he wants. He's trying to pull me across the gear stick and onto his lap. I could resist his tugging. I know he would stop trying to pull me onto him if I did, but I'm done resisting him. I don't want to deprive myself of this any longer. I'm done listening to my head. It's time to give my body what it wants.

The decision is made in a split second and I move with him, pushing myself up and across the gap between us. I clamber onto Ashton's lap, straddling his thighs, without breaking our kiss. My pussy presses against his cock, only the thin layer of my panties and his pants between us now. I can feel how hard his cock is, how big it is, and it just makes me want him more.

Knowing this is turning him on as much as it is me, it empowers me further, giving me the upper hand, and knowing this makes me feel giddy inside. I am driving him wild and I know it. It's not just his hard cock that gives it away, it's in the way he groans longingly as we kiss... the way his hands are moving up and down my back, my sides, like he wants to explore every part of my body.

I can't help myself. My pussy is in control now, and it's driving me too crazy to resist it's pull any longer. I start to move my hips slowly backwards and forwards, moving myself up and down Ashton's length. It teases me, bringing me even closer to the edge, but it offers some relief too, as his cock presses against my clit, giving me the touch my body is craving.

Ashton groans again, louder this time. He pulls his lips from mine and looks into my eyes. I can see the longing in his eyes. His chest is heaving where he's panting for air.

"Oh God Elena, you have no idea what you're doing to me, do you?" he says in a low, almost tortured voice.

I have every idea what I'm doing to him. It's exactly the same thing he's been doing to me since he grabbed my wrist and kissed me. I don't reply. I just smile at him and keep moving, grinding myself harder onto him.

His hands pause on my hips for a moment and then he leans closer to me, running his tongue lightly over my neck. It's my turn to moan and groan as tingles spread down my neck and over my chest, bringing my nipples to attention. He keeps licking my skin, and then he runs his wet lips down my neck, kissing and suckling at me.

His hands start to move again, pushing my dress up and moving beneath it. They move over my bare back and then he runs his nails down my sides. I suck in a breath as my skin puckers into rows of tingling goose bumps beneath his touch. He moves one hand around to the front of my body, cupping one of my breasts and kneading it. My bare, hard nipple rubs over his palm and I feel a shock of electricity flood down my stomach, meeting the longing need from my clit in the center of my body.

I bite my lip to keep from crying out when Ashton rubs my nipple hard between his fingers and his thumb, making it even more sensitive. He pinches it gently and holds it clamped in place for a moment, then he releases it, and the blood rushes back in. This time, I can't stop the strangled cry from leaving my lips as more electricity courses through me, bringing more of my nerves to life.

Ashton moves his hand back down my body, trailing his fingers over my stomach and then moving lower. He runs his fingers over the outside of my panties, setting off my clit tingling again.

"You're so wet," he whispers as he feels the damp material clinging to me.

His words only make me wetter as my pussy clenches, begging to be filled. Ashton runs his fingers over my panties again, and then he pushes his fingers under the waistband. He looks me straight in the eye as his fingers move lower. I can't look away from his eyes, and knowing he is seeing me as he moves his fingers closer to my pussy, really seeing me, only turns me on more.

He pushes his fingers between my lips, rubbing them over my clit and fire floods through me. He growls as his fingers rub over me, spreading my juices around. I moan as his touch makes my pussy clench again. His fingers find my clit and he starts to work it from side to side. My insides are going crazy as my orgasm builds up.

Ashton leans forward as he works me. He runs his lips gently over mine, not quite a kiss, just enough of a touch to tease me and make me want his mouth on mine again. He runs his tongue over my lips and then he nips my bottom lip between his teeth, tugging it sharply while making me cry out as the slight pain in my lip becomes a tingle that moves through my body, accentuating the delicious feeling in my clit and in my pussy.

He releases my lip and pushes his mouth against mine again in a kiss so desperate, so filled with need, that I almost unbutton his pants and ride him right here at the curb outside of my house. I kiss him back with equal fervor, pushing my hands into his hair once more. I keep my hands in his hair, partly because I like the way it feels, and partly to stop myself from going through with the idea in my head — the one where I fuck his brains out in my front street.

His hand keeps working my clit and I move my hips, getting more purchase against his fingers and upping the pace of his teasing touch. I feel him smile against my lips, amused by my eagerness.

Ashton moves his hand off my hip and strokes his way to the back of my panties. He pushes his hand beneath the waistband and cups my bare ass cheek. His touch is soft, gentle. It only makes me want him more. He moves his hand over my ass, getting lower, and I tense up slightly as his fingers move through my ass crack. Is he going to attempt to try ass play on me? His fingers keep moving and I relax again.

He pushes them into my pussy from behind and I gasp. I pull my mouth away from his, gasping and panting, trying to suck in some air. The feeling of his touch in two places at once like this is so intense and I feel like I can't breathe while he's kissing me. I press my face against Ashton's neck, breathing in his scent and grounding myself for a moment as my body absorbs the new level to my lust.

His hands move in perfect harmony together, one working my clit, one working my g-spot. My body takes over completely and I buck my hips, wanting to get more from Ashton, needing to come before I explode.

My orgasm finally hits me, an intense feeling of heat and pleasure starts in my pussy and my clit then moves up to my stomach, making my muscles clench as my insides clench and unclench. My pussy tightens around Ashton's fingers, but it doesn't stop him from working me, pushing me deeper into the whirling storm of my pleasure.

I stop moving my hips as my back goes rigid, pulling my face away from Ashton's neck. I throw my head back, my mouth hanging open, searching for a breath that isn't coming. I can feel the tendons in my neck stretching as my pussy clenches tightly around Ashton's fingers again. My clit is pulsing so hard I think it might actually be physically vibrating.

Another wave of pleasure sweeps over me, and I feel a rush of warm liquid running from my pussy, coating Ashton's hand. He moans as my juices crash over him. His fingers stop working me and finally, I can breathe again. I suck in gasping breath after gasping breath, trying to get myself back under some sort of control.

My head comes back up as my muscles finally relax. Ashton slips his hands back out of my panties and I scramble back into my own seat, no longer able to meet Ashton's eye.

Oh my God, what have I done?

I've let us go too fast, let my body take control of my head which essentially means I lost control altogether. And now Ashton is going to expect more. And if I say no to more, he's going to think I just led him on, used him to get my own orgasm.

"Elena?" he says softly.

I force myself to look at him – I don't owe him sex, but I do owe him some respect.

He looks at me with concern in his eyes. "Are you all right?" he asks.

"I — yes. No. I'm sorry," I say with a loud sigh.

"What for?" Ashton asks. He's frowning now, but he doesn't look annoyed. He still looks concerned.

"We shouldn't have done that. I shouldn't have done that. I just got caught up in the moment and..." I trail off.

"And now you regret it," Ashton finishes for me.

"Not regret it as such. I just — I'm not ready to go any further and I don't want you to think I'm just messing with you," I finally admit.

To my surprise Ashton laughs.

I stare at him questioningly.

He shakes his head slightly. "Would I like to come in and make love to you all night Elena? Of course, I would. Can I wait until you're ready to do that? Yes, one hundred percent. And if you decide you're not ever going to want that, then I'll understand."

"Really?" I can't help but whisper.

Ashton laughs again and nods his head. "Really. Elena, I've waited over a decade for this moment. I can wait a little longer," he reassures me. "You mean a lot to me, and I already know that you're more than worth waiting for."

I smile a little tentatively and when he returns my smile, I feel myself smiling back at him properly. "For what it's worth, I'm glad I gave in and we did that," I say.

Ashton winks at me and then looks pointedly at his hand that's glistening with moisture. "Oh trust me, I know you enjoyed yourself," he smiles.

I feel myself blushing but I return his smile. Maybe this wasn't such a mistake after all. I know I have to get out of the car though. If Ashton kisses me like that again, I really don't think I'm going to be able to stop myself from going any further. "Well, goodnight then," I say awkwardly.

"Sweet dreams, Elena. See you tomorrow." He leans in for a kiss.

I turn my face to meet it. It's not a lust filled kiss. It's a soft, tender kiss. Ashton doesn't linger, and when he pulls his face from mine, I'm relieved that he hasn't kissed me hard enough to make me lose control again. I'm also a little disappointed that he's kept his word, not pushed me, because if he did push me, I would have given in, and had an excuse for letting myself get lost in the moment again.

I get out of the car before I can say or do anything I might regret. I walk up the path to the front door, waiting for the car engine to roar into life behind me, but it doesn't. Ashton stays where he is until I open my front door and push it open. I step inside and then I turn and wave at him. He blows me a kiss and I smile to myself. Only as I'm closing the door does the engine finally roar to life and Ashton drives away, and I get the feeling he didn't stay because he hoped I'd change my mind, but that he stayed to make sure I got inside safely. It's sweet and I like that he cares about me on more than just a physical level.

I close and lock the front door and then I stand behind it, my back pressed against it. I am filled with regret about what just happened, but I surprise myself, because I don't regret what we did. I regret that we didn't do more.

Chapter Twenty-four

Ashton

I had another long and sleepless night last night. I got home from dropping Elena off, showered and went straight to bed, but I knew even before I closed my eyes that sleep was going to elude me. My cock is still craving Elena's touch.

I want her so much it's fucking painful and the feeling never goes away. Even after the time we spent together tonight, in the restaurant and then in my car, I want more. I feel like no matter how much time I spend with Elena... it'll never be enough. I'll always want more.

I jerked off as I lay awake in the darkness, my mind taking me back to the moment Elena came on my hand, but it gave me very little relief. Even as I came, I started thinking about what it would feel to come inside of Elena, and within seconds, I was hard again.

I spent the night trying to ignore the longing I feel, but it was useless. I kept seeing Elena throwing her head back with wild abandon as she came on my hand. I kept feeling the sticky silkiness of her juices coating my skin. And I kept imagining the sweet taste of her kisses.

As morning rolled around, other thoughts began to penetrate my brain, thoughts that kept me awake for a different reason. I kept seeing Elena's face after she clambered off my lap. The regret there had been clear to see. And all I can do is hope my reassurances are enough, and that she was telling the truth – she only regretted going too fast – not that she regretted being with me at all.

I cling to the tiny shred of hope she gave me when she told me she would at least try to let go of all the old resentments and give us a chance. I really hope she can. My God, do I hope she can let it all go and give us a chance to start over. But if she can't, then I'll have no one to blame but myself. I'm the one who made her feel that way in the first place, and I'll just have to learn to live with knowing Elena can never be mine. Something tells me it's easier to think this than it will be to actually do it, but what choice will I have?

I think I finally managed to drop off to sleep at about 5.30. My alarm is set for six and it blares out now, dragging me back from the sleep I've craved all night. I wake up feeling hungover, despite only having drank half a bottle of wine. I sit up and run my hands over my face, trying to wipe away the tiredness hanging over me. It's no use. The only thing that might help me feel more awake is Elena.

I smile to myself when I realize her car is still at the office. It gives me an excuse to text her. Hopefully, even to see her if she accepts my offer. I reach across to my bedside cabinet and pick my phone up, instantly feeling more awake. I type out a text message and read it back.

Good morning, Beautiful. I've just remembered your car is still at the office. Want me to swing by and pick you up around 8.30? x

I put the phone down on the bedside cabinet again and get out of bed. I'll drive myself crazy just sitting here waiting for a response. If I even get one, that is. God, what if she just ignores my text altogether? What then?

I go downstairs and down the hallway through to the kitchen to make coffee. While I wait, I put sugar in my cup and grab the milk from the fridge. I pour a cup and then force myself to go and sit down at the table rather than going back for my phone. I debate pouring out some cereal, but my stomach is churning and I know I won't be able to eat anything.

I finish my coffee and rinse my cup out in the sink, and then I finally go back up the stairs to the bedroom. It feels like forever has passed, but when I pick my phone up, there are no new messages. My heart sinks and I slam it back down a little harder than I would have liked to. I mean I get it if she doesn't want me to pick her up, but would it have killed her to text me back, even if she was just saying no thank you?

With my hopes of hearing from Elena dashed, I can feel how tired I am once more. My eyes feel gritty as I open up my wardrobe and start getting dressed. I debate not going into the office at all today, but I decide against it. It might soon be the only place I get to see Elena at all, and the last thing I want is her thinking I'm freaking out about last night.

I am almost dressed when my phone beeps. I practically dive across the room and snatch it up, well aware I'm acting like a teenager who has asked his girl to the prom and is desperately waiting for her answer. My heart skips a beat when I see Elena's name on the screen. I guess I was just being impatient. I smile to myself when I read her text.

Sorry it took me so long to answer, I was in the shower. That would be great, thank you x.

I punch the air in joy. She doesn't hate me. She's not avoiding me. She was just in the shower. This brings up an image that makes my cock pulse with desire. Elena naked, soaping herself, her hands rubbing over her skin, making herself slippery with the soap. I swallow hard and try to push the image away. It doesn't work, but I no longer care. I can live with being frustrated now, since I know I'm going to see her sooner than I dared to hope. I no longer feel tired. I feel like I'm more alive than I've ever been. Like I'm walking on air.

I finish getting ready quickly and go for another coffee. This time, I take my phone with me, and when it stays silent, I don't mind at all.

The time is dragging now. Maybe it's a good thing. I need to get a grip of myself. I can't turn up at Elena's like an excitable wreck. I need to get this out of my system before I see her.

Finally, it's eight o'clock and I can leave the house. I want to pop back to the florist's place before I collect Elena and order her some more flowers. I drive to the florist's shop and go inside.

The little bell rings and the same florist appears. She gives me a warm smile when she sees me. "She liked the orchids I take it?"

"Well, we went on our first date last night, so I'm thinking yes," I say, unable to take the goofy grin off my face.

"Fantastic," she says. "So what can I do for you today?"

"I'm thinking something cheerful and bright," I say. She purses her lips for a moment and then she begins leafing through a catalogue. "How about this one?" She turns the catalogue towards me and shows me a beautiful arrangement of large daisies, sunflowers and greenery.

I nod. It's perfect. "Yes, she'll love that one." I grin.

The florist hands me a card to write my message on as she loads up a screen on her computer. She double checks my name and waits for a second. "Are all of the delivery details the same?" she asks.

"Yes," I say.

I think for a moment and then I write on the card.

"If I wait for eternity for you, you'll still be worth the wait A x."

I pay for the flowers and leave the shop with a genuine spring in my step. Whatever happens today, I have a feeling it's going to be a good day.

Chapter Twenty-five

Ashton

I drive across town and pull up outside of Elena's place at around eight twenty-five. I don't know what to do now. Do I text her? Beep the horn? Go to her door? I'm afraid going to her door will look too formal and pushy, and a beep or a text will be too much, like I'm trying to hurry her up. I am saved from having to make the decision when Elena's front door opens and she steps out.

She looks amazing. She's wearing a pale pink knee length dress with a white jacket and white strappy shoes. Her hair is loose around her face.

I want to push my hands into her hair and kiss her hard to greet her, but I hold myself back as she gets into the car. "Morning," I say.

"Morning," she replies. She looks at me and smiles a little uncertainly.

I realize it's because I'm just sitting here and she's wondering why we're not pulling away. I return her smile and pull away from the curb and she relaxes a little bit. This tells me she probably doesn't want to talk about last night, which is all I want to talk about, to relive. I suddenly find myself completely lost for something to say to her that won't either make her uncomfortable or be about work.

Again, she saves me from having to come up with something. "You'll never guess who sent me a friend request on Facebook this morning. Archie Maynard," she says.

I never would have thought of him at all before now. "Archie Maynard as in the dumb kid whose parents donated so much money to the school that they didn't dare suggest he leave for a less academic school?" I say, surprised.

"Yeah," Elena says. "I guess he got the last laugh on that one though. He's an actor now and he's just landed a role in a big movie."

"Good for him," I say, meaning it. Archie was like me at school; the kid everyone knew didn't really belong there. Unlike me though, he didn't find a way to fit in, a way to make the other kids like him, and he was always a bit of a loner. It's good that he's found his place in the world, and yeah, it's good that he can give the middle finger to all of the staff from Franklin School who all thought he'd never make anything of his life.

We chat a bit more about Archie and a few of the other kids who we went to school with, and by the time we pull up in the office car park, any awkwardness between us is gone. We still haven't talked about last night, but I don't think that's a bad thing. If Elena regretted it and didn't want to give us a chance, she would surely have said something by now and not just pretended everything was normal and kept me hanging. Right? I sure hope so.

We get out of the car just as Beatrice's car pulls up.

Beatrice and Karen get out of the car. Karen doesn't seem too interested in Elena and me, but Beatrice grins widely when she sees us together. I guess she knows who my date last night was with now. That will be around the office before I've even have a chance to take my jacket off. I don't care. I don't care who knows Elena and I went out together. Hell, look at her. I want the whole world to know this perfect woman chose to give me a chance.

"Well, it looks like someone chose the right restaurant." Beatrice grins after we say good morning and are heading towards the office doors.

Elena blushes slightly next to me.

I look at Beatrice sharply. "Beatrice, that's not really an appropriate thing to say," I tell her.

"Oh relax, I'm just messing with you." She laughs.

I want to say more, to make her see that Elena and I are not going to become a piece of office gossip, but if I say anything now, it's only going to make Elena more uncomfortable, so I bite my tongue. At least Elena and I are both wearing different clothes from yesterday. If I had stayed over at her place, it would be totally obvious now.

Beatrice rummages in her hand bag for a moment. "Oh dammit," she says. "I left my phone in the car. You three go on and I'll catch up to you." She turns and walks away. She's acting strangely again. Her voice sounded kind of shaky and she wouldn't look at any of us.

I have no idea what's going on with her. Maybe she's just embarrassed because she realized her comment crossed a line.

"Which restaurant did you go to?" Karen asks as we cross the lobby. "I swear, I'm not looking for gossip fodder. I have a date this weekend and I want to go somewhere nice."

I tell her where we went.

Elena just walks, looking straight ahead of her.

We get into the elevator and I'm glad when a few other people get in with us. By now, Beatrice has likely retrieved her phone and texted half of the company about our arrival here this morning, but it doesn't seem as obvious when we step out with a throng of other people. We head along the corridor and Karen stops at her desk.

Elena and I keep walking.

"Are you ok?" I ask her when we're out of earshot of the secretaries' cubicles. "I'm sorry about that back there."

"I'm fine," she says. "And it's not your fault Beatrice has nothing in her life except gossip. I guess I'm just a little embarrassed. How long before everyone here thinks I only got the job because something was going on between us?"

"Screw what anyone else says. You got the job because you're good at what you do," I say. Is that entirely true though? I mean she is good at her job, but would I have entertained someone who tanked their interview like that when I had other candidates who were as well qualified as her if she hadn't been the love of my life for as long as I can remember? Maybe. Maybe not. But it doesn't matter. It's no one else's business.

"Yeah, fuck them." Elena smiles. "There'll likely only be Beatrice that has a problem with it, and she seems like the sort of person who finds a problem with everything and everyone."

"You don't sound like you like Beatrice much," I say.

Elena shrugs. "It's nothing personal. I just don't like her type. You know the gossipy type who seems to know everything about everyone."

"She's harmless really," I say, more to try and make Elena feel better than from any loyalty to Beatrice.

"Yeah, people tend to take those types with a pinch of salt anyway. If she sees two people in a car together and assumes they must have had sex, that really says more about her dating life than mine," Elena says.

"You think maybe her and Karen were getting it on last night?" I grin, wiggling my eyebrows.

Elena laughs and gently shoves my arm. "That's not what I meant and you know it."

She's still laughing when we reach the end of the corridor and split off to go into our separate offices.

Chapter Twenty-six

Ashton

I run over my day's calendar and notice the first thing on the agenda is a meeting with the secretaries. I gather up my notes for the meeting and make my way through to the smaller conference room, conference room B. The secretaries and Elena are already in there when I arrive. Someone has poured me a coffee which I pick up and sip gratefully. "Thank you whoever did this," I say, holding the cup up a little.

"You're welcome," Beatrice purrs.

I begin to run through the points on my list. Elena takes notes beside me and I'm more than aware of her knee occasionally brushing against mine beneath the table. I'm tempted to put my hand beneath the table and run it up her thigh, beneath her dress, but I'm not sure how she'll take it and so I don't.

The meeting goes smoothly enough, although I do notice Beatrice giving Elena and me some strange looks through it. I just can't fathom her out. She's definitely acting like she's jealous of us, but I can't decide if it's because she does have a thing for me after all, or if it's more like what Elena said, and Beatrice is worried that Elena will get preferential treatment.

I don't have time to dwell on it. After the meeting, I have a brunch appointment with a client. The meeting goes well and I come back into the office in a good mood. To be honest, if the meeting had gone badly, I think I still would have come into the office in a good mood because of Elena. I return to my office and begin responding to emails.

There's a quiet knock on my door and I look up. My heart skips a beat when I see Elena standing there. I smile and beckon for her to come in.

She comes in and gives me a smile and then she bites on her lip for a moment. "I just wanted to say thank you. For the flowers," she says. "They're beautiful."

"No. You're beautiful," I say.

She blushes a little but she looks pleased.

I decide now is as good a time as any to broach the subject of Elena and me "I had a great time last night Elena," I say.

"Me too," she agrees.

I decide to take a chance and I get up and move over to my bookshelves. I beckon to Elena. "Come over here a minute. I want to show you something."

She walks over towards me and looks up at me.

I grin at her.

"What?" she asks.

"This here is a great little corner," I say. "Because no one can see us through the glass."

"Really," Elena says, smiling up at me. "It would be a terrible shame to waste that knowledge."

I'm still smiling as I lean down and kiss her. Our lips meet and it feels right, like they were always meant to fit together this way. She moves closer to me, pressing her body tightly against mine. Her hands roam over my back, tugging my shirt loose and moving underneath it.

My cock is instantly hard at her touch and the tighter she presses herself against me, the more turned on I am becoming. I want so badly to turn her around, bend her over and take her right here. I can't do that though. It would be awkward enough if a member of staff, or worse, a client, catches us kissing like this, let alone anything else.

Elena seems to come to the same realization because she pulls away from me.

I groan, a sound of frustration. I want her back in my arms... to have my mouth back on hers.

She giggles slightly when she sees the effect she's having on me.

I shake my head but I smile. "You're making me crazy, Elena."

"Oh, okay. Maybe we'd better stop meeting like this then," she says.

I shake my head quickly. "I didn't say being crazy was a bad thing did I?"

She laughs softly and starts to move away. "Well, some of us have work to do."

I can't take my eyes off her ass as she walks towards the door. She's swaying her hips more than usual, inviting me to watch her walking away.

Pausing at the door, she looks back at me and grins. "You might want to tuck your shirt in."

Then she's gone as quickly as she came, leaving me reeling once more.

I SIT NERVOUSLY WATCHING my phone, waiting for it to beep. I'm waiting for Elena to text me. I know she will. I'm just nervous about what she will say.

I did something stupid, something daring. It felt like a great idea at the time, but now I'm not so sure it was. I ordered some lingerie for Elena and had it delivered to her home. I paid extra to have it delivered by 10am Saturday, and it's now 10.30. I've had a message from the company confirming the package was handed to the resident, so I know she received it.

The lingerie is sexy, but in my opinion, classy too. I didn't want to send her something she might think looked trashy. I opted for a pair of cute little lacy black panties with deep purple detailing and a matching, low cut bra. I was very tempted by the corset, but I'm not sure if Elena would be into that kind of thing. At least by playing it relatively safe I know she'll at least be able to wear my gift – even if it offends her that I took a leap of faith and sent her underwear.

I don't think it will offend her though. I really hope it won't. It's not like she's been shying away from me. Since we went to the restaurant, we've had many stolen kisses in the office and we've been out for dinner two more times. I know she's starting to let her guard down around me. It's driving me crazy being around Elena, holding her, kissing her, and not being able to go any further.

I don't want to rush her, but she just turns me on so much, and holding myself back from her all of the time is killing me.

Once I knew Elena had received the gift, I sent her a text message telling her I would love to see her wearing the underwear. That was twenty minutes ago and I haven't heard back from her yet. It's worrying me a little bit, but I try to keep myself in check. Maybe she was on her way out and hasn't had a chance to open it yet. Or maybe she just hasn't seen my text message yet.

I'm confident she'll reply. Even if it's just to tell me there's no chance of that. This is what I'm really afraid of. If she feels like I'm pushing her too fast, panics and takes a step back.

Come on Elena. Just put a man out of his misery I think to myself as I continue to stare at my still silent phone. The blank screen stares back at me, and I feel like it's mocking my torment.

Chapter Twenty-seven

Elena

I have just stepped out of the shower when my doorbell rings. Dammit. I'm not expecting anyone and I debate just ignoring the door, but I know if I do that, it will bug me not knowing who it was or what they might have wanted.

I pull my robe on and belt it shut as I run down the stairs. The doorbell blares again, as I run down the stairs. Now I'm definitely glad I decided to start coming down to answer it. It really would have bugged me who I'd missed when they're this insistent. I reach the door after what feels like forever but really can't have been more than a minute or two, and pull it open.

A man stands before me with a box in his hands. "Elena Woods?"

"Yes," I say, a little cautiously.

"I've got a delivery for you."

"I didn't order anything," I say. My suspicions are being raised, and I'm conscious of the fact I'm naked underneath my thin robe.

The man doesn't seem in the least bit fazed by my caution. He shrugs his shoulders. "Says here it was sent by an Ashton Miller," he informs me.

I relax. It's a gift from Ashton. I nod, acknowledging I'll take the delivery.

The man hands me a small machine that looks like a card reader. "You just need to sign that to say I delivered the package."

I awkwardly scribble my name using the little grey stylus he pushes into my hand, although my scribble comes out looking nothing like my real signature. The man takes the stylus and his machine back and hands me the box. It's light, so light, I can't even begin to fathom out what might be in here.

"Have a good day," the man says, walking away from the door.

"Thanks, you too," I call after him.

I close the door and go through to the kitchen, excited at what might be in the box. I get a knife and cut carefully through the packing tape and then I put the knife to one side and open the box. Layers of snow white tissue paper sit on the top of the box. I push them to one side and gasp slightly when I see what Ashton has sent me. Inside the box is a gorgeous black and purple lacy lingerie set. I pull them from the box and hold them up to look at them. I love them. They're sexy in an understated way. They say classy woman who wants to look good in the bedroom rather than whore who just wants to fuck. Ashton seemingly has very good taste.

As I'm studying the underwear, I hear my phone beeping from upstairs. I smile to myself, almost certain it will be Ashton asking if I like the gift. I put the underwear back in the box and take it upstairs with me. I go to the bedroom and grab my phone. It is indeed a text message from Ashton. My pussy clenches when I read it, my breath catching in my throat.

I'd love to see you wearing those x.

I sit down on the edge of the bed to think. I was determined to take it slow with Ashton, and already, things are moving faster than I imagined they would. But it's not as though Ashton is pressuring me. I'm as into him as he is into me, and he's not the only one who instigates stolen kisses in the office. And he's not the one who spent dinner last night running his toes up my leg. Nope. That was all me. I knew the effect it was having on him, and I loved it, but the truth is, it's having the same effect on me. I'm not sure I want to go slowly anymore. I don't think I want to keep waiting. I'm not sure I can.

Did I ever imagine myself here with Ashton? Nope. Well, not in any realistic way, only in a teenage fantasy way. But now I am, and although I know I'm falling for him fast, is that really such a bad thing? Would it hurt to indulge myself a little?

I mean Ashton has definitely grown up. He's not that same little kid who was so desperate for my attention that he made me feel like crap. He's even apologized for all of that, and I knew when he was explaining it to me that he regretted handling it the way he did.

Fuck it, I think to myself. I'm going to do it. If he wants to see me wearing this, then he will.

I'm smiling to myself as I go to my dresser. I dry my hair and apply a little bit of makeup, and then I slip my robe off and put the lingerie on. It's a perfect fit and as soon as I put it on, I feel empowered and sexy. I look at myself in the mirror. I look good, even if I do say so myself. But something is missing. I think for a moment and then I go to my underwear drawer.

I pull out a suspender belt in black and a pair of black stockings. I put them on, my heart racing and my pussy wet. The silk of the stockings against my legs feels good, but not as good as I imagine Ashton's fingers would feel running up my legs. I move to my wardrobe and take out a pair of patent black leather high heels. I slip them on and go back to the mirror.

I nod to myself. Now my look is complete.

I think for a moment and then I move to my bed. I pull the duvet straight and run my hands over it, getting out any creases. I grab my phone and lay down on the bed. I pull my knees up and open my legs a little and then I take a picture. I get to my knees and bend forward, posing on all fours. I have to raise one hand to take the picture, but I don't think the effect is lost. I arch my back and pout then take another picture.

I am quite enjoying this little impromptu photo shoot now and I take a few more photos, one a full length shot of me in the mirror, and another couple where I'm draped over the ground or the bed. I take one with one leg on a chair.

I sit back down on the edge of the bed and begin to look through the photos. I choose the chair shot. I smile to myself as I text Ashton back.

Your wish is my command x.

I send the text message and then I send the photo. I wait, anticipation throbbing through my whole body. I don't have long to wait before my phone beeps.

The things I want to do to you x.

Like what? I send back.

Like lick your pussy until you come in my mouth and then fuck you raw.

A shiver goes through my body at the thought of Ashton licking my pussy, at the thought of him fucking me, stretching my pussy out and filling me up. I think for a second, and then in a moment of daring, I send Ashton the photo of me on my knees bending forward. *I'll be waiting x,* I send.

I can almost taste you. Ashton sends back almost instantly.

I am so wet now I can feel my juices soaking into my new panties and dampening the tops of my thighs. I lay back on the bed and push my hand into the panties. I start to stroke my clit as I send a text back to Ashton with my other hand. *I'd like to taste you too.*

Imagining Ashton's reaction to the text makes me even more turned on. My fingers are moving faster and my breath is coming in short pants. My clit is throbbing deliciously and my whole body feels warm and alive. I drop my phone onto the bed and grab the duvet with my now spare hand, twisting it into my fist as my stomach contracts and my pussy clenches.

I am working myself faster and harder, on the brink of orgasm when my phone beeps again. I can't stop now. I keep going, momentarily ignoring the phone. Knowing that Ashton's text is waiting for me spurs me on and I let myself go over the edge. My orgasm blooms through me, spreading heat through my body and out into my limbs. I let out a quiet moan as pleasure bursts inside of me. My pussy tightens and relaxes and I start to coast down from my pleasure.

I pull my hand out of my panties and lay in place for a moment, getting my breath back. My limbs feel heavy, my body sated, yet at the same time, I feel light, like I might just float away.

Chapter Twenty-eight

Elena

Once I get my breath back, I reach for my phone and read Ashton's text.

I can't wait until dinner to see you. Let's have lunch. I'll pick you up in half an hour.

A delicious tingle runs through me at the thought of seeing Ashton so soon. I smile to myself and push my hand back into my panties. I lift my ass up from the mattress a little and close my eyes and then I raise my phone and snap another picture. I check the picture and smile.

I sit up and debate for a moment and then I type out a text. *I am a little hungry from my workout.* I send the text and wait a couple of seconds, long enough for Ashton to read the message and be a little confused by it. I send the picture. That will clear up his confusion I think to myself with a grin. His reply comes back almost instantly and it's just one word.

Fuck.

I think it sums this up nicely.

I decide to leave the new lingerie on. It would be rude not to after Ashton went to the trouble of sending me it, and maybe I can give him a little peek of what's to come in the car on the way to lunch. I remove the suspender belt, stockings and high heels though.

I go to my wardrobe and throw it open, deciding what to wear. I settle on a short navy blue sundress and a pair of matching wedges. I get dressed and pull a brush through my hair. I tidy up my makeup – having an orgasm really messes with your eyeliner game it seems.

I've just finished getting ready when I hear a car pull up outside. I pick up my phone, hurry down the stairs to grab my handbag and keys. I'm pulling the door open as Ashton opens the gate. I pause. If I let him come to me, he could come in, and I know exactly where that would lead.

Instead, I step out of the door. I'm done taking it slow, playing hard to get. But I am hungry and I think knowing what's coming after lunch will make it all the more delicious. Both lunch and the feeling of anticipation inside of me.

I pull the door closed and lock it then I turn to walk down the path, but Ashton is right behind me, blocking my exit. My breath catches in my throat at the sight of him. He's wearing jeans and a plain black t-shirt and he is totally rocking the look. His hair is in its usual messy style and I just want to run my hands through it.

He doesn't speak, he just pulls me into his arms and presses his lips against mine.

I melt into his kiss, wrapping my arms around him and pressing myself against him, needing to feel his body against mine. I kiss him back with the same intensity he has when he kisses me, and somewhere in that kiss, a silent understanding passes between us. An understanding — today, anything can and will happen.

Ashton finally pulls his lips from mine. He keeps his arms wrapped around me and moves his head back slightly so he can look at my face. He smiles. "Hi," he whispers.

"Hi," I reply with a soft laugh.

When I was sending him those pictures, I was a little worried that I would feel awkward or embarrassed with him when I saw him again, but in fact, the opposite is true. I feel completely relaxed and I know I'm starting to trust Ashton. I'm finally letting my walls come down and letting him in.

He leans forward and kisses the top of my head and then he releases me. "Let's go."

I follow him to his car where he pauses to open the passenger side door for me. I smile my thanks to him and get in. He waits until I'm settled and then he closes my door and walks around to the driver's side of the car and gets in. He starts the engine and pulls away, heading away from the town center and instead, towards the outskirts of town.

"Where are we going?" I ask, thinking he must have found somewhere nice in the next town.

"The park," he says.

"The park?" I repeat. "Didn't the café there shut down like three years ago?"

"Yeah." He glances at me and then his eyes go back to the road.

For a fleeting second, I'm jealous that the road has his attention.

"I brought a picnic," he says.

"That sounds perfect." I smile.

It's a warm, sunny day, and a picnic really does sound good, although that's not why I think it sounds perfect. I'm imagining a secluded little spot somewhere where we can be alone and I can show him what I'm wearing beneath my dress. It also tells me something about Ashton. It tells me that he really does listen to me and takes in what I'm saying to him. The other night at dinner, we got to talking about the local area, and I told him that the park was one of my favorite spots.

Ashton glances away from the road and looks at me again. He sees my smile and returns it. He glances back at the road and laughs a little. "I was worried you would be disappointed," he says.

"Disappointed? No, of course not. I couldn't think of a better way to enjoy lunch."

"I remembered you saying how much you liked the park, but a picnic is always a risk isn't it? Some people just aren't the outdoorsy type when it comes to eating," he says.

"Oh, I definitely am," I hurry to reassure him. "I love picnics, barbecues, eating on the terrace of restaurants."

"Me too," Ashton agrees.

We reach the car park adjacent to the park. Ashton finds us a parking spot and we get out of the car. He goes around to the back of the car and opens the trunk. I can't help but watch as he bends down slightly, his ass perfect in his jeans. I think it would be even more perfect out of them.

He reaches in and pulls out a large checkered blanket and a cooler.

"Well, look at you with all the right equipment," I say.

He glances back over his shoulder and smiles at me.

I feel myself blushing slightly when I realize the double meaning of what I've said. I return his smile.

"Oh I definitely have all of the right equipment," he says. "And don't worry. I know how to use it too."

My blush deepens.

Ashton is almost laughing as he closes the trunk and locks the car.

We start to walk and he takes my hand in his. My skin tingles where it touches his and it suddenly hits me that I'm no longer just driving him crazy. I'm driving myself crazy too. It's going to be hard getting through this picnic without jumping on Ashton right here in broad daylight and riding him.

Chapter Twenty-nine

Elena

We enter the park. It's busy, full of families with small children and other couples out for a stroll, everyone enjoying the sun. We walk past the small lake. Families crowd around it, feeding the eager ducks. Children scream with delight as the almost tame ducks eat bread from their hands. A few remote-controlled boats float lazily across the water.

By unspoken agreement, we pass the lake, both of us looking for a slightly more secluded spot. I lead Ashton past the bandstand where a group of teenagers sit on the steps sunbathing. We cross a large open expanse where several ball games are underway and children run around. I lead Ashton through a gap in the trees and into the flower beds. We weave through them, pointing out pretty flowers to each other. I keep walking past the flower beds.

"Do you have a spot in mind?" Ashton asks me.

I nod as we leave the flower beds behind and cross another grassy expanse. At the end of the grass, a little brook trickles lazily. Trees line the area behind the brook. I point to a spot beside the brook. "Here." I smile.

Ashton smiles back at me and spreads the blanket out. I move to help him and we get it laid down flat. I step onto it and sit down. Ashton sits beside me and we look out across the grassy area. It's quieter here, although there are still families engaged in ball games and games of tag. Their laughter floats on the air, and instead of making me feel like we're not in as private a spot as I would like, the sound makes me happy.

I've waited this long for Ashton. I can get through a picnic and wait until we get home for anything more.

Ashton opens the cooler. He pulls out a bottle of sparkling white wine and two glasses which are almost frosted from their time in the cooler. He opens the wine and pours two glasses of it out. He hands one of the glasses to me. He smiles at me and raises his glass. "To us," he says.

"To us," I repeat, clinking my glass against his.

We both take a sip of the wine. It's cold, crisp and refreshing. I take another sip as I watch him.

Ashton sets his glass down beside the bottle and goes back into the cooler. He pulls out a tub of salad and two large chicken breasts. He digs back in and comes out with two plastic plates and plastic cutlery. He's humming to himself as he puts a chicken breast on each plate then adds lettuce, tomatoes and cucumber slices to each of them. He hands one to me, along with a knife and fork.

I put my wine glass down and take the offered plate. I take a bite of the chicken and smile. "It's yummy."

Ashton takes a forkful of his and nods his head as he chews. "It is," he agrees when he swallows.

"You cooked it. You must have already known that," I say.

"I bought it at the deli down the road from your house." Ashton laughs. "Seriously Elena, how quickly do you think I could have cooked these?"

I laugh with him. Of course, he's right. He only gave me half an hour from the moment he texted me.

"I don't think I've ever been here," Ashton tells me. "It's beautiful here."

"You've never been to the park?"

"Oh no, I've been to the park. We used to come here after school sometimes and play football. I mean I've never been over this side of the place. We always stayed around the lake area or on the first field."

"I used to come here in the summer holidays with my friends," I tell him. "We'd come out here to the brook and spend the day reading, gossiping, and working on our tans."

"That actually sounds more appealing than running around playing football." Ashton grins.

"Maybe now." I laugh. "But I can't see it having much appeal to a teenage boy."

"I think it would. They would just never admit it," he replies.

"We used to sit here and plan our weddings, Lottie and me. You remember Lottie?" He nods and I go on. "We were going to have a joint wedding, where we both married our true loves. The ceremony was going to be in the bandstand, and we'd have tables and chairs set up and we'd all dance until it got dark, and then we'd have strings of fairy lights so we could keep going before we went off on our joint honeymoon. It sounds kind of stupid now doesn't it?"

"No," Ashton says. "I could see it. Ok, maybe not the joint wedding and honeymoon, but this place would look pretty good strung up with fairy lights, with a band playing and people dancing."

"I see you have given this some thought," I tease him.

"Oh, no." He laughs. "Wedding planning? That's one thing teenage boys don't do. Or even wish they could admit to wanting to do."

I laugh with him. "No you're all too busy dreaming of being professional footballers."

"That's so cliché," Ashton mock-scolds me.

"Oh, really?" I laugh. "So you're telling me that wasn't your dream as a kid?"

"No. I wasn't a cliché at all." He pauses and smiles. "I wanted to be an astronaut."

We both laugh.

"What about you? What did you want to be when you grew up?" Ashton asks me.

"I always wanted to be a teacher. I changed my mind right before college. I'm glad I did now."

"You don't like kids?" Ashton asks me.

"Oh, I love kids. Just not thirty at once. And not the ones with attitude problems. I wouldn't have lasted two minutes in a school. The first cocky little shit who pushed his luck would have had me fired when I told him exactly what I thought of him."

"If it makes you feel any better, I'd have been no good as an astronaut either. I hate flying."

"You're scared of flying?" I ask.

"I said hate, not scared," Ashton corrects me. "I don't have panic attacks or anything. I just don't enjoy it. And I'm always a little bit relieved when the plane touches down."

"Yeah, I'm thinking that's not a good qualification for an astronaut." I laugh.

"I think maybe it was a good thing that life had other plans for us though. Imagine now if you were a teacher and I was an astronaut. What would have been the chances we'd have met again?"

"Slim," I agree. "But I guess if something's meant to be, the universe would have found a way."

"Yeah maybe, I could have come to your school to give the kids some sort of talk about outer space. We could have had our first date on a rocket."

"That doesn't sound so bad." I smile. "And it's not like I'd had to have been nervous. You were hardly going to launch the rocket being that you're afraid of flying."

He laughs and shakes his head. "I knew I shouldn't have told you that."

I smile at him as I put my plate down.

Ashton has already finished his. He pulls a little carrier bag from the cooler and scrapes the left overs into it.

"Is that your doggy bag?" I tease him.

"Hey, it's one thing mocking me about my dislike of flying. But having a trash bag is just the socially responsible thing to do," he says, with a stern tone that's given away by the way his eyes sparkle with amusement. He puts our used plates and cutlery back into the cooler. He pulls out a container of strawberries and opens it. He offers it to me and I take a strawberry. He tops off my wine glass and then he takes a strawberry for himself. We eat them and he takes another one. This one, he holds out to me. I go to take it, but he shakes his head, bringing it up to my mouth.

I laugh and shake my head, but I play along, biting into the strawberry.

He eats the other half and then picks up another one. He holds it up and I bite it. He watches as I chew it and then he brings the remaining half up to my mouth again. I go to take a bite, but Ashton rubs it over my lips. "Aww well, would you look at that. You have juice on your face," he grins as he leans towards me. He runs his lips gently over mine, and then he licks the tip of his tongue over my lips, lapping at the juice and licking me clean.

As his tongue moves across my lips, I feel desire flooding through me. I want Ashton so badly, and the more time we spend together laughing and joking like this, the more and more I want him. I have definitely let myself fall for him.

I bring my hand up and place it on Ashton's cheek and when he starts to move his head back from mine, I push my hand back into his hair, holding his mouth in place on mine. I kiss him slowly at first, a soft, tender kiss, that soon becomes deeper and more passionate. It takes everything I have not to start stripping him on the spot, but I'm still aware of the voices in the distance and I don't think being arrested for public indecency would be a good ending for our date.

Still, I do nothing to stop him when Ashton slowly lays me down on my back and comes with me. He's not exactly lying on top of me, he's more beside me, his upper body raised and turned so he can keep kissing me. His hand goes to the bare skin of my thigh, running over my skin and going underneath the hem of my dress.

He runs his fingers over my inner thigh, making my skin tingle and my breath catch in my throat. His touch is light, just enough to make me want more. I can feel myself getting wet at his touch, his kiss. Maybe we could get away with going further here. No one has been close enough to know what we're doing the whole time we've been eating.

I run my hands down Ashton's back and over his tight ass, kneading it. His tongue pushes deeper into my mouth, my own tongue snaking around his, tasting the wine and the strawberries.

"Dad said we could try to catch some little fishes in the brook. Is that the brook?" a high, childlike voice says loudly.

Ashton and I jump apart just in time as a family of three – a mom, a dad, and a boy of about four years' old – come through the trees behind us. We look at each other and laugh as the mom assures the boy this is indeed the brook. The little boy is carrying a small net which he proudly thrusts into the brook.

"I feel like a kid caught doing something they shouldn't," I whisper to Ashton.

"Me too." He laughs. "It's just a good thing the kid was so excited or we might not have even heard them coming."

"Maybe that was our cue to leave," I say.

Ashton nods, although he looks disappointed. He gathers up the rest of our things and puts everything back in the cooler except the rubbish bag.

I smile to myself. I know how I can stop him being disappointed. "Ashton?"

"Hmm," he says.

He turns when I don't speak. I smile at him and push my dress off my shoulder slightly, showing him the black bra strap with purple detailing.

He makes a low growling sound in the back of his throat when he realizes I'm still wearing the underwear from the photos I sent him, the same underwear I was wearing when I touched myself thinking about him.

"God Elena, what are you doing to me?" he asks in a husky voice that is so dripping with lust it makes my clit tingle.

"I'm not sure?" I smile. "But you're doing the exact same thing to me."

Ashton jumps to his feet and practically runs to the nearest bin with the trash.

I get up and move the cooler and start folding the blanket up.

Ashton comes back and helps me. He picks the cooler up and slings the blanket over it, and then he takes my hand in his and we make our way back to the car. It's not the leisurely stroll we took to find the spot. It's a fast walk, urgent and insistent. Just like the need for him that's growing inside of me.

We get into the car, and without asking, Ashton heads straight back to my place. We barely speak in the car, the electricity sizzling in the air makes conversation unnecessary. We don't need words at this moment to understand each other. We both know exactly what we want and exactly what we're going to do next. Ashton pulls up outside of my house and cuts the engine.

"Elena wait," he says as I go to get out of the car.

I feel my heart sink. He's going to tell me he doesn't want to come in, that he has somewhere else to be.

"Are you sure you're ready for this? Because I'm telling you now, if we go in there, I'm not going to be able to hold myself back," Ashton warns.

His voice is serious and I know he means it, although his eyes beg me not to send him away. I have no intention of sending him away. Not this time.

"Then what are we waiting for?" I grin and get out of the car.

Ashton scrambles out of his side. I move down the path to the door with Ashton only inches behind me. I fumble my key out and get the door open. I step inside. I have barely crossed the step when Ashton grabs my wrist and turns me to face him. He leans in and our lips come together in a frantic, desperate kiss. He kicks the door shut as I pull his t-shirt over his head and throw it to one side.

Chapter Thirty

Ashton

My heart is pounding in my chest, matching the pulsing feeling that bangs through my cock as it swells, pushing against my jeans, searching for freedom. The denim is tough, hard, and it only adds to the growing lust inside of me.

I take a second to look at Elena, really look at her, as we break our mouths apart long enough for her to drag my t-shirt over my head. I raise my arms and it's off me. Elena throws it to one side and I kick her front door shut.

I can see the lust I feel for her mirrored on her face. Her eyes seem to have become a shade darker as she meets my gaze and holds it. Her chest is heaving with the anticipation of what is to come. She looks hotter than she's ever looked before and I can't wait to touch her, to taste her. I need to have her, right here, right now.

Our mouths come back together, our tongues colliding, our hands all over each other. We've both held ourselves back from each other for so long, so now when we are finally giving in, we're both frenzied.

I reach behind Elena and open the zipper on her dress. She untangles her arms from around me for long enough for the straps to tumble down her arms, over her wrists, and off the ends of her hands. Her hands go back to my body as the dress falls to the ground. Elena steps out of the dress, kicking it to one side. Her hands go to my jeans and start to open the button and the zipper there. She pushes them down roughly, coming back for my briefs.

I feel the air wrapping around my cock, the restriction of denim gone and my underwear falling away. It feels good to be free of the denim prison. Elena's hand wraps around my cock and I gasp in a breath. Again, I find myself holding myself back, but this time it's not because I can't touch Elena, it's because I don't want to come too soon and have this delicious moment be over.

I kick my shoes off as Elena works her magic on me. I kick off my jeans and briefs then wriggle my feet out of my socks. I manage to do it all in a way that doesn't slow Elena down for a moment and doesn't break our contact.

Elena works my cock slowly at first, teasing me. Her other hand is roaming over my back, stroking my skin. Her fist begins to move faster and I find myself riding on a wave of pleasure that fills my stomach and spreads out through my body. I don't want her to stop, but I know I have to stop her or I'm going to come too quickly. I run my fingers down her arm until I get to her wrist and then I gently pull her hand away from me. I feel both relieved to relax for a second without the risk of coming on the spot, and disappointed that her touch has gone away.

Elena pulls her mouth from mine and looks up at me with a frown.

I smile down at her and start to walk her backwards towards the stairs. I wrap my arm around her waist and gently lower her onto the third step. "Your turn." I grin, kneeling down in front of her.

She looks amazing in the lingerie I bought her. She's every bit as sexy and as classy as I imagined she would be in it. I kiss her again and then I pull back. I put my fingers in the waistband of Elena's panties and she lifts her ass off the stair long enough for me to pull them down. I add them to our pile of clothes and then I turn back to Elena and smile at her.

I motion for her to go up and she scoots up a few stairs, leaving my face in line with her pussy. I moan as my cock twitches at the sight of it. She's dripping wet, the moisture catching the sun's rays and making her pussy seem to almost sparkle. I put my hands on her knees and push them outwards.

Elena makes no effort to stop me, in fact, she works with me, opening her legs wide and grabbing my shoulders and pulling me in.

I run my tongue through her slit, starting at the top and working down to her pussy, and her juices coat my tongue, my chin. She tastes every bit as good as I imagined she would and I groan into her pussy as my tongue tingles with her taste. I lick back up her slit, moving away from her pussy as the tip of my tongue seeks out her clit. I feel her shift slightly as my probing tongue finds her sweet spot and works her clit from side to side. She lays back on the stairs, spreading her legs as wide as the gap will allow her to.

I feast on her, lapping up her juices and making her writhe beneath my tongue. I keep the pressure light, teasing her, wanting to draw her orgasm out of her slowly so that when she comes, she really comes. She moves her hips, pressing her mound tightly against my tongue and getting more friction on her swollen clit. I start to move back a little, wanting to make this last, but Elena isn't letting me go anywhere. She wraps her legs around my neck, holding me in place against her pussy.

Her assertiveness turns me on even more and I feel my cock pulsing, screaming to be touched. I ignore the feeling, concentrating only on Elena and her pleasure. We've both waited so long for this, and while I already know Elena was worth waiting for, I want to make her body mine, and make her feel things she has never felt before. I want to show her I was worth waiting for too.

I stop holding back, stop teasing Elena. It's time to show her the magic I can work on her, the way I can make her body sing. I suck her clit into my mouth, sucking it hard, stretching it out. I press it with my tongue, flattening it against the roof of my mouth. Elena moans, a low sound so full of desire it almost makes me come on the spot. She whispers my name as I move my tongue up and down slightly, vibrating it against Elena's throbbing clit.

I release her clit and go back to licking her. She's close to her orgasm now. Her breath is coming in a series of gasps, her thighs around my neck have gone rigid. Her spine is arched, pushing her pussy more tightly against my face. Her hands come down to push into my hair and she holds my face even tighter against her pussy, tugging at my hair, making my scalp sting deliciously.

I can barely breathe now, but I don't care. Elena is filling me up. She's all I can smell, all I can taste, all I can feel, and right here is exactly where I want to be. I press down on her clit hard with the tip of my tongue and I wiggle it, moving it in a circular motion, making her clit move side to side and back and forth. Elena sucks in another gasping breath which she releases in a strangled sound that is almost a whimper.

Her back arches further and her fists in my hair tug harder than before. Her legs tense up and hold me tightly in place as her orgasm ravages her body. I don't stop licking her. I want her to know how good she can really feel. I keep pushing her and her second orgasm hits her just as her muscles are relaxing from the first one. Again, she goes rigid, her body awash with pleasure.

When her legs relax as her second orgasm recedes, I reach up and gently remove them from my shoulders so I can move back a little. I still work Elena's clit with my tongue, and now, I push two fingers inside of her pussy too. She is dripping wet with her juices coating my fingers instantly, running down my hand and over my wrist.

She calls out my name in a voice that barely sounds like her own as I move my fingers inside of her in time with my lapping, licking tongue. I find her g-spot and massage it. She screams my name again, and then she sucks in another breath. She holds it as pleasure assaults her. I move my tongue away from her clit, replacing it with the fingers of my other hand.

I come up onto my knees and look down at her as I work her clit and g-spot together. Her mouth is hanging open, her eyes glazed. Her face contorts in ecstasy that's so intense it looks almost painful. She still hasn't taken in a breath although her open mouth is gasping. I keep working her. I know the moment she goes completely over the edge. Her muscles go floppy and her eyes roll back in her head. For a second, she blacks out, but then her eyes roll back into place, looking slightly dazed. Her eyelids are heavy with lust. She sucks in a huge breath that shakes her full body and she lets it out in a series of unintelligible sounds. Liquid pours from her pussy, covering my hands and soaking her thighs.

Her body is still shuddering from the orgasm tearing through her when I take my hands away from her pussy. I push myself up on top of her, resting on my elbows and kiss her. Her mouth is slack, and for a moment, I am worried I've pushed her too hard, but after a second, her arms come up and lock around my neck and she responds to my kiss, pushing her tongue into my mouth and massaging mine with it. A spark of excitement goes through me at the thought of her tasting her own orgasm on my tongue.

I push my arms beneath her legs, wrapping them around my waist and holding her to me. I flip over and land on my ass with Elena held tightly against me, sitting in my lap. I can feel how wet she still is. Her juices are coating my thighs now. She shifts forward slightly, moving her hips, rubbing her pussy over my cock, and I know I can't wait much longer to be inside of her.

I unhook her bra and pull it down her arms, throwing it over the bannister onto the ground. I kiss her again and move my hands to the front of her body, kneading her pert little breasts. She moans as I pinch her nipples between my fingers and roll them through my fingers, bringing them to two hard little points.

I keep working the nipple of her right breast with one hand. I reach down with the other one and run my fingers through her slit. She gasps when I make contact with her clit. It's still swollen, tender from the orgasms and I imagine it must feel like electricity running through her body. I spread her juices around, and then I grab my cock and press it against the opening of her pussy.

I pull my mouth back from hers and look her in the eye as I penetrate her. I feel myself sinking into her delicious warm folds as her pussy opens for me. I can feel her stretching, accommodating me as I claim her pussy as my own. I move my hand from her breast and rest both hands on her hips as I begin to thrust into her.

She moans again and I lay back on the stairs, watching her as she begins to match my thrusts with thrusts of her own. She is majestic, quite the sight to behold. Her skin is pink, flushed with orgasms and exertion. It glistens where a thin sheen of sweat coats it. Her breasts bounce as she thrusts. I keep my hands on her hips, moving her up and down faster and faster, enjoying the view I've been given, wondering how I got so damned lucky.

She moans again and she reaches down with one hand and pushes her fingers between her lips, rubbing them over her clit and gasping again. The sight of her riding me, touching herself with her head thrown back, her mouth hanging open is almost too much and I feel my cock twitching inside of her. I bite down hard on the inside of my cheek, stopping myself from coming. I don't want this moment to be over. Not yet. Not when Elena is enjoying herself so much.

My whole body is on fire, the sight of Elena is almost too much, and the way her tight little pussy grips me, moving over me, pushing me closer to the edge makes me suck in a tortured breath that sears my throat.

Her hand is moving furiously and she cries out as another orgasm rips through her. I feel her pussy clenching around me, a rush of warmth flooding over my cock as she comes. I can barely control myself now. I am panting, pounding into Elena, needing the release of an orgasm. Elena goes rigid for a moment as she hits the peak of her orgasm and her pussy clenches so tightly that she holds my cock still inside of her for a moment.

She relaxes again and I pound into her once more. She gasps with each thrust, letting her breaths out with little *oh* sounds. I keep moving and now Elena is moving again, wiggling her hips from side to side, as she slams up and down on me.

I can't hold back any longer. Fire floods through my cock and up into my body as I come. I spurt into Elena, my come mixing with hers, my cock twitching wildly inside of her. I close my eyes as my mouth twists with ecstasy and I slam into Elena again, filling her up and holding myself in place, my ass in the air off the ground. Elena moans as I fill her all the way up and I spurt again. She screams my name as she comes with me, and then my muscles turn to jelly as I flop back onto the stairs.

Elena crumples forward landing on my chest. My cock slips out of her and I instantly need to be back inside of her. My body feels heavy and it takes a lot of effort to bring my arms up, but I do it anyway. I wrap them around Elena and hold her as she lays spent on my chest, her body shaking as she pants for air. I am no less of a wreck than she is. I too, am panting and I can feel my heart racing. I tighten my hold on Elena, not wanting to ever let her go.

I am starting to feel a little bit more in control now.

Elena lifts her head from my chest. She smiles at me. "Was I worth waiting for?" she asks with a grin.

"Nah," I say.

Elena gently slaps me on the chest.

I laugh and then I turn serious again. "You were worth every second of it."

She smiles and then she pushes herself up from me. "We should go into the sitting room where it's a little more comfortable."

I miss her warmth, the closeness of her skin against mine.

She is already walking away as I stand up. She gathers our clothes and heads into the sitting room. I take in her large leather couch, her glass coffee table, the little shelf of books beneath the wall mounted TV. But mostly... I take her in.

"I don't think we're going to be needing those clothes anytime soon," I tell Elena.

She turns back to me. "Is that so?"

I nod and reach out for her. She drops our clothes and steps over then and into my arms. Our lips meet and fire floods through me once more. My cock comes instantly back to life as I remember how it felt to be inside of Elena. I'm soon going to be inside of her again. My whole body is tingling at the thought of it.

I move my lips from Elena's and kiss down along her neck. She lifts her head, and moans softly as I kiss her. I turn her around and pull her body back against mine. I can feel her ass pressing against my hard cock and she moans again, when she feels my hardness pressing against her.

I run my tongue down the side of her neck and my hands roam all over her body, concentrating on her breasts. I put one hand on her hip and move my other hand slowly down the front of her body, running my fingernails down her stomach feeling her skin puckering up into goose bumps at my touch.

I move my hand lower and push my fingers between her lips once more. I work her clit, loving the sound of her whimpering as I bring her body back to life. Her moaning vibrates through her back and into my chest as I feel like we are truly becoming one. I keep moving my fingers over her clit, hard and fast, so it doesn't take long for her to reach her orgasm. She presses herself more tightly against me, her body writhing against mine as she whimpers while her climax courses through her body.

I feel a rush of warm liquid flooding from her pussy. Her breathing is fast now, and her skin is hot against mine. I kiss her neck again as I keep working her clit, pushing her over the edge again. She moans my name as she loses herself in her pleasure. Her hands clench up into fists at her sides as she gasps.

I move my fingers from her clit, my hands on each of her hips and I gently nudge her forward. We walk to the arm of the couch, and I run my hands up Elena's sides. I put them on her shoulders and push her forwards, bending her body over the arm of the couch. She's following my lead and she sets her feet to the sides, opening herself up to me.

I stroke my fingers through her slit, spreading her juices around. I move my hands over her ass cheeks too, leaving a trail of glistening dampness behind. I run my nails along her spine, watching as her skin erupts in goose bumps once more. I can't wait any longer. I need to feel her pussy wrapped around my cock again.

I take her ass cheeks in my hands, gently pulling them open and exposing her dripping wet pussy. I slam into her in one hard thrust that makes her cry out. I release her ass cheeks and move my hands back to her hips, pulling her on to me, moving her in time with my thrusts, making each one longer and deeper than the one before it.

Elena is going wild beneath me, writhing and moaning as I fill her up, making her body come back to life. I keep thrusting, pulling her back onto me until I am almost on the edge of my climax and then I pull one hand from her hip. I keep thrusting as I move my hand around to the front of her body and massage her clit. I massage it until I know Elena is about to come and then I stop. I run both of my hands up her sides and grab her by her upper arms. I pull her up off the couch, straightening her and holding her against my chest once more.

I hold her around the waist with one arm and my other hand finds her clit again. I pump into her as I massage her clit once more, bringing her back to the edge of her orgasm. This time, I don't stop. I keep rubbing her clit until I feel her already tight pussy get tighter, gripping my cock in a vice like grip that is so intense it's almost painful.

Elena shudders against me, screaming my name as her climax tears through her body. She goes rigid, her head coming back to rest on my shoulder, her chest heaving. She relaxes again as her orgasm begins to recede. Her knees buckle and I feel her start to fall. I tighten my hold on her waist and bring my other arm around her just above her breasts, keeping her from falling.

I pump into her faster, harder. I can feel my climax is right there and with one final push, I explode inside of Elena as fire spreads through my veins. My whole body is a tingling mess of pleasure and for a second, I can't catch my breath. I stand, suspended in space and time with Elena in my arms as I spurt into her again and again. Each spurt sends electrical pulses around my body, making every nerve throb with the intensity of my orgasm. It holds me in its grip for a moment and then I feel it starting to fade, leaving behind the leaden warmth of sated muscles. My cock slips out of Elena and I start to let my body relax. Elena begins to stumble and I catch her.

I turn her in my arms and pull her against me. She looks up at me with a lazy smile as I lean down and kiss her. After I kiss her, I scoop her up in my arms and carry her to the couch where I deposit her. I sit down beside her and pull her head into my lap.

She looks up at me, a dazed, sated smile on her lips. Her eyes are starting to close.

I've worn her out. I smile to myself as she closes her eyes and sighs with contentment. I am tired myself. After being

awake for most of last night and then our love making session, I am not really surprised, but I don't want to sleep. I
want to stay awake and just enjoy the weight of Elena's head
in my lap.

She turns onto her side and brings her hand up, putting
it on my leg next to her face. I place my hand on the top
of her arm, holding her as she finally succumbs to sleep. I
plan to stay awake, drinking in her scent, marveling at the
fact that this perfect creature has chosen to be with me, but I
soon feel my eyes closing.

I pull them back open, but the effort it takes to keep
them that way is too much.

In the end, I surrender myself and drift off to sleep.

Chapter Thirty-one

Elena

I wake up slowly, aware of a deep aching feeling in my muscles. My body feels battered and raw, almost like I've ran a marathon. My pussy feels tender and bruised, and my clit is swollen and sensitive. I smile to myself as the memories come back to me and I know why I feel this way. I finally let Ashton in, gave myself over to him, and my God — was it worth it. Ashton is a considerate lover who clearly wanted me to enjoy the sex as much as he did. I lost count of the amount of orgasms I had, but I know it was a lot. Definitely more than I've ever had in one session with anybody else.

I am laid on the couch, the leather sticking to my skin. My head is resting on something soft and I realize it's Ashton's thigh. I unstick myself from the couch, wincing at the stinging sensation and I roll onto my back to look up at Ashton.

He's asleep, his head propped up on his hand, his mouth slightly open. He's breathing slowly and deeply.

I watch his chest expanding and deflating for a moment. I smile to myself. I guess I wore him out as much as he wore me out. He looks so peaceful and I hate to have to wake him, but my stomach is growling and we have a dinner reservation soon.

I decide to go and get in the shower and get ready and then come back and wake him.

As I sit up, Ashton stirs. He rubs his hands over his face and then he stretches. He smiles at me. "How long were we asleep? I guess we deserved a nap after that session." He grins.

"True," I smile. "I'm going to go and get in the shower and get ready so we can go for dinner." I stand.

Ashton stands up with me. He grabs my hand before I can walk away and pulls me to him, kissing me on the lips. "I could come and shower with you," he says, as he moves his lips from mine and kisses down my neck.

My body is already responding to his touch but I shake my head and laugh, gently pushing him away. "We'll never make dinner if you come into the shower with me," I point out.

"It wouldn't be the worst thing in the world if we missed dinner." He grins.

My stomach growls as he says it and we both laugh. "Ok, maybe it would be. Let's go for dinner. We can always continue this after." He winks at me.

A shiver of desire goes through me. I practically run from the room, knowing if I stay even a second longer, I won't be able to stop myself from jumping on him, instead of getting ready.

By the time I get out of the shower and go through to my bedroom, Ashton is waiting in there for me.

He has neatly folded my clothes from downstairs and he's sitting on the bed with his briefs back on. "Do you mind if I hit the shower?" he asks.

I shake my head as I go towards my dressing table.

He gets up from the bed and heads for my bathroom door. As Ashton and I cross paths, we pause for a kiss and then he's gone and I concentrate on getting ready, not letting myself think about the fact he's only feet away from me, naked, wet and slippery. It's hard not to think about it, but I try. God... do I try.

WE MAKE IT TO THE RESTAURANT at seven o'clock straight up, just making our reservation. It was touch and go for a moment as I dithered over what to wear. I finally settled on a red body hugging dress with matching heels.

Once we got seated and ordered our meals, we soon relaxed after the frantic rushing around, and Ashton and I spent dinner alternating between laughing together and flirting outrageously with each other.

I put my spoon down after putting the last slither of my ice cream into my mouth. I smile at Ashton.

He hasn't taken his eyes off me all night.

"What?" I ask.

"Nothing." He shakes his head ruefully. "You just look so beautiful."

I feel myself blushing under his compliment.

He takes a long drink of his wine and then he grins at me and before I know what's happening, he begins to sing Lady in Red to me. He sings it loud enough for the people at the nearing tables to glance in our direction.

I feel heat flooding my cheeks. "Ashton, stop it." I laugh, looking to my left and then my right in utter horror.

He laughs and stops singing. "Is my singing really that bad?" he laughs.

"Yes," I laugh with him. "And everyone is looking at us."

"Screw them." He beams at me. "When you look as good as you do tonight, who cares who knows it?"

"I care." I giggle. But I realize I really don't care who's looking at us. I don't care who knows that I have fallen completely under Ashton's spell. "I do like that song though," I concede.

"Then it's settled," Ashton announces. "That's now officially our song."

I feel warm inside at the thought of having our own song. I smile at Ashton. "I like that."

Ashton drinks the rest of his wine, not taking his eyes off me as he swallows. "So do you want me to finish serenading you, or do you want to get out of here?" he asks when he puts the glass down. His eyes are sparkling at me.

I know exactly what he's asking me. "Let's go." I nod with a smile.

Ashton waves down our waiter and asks for the check.

I excuse myself to go to the bathroom. I pee quickly then I stand in front of the mirror washing my hands and looking at my reflection. My cheeks glow pink. My eyes sparkle. I am a woman in love and it's written all over my face.

I dry my hands and go back to our table.

Ashton stands up as he sees me approaching. "Ready?"

I nod. I don't think there'll ever be a time when I'm not ready for Ashton.

We leave the restaurant and Ashton starts walking.

I hurry to catch up with him. "Where are we going?"

He looks over at me. "I thought it was about time you saw my place. It's not far from here. Are you up for it?"

"Lead the way," I reply. It'll be nice to finally see Ashton's place, but it's really Ashton himself I want to see. Specifically, I want to see what's beneath his clothes all over again. God, I'm insatiable. He's got me craving his touch every second I'm with him and indeed every second, I'm not with him too.

Chapter Thirty-two

Elena

We walk through a pretty neighborhood, my hand in his. He leads me around a corner and into a small cul-de-sac. I can see just by looking at the houses here that they're all worth a fortune. Each one is set right back from the road, surrounded by a large garden.

Ashton takes me to the house right at the end of the little street.

It's a three-story house that puts my tiny little house to shame. The garden wall is lined with conifers that are still quite small, but which, in a few years' time, will make Ashton's garden completely private. I can still see the upstairs rooms above the conifers and I notice that each of them have balconies on them. Aston pushes the garden gate open and I follow him up the path, noticing the neatly mowed lawn and the flowers lining the pathway.

He opens the door and stands aside, motioning for me to enter.

I find myself standing in a large, high ceilinged entrance way. On my left is a closed door. Ahead of me is a long hallway with more closed doors. And to my right is a stunning, white marble sweeping staircase.

Ashton closes the door behind himself. He switches on a light and a soft yellow glow shines over the entranceway and the stairs. "Would you like a drink?" Ashton asks.

I shake my head. "No, I'm good thanks. I'd love a tour though."

"Elena, if you want to see inside of my bedroom just say so." Ashton winks at me.

"I most definitely do want to see the inside of your bedroom before tonight is out." I laugh. "But I really would like a quick tour first."

"Your wish is my command, Lady in Red," Ashton says with a bow.

I laugh and he takes my hand and leads me to the door on my left. He opens the door and flicks the light on. The room is a huge lounge, tastefully decorated in pale cream with a turquoise and silver feature wall and a big fireplace set in it.

"It's beautiful." I smile.

"I wish I could take the credit for it, but I have to admit I had an interior designer do most of the décor."

"She's nailed your personality," I comment as I take in the extra detailing across the room.

"How did you know it was a woman?" Ashton asks.

"The little touches. Like the cushions and the curtains."

Both are made from turquoise velvet and have threads of silver running through them.

Ashton nods his head and leads me to a different door. "This is the dining room," he says as we go in and he flicks on the light.

It's another big room, dominated by a huge mahogany table with ten chairs. The table has a silver candelabra in the center and it's set for dinner. Ashton keeps moving through the room and I follow him. There are two doors on this wall.

Ashton points to one of them. "That's just my office. You don't want to see that, it's a mess of paper and files." He laughs. He opens the other door and turns on the overhead light. It flickers on and off twice, then it pings into life and stays on.

I find myself in a modern kitchen. It's decorated in black and white, full of sleek edges and shiny surfaces. In the center is an island. At one end, is a sleek white breakfast bar with black high stools and at the other end is a small table with two chairs. The table and chairs look like pine while the chairs have bright red cushions on them. They look strangely out of place here.

Ashton sees me looking at them and he smiles wistfully. "Camilla, my interior designer, hated that table and chairs," he explains. "She said they don't match the tone of the house in any way shape or form. I mean she's right, but you saw the dining room. There's no way I'm eating at a table that size every night. I insisted on this homely little thing, a place where I can actually feel at home to eat."

"I love it!" I smile.

"Maybe you should have designed the house." He stares at me with a wistful look in his eyes.

I think of my own place. It's nothing like this modern palace, but if Ashton likes things that are homely, my place feels lived in, a home rather than a house.

Ashton leads me through another door and we're back out in the hallway. He points to the closed doors on the other side of the hallway as we walk back towards the stairs. "That's the laundry room. Then a small bathroom. And that's just a coat closet." He leads me to the stairs and we begin to climb them.

I can feel anticipation bubbling up inside of me as we climb higher. The staircase really is stunning and as we reach the top, the hallway there branches off into two halves. One half is the staircase twirling away and up to the third floor. The other half is an open hallway with a waist high railing running along it. Four doors lead off it.

"The end door is a linen closet," Ashton explains. "The one next to it is a bedroom. That one is the bathroom. And this one is my bedroom." He nods to the door closest to us.

"What's on the third floor?" I don't even know why I asked. I don't care what's up there. I care what's behind door number one... Ashton's bedroom.

"A couple of rooms that are officially bedrooms but that I use for storage and what I call a home gym but is really just a treadmill stuck in the middle of a room," Ashton says with a smile. "Do you want to take a look?"

"I'd rather look in there." I nod to Ashton's bedroom door.

"Good choice." He smiles, pushes the door open, and gestures for me to enter. He flicks a switch and a soft light comes on. It's not the overhead light; it's a lamp by the bed-side. He flicks another switch. Nothing happens.

"What was that one meant to do?" I ask.

"Look behind you," Ashton says with a smile.

I do and I gasp when I see the rest of the house is now in darkness.

"I was forever getting into bed and remembering I had left a light on somewhere, so I installed a master switch," Ashton explains.

It makes sense and I nod. I wouldn't mind one of those myself. I look around the bedroom. It's neat and tidy. A large wardrobe and a chest of drawers' line one wall. A desk and computer chair sit at another. Ashton's bed is pushed up against the third wall, the headboard almost touching it. His bed is huge, a king size for sure. It's dressed in black satin sheets with a matching duvet cover and pillow cases. On each side of it is a teak bedside cabinet. Beside one of them is a glass door that must lead out onto one of the balconies I saw on the outside of the house.

I feel nervous suddenly now, since I'm being presented with such a beautiful place. It reminds me that Ashton is a millionaire and only a couple of months ago, I was one month's salary away from being homeless. We've always come from different worlds, but maybe this is a bridge we won't be able to cross now since we're older.

"What's wrong?" Ashton asks, studying my face.

"Nothing." I shrug.

"Come on, Elena. What is it?" he presses me, looking at me with concern.

"I just... I'm almost afraid to touch anything in case I break something. Your home is beautiful, but it's a little overwhelming," I admit. "Everything you have looks like it's worth a fortune."

"The only thing in this house that I can't replace is you." He smiles at me. "If you break something, I don't care. It's only stuff Elena and it's not important to me."

I feel myself relaxing at his words, and when he comes closer and pulls me into his arms, I let go of my nervousness at the huge house and the impressive décor to melt into his kiss. Within minutes, our clothes are off and we're moving closer to Ashton's bed. My pussy is wet and my clit is pulsing with desire all over again.

I am feeling brave suddenly and I pull my mouth from Ashton's. I take his hand and lead him towards his bed. I stop when we reach it to put my hands on Ashton's shoulders and push him backwards. His knees hit the bed and he falls onto his ass. He grins up at me as I remain standing. I step between his knees and wrap my arms around his shoulders, kissing him again. He puts his hands on my ass and then his hands roam over my body, finally settling them on the small of my back.

I kiss Ashton deeply, passionately, wanting my kiss to tell him I forgive him, that I've fallen deeply for him, and I don't plan on running from this.

Chapter Thirty-three

Elena

Finally, I pull my mouth away from Ashton's. I reach behind me and take his hands from my back. He looks at me questioningly as I smile down at him, and then I fall to my knees between his thighs. I take his hard cock in my fist and pull it towards my face and then I push my lips over the tip and suck him into my mouth.

I move my lips down his length, sucking him further into my mouth. I move my mouth back up, releasing him. I keep my grip on the base of his cock and start to flick my tongue over the tip of it, teasing Ashton and working him into a frenzy. I can hear him moaning, and his hands are gripping the duvet in tight balls on either side of his legs.

I know I'm driving him wild and I start to lick along his length, lapping at him, enjoying the taste of his cock and the scent of his lust. I lick back up along his shaft. A dribble of pre come runs from the tip and I lick him clean, swallowing the liquid down. I open my mouth and wrap my lips around the tip of him, sucking hard, lapping at him, sucking up every last drop.

I take him back into my mouth, suckling noisily on his cock. I make *mmm* sounds, wanting him to know I'm loving this. His growls tell me he knows it and I stop teasing him, moving my head quickly up and down, working my tongue over him as I suck on him like my life depends on it.

His breathing is speeding up now, he's almost panting and he says my name in a low, lust filled voice that makes my clit tingle and my pussy clench deliciously. A shiver goes through me, leaving a trail of goose bumps running up and down my spine. I keep sucking, knowing Ashton is almost there now. His cock starts to twitch slightly and suddenly, his hands are on my face, gently pulling my head back away from his cock.

I look up at him, suddenly afraid I misread his reaction to my blow job and he wasn't enjoying it as much as I thought he was. He grins at me and I know it's not that. I can see the lust in his eyes.

"I was ready to come and I want to come inside of your pussy," Ashton says, answering the question I haven't asked out loud.

His words send another shiver through me and I feel my pussy getting wetter. Ashton takes my hands in his and helps me to my feet. I place my knee on the mattress beside him and straddle him. I cup his face in my hands and kiss him full on the mouth. He wraps his arms around my waist, pulling me closer to him. Our chests press against each other and I can feel electric pulses moving through my skin where our bodies touch.

He deepens our kiss and my stomach flutters in excited anticipation. I can't wait any longer. I need to feel Ashton inside of me, filling me up. I reach down for his cock, but before I can grab it, Ashton stands up from the bed. He holds me against him and I come up with him. He turns quickly and lays me on my back, clambering up onto the bed between my legs. He runs his fingers through my slit and I hiss in a breath as his fingers run over my sore, throbbing clit.

He leans forward and plants a kiss on my stomach and then he enters me, his cock stretching my pussy as a strangled gasping sound leaves my lips while a stinging pain bursts through me, turning into pleasure as it reaches my stomach. Ashton thrusts, pushing himself all the way into me and I feel the stinging sensation shooting through me again as I stretch to accommodate him. My tender spots pulse angrily, but the insistent pain only turns me on more, and when Ashton starts thrusting inside of me, I wrap my legs around his waist, pulling him in deeper.

I move my hips in time with his, feeling his large cock rubbing over my g-spot and slamming against my cervix. I can feel my body responding now, my tender spots getting used to being stimulated once more. My orgasm builds inside of me spreading through my body, as a delicious, tingly warmth wakes up all of my nerve endings and makes my head spin.

Ashton keeps thrusting, long, deep strokes that fill me up and drive me wild. My climax explodes through my body, carrying me away on a sea of pleasure. I feel like I am floating as I lose myself in the ecstasy of the moment.

I hear myself screaming Ashton's name, begging him not to stop fucking me. He obliges, his thrusts speeding up now. My orgasm has just started to fade when I feel another one washing over me, the wave of ecstasy takes me by surprise. Pleasure floods me and I try to scream Ashton's name again but no sound comes out of my mouth as my body goes rigid. I can't think. I can't breathe. I can only feel the pleasure.

I hear Ashton moaning, his breath tickling my neck as he presses his face against it. I feel his cock twitching inside of me and then a rush of warmth as he comes. He whispers my name as his cock throbs inside me and spurts again. I find I can move again and I gasp in a much needed, desperate breath. I cling to Ashton, digging my nails into his back as I come slowly coasting down. His cock gives one final pulsing and then I feel it slip out of me.

He rolls off me and we lay side by side, getting our breath back for a moment. I'm just starting to feel normal again, when Ashton stands up from the bed. He pulls the duvet back and motions for me to lift up. I lift my ass and he pulls my side of the duvet out from beneath me. I lower myself and he covers me up. He goes and turns the light out and then he comes back to bed, slipping in beside me. I turn to face him and we look into each other's eyes for a moment as Ashton wraps his arm around my waist. I snuggle closer to him enjoying the warmth of his body against mine.

I put my arm around his waist too, pulling myself even closer to him. I want every part of me to be touching a part of him. I want to feel closer to him than I ever have before for what I'm about to say to him. "I forgive you," I whisper after a moment.

"Huh?" Ashton says, his voice sounding muffled.

I realize he was already half asleep.

"You asked me if I could ever forgive you for bullying me," I say.

He winces at the term.

Although I feel bad for saying it so bluntly, that's what he did and it needs to be acknowledged. "I told you I wanted to forgive you but I didn't know if I could. Well, I can. I have. You've shown me every day since I came to work for you that you've changed."

He leans in and kisses me, his hand stroking my back. "You have no idea how good it is to hear you say that Elena," he says quietly. "It means we have a chance."

"A good chance I would say," I tell him. "But I can feel myself falling for you Ashton, so if you have any reservations about this, about us, please say so now."

"I have no reservations about this whatsoever," he says instantly. "I fell for you the moment I saw you and that's never changed. Those feelings never quite went away. I'm hopelessly in love with you and I have been for years."

"I-I love you too," I say quietly.

Tears shine in Ashton's eyes as he rubs his lips over mine.

I can feel tears in the corners of my own eyes too. I didn't mean to say it. I didn't mean to tell him I love him, but I do and now I've said it. I'm glad I did. It's not too soon. It's not like we were strangers. I've known him for most of my life.

"I'm going to spend every day of the rest of our lives trying to make you as happy as you make me Elena. And if I'm even half as successful at it as you are, then I'll rest easily knowing you're happy."

I smile at him and he kisses me again. We fall into a comfortable silence, laying in the darkness studying each other's faces. I can see the joy on Ashton's face and I know I was wrong. People can change. I'm just glad I realized it before it was too late and I lost Ashton for good.

Chapter Thirty-four

Elena

Ashton and I spent a lovely, lazy Sunday together. We woke up early and spent the morning in bed. I was still so sore from the love making the night before, but I couldn't keep my hands or my mouth off Ashton. He was gentle with me and I soon forgot about the tenderness and threw myself into it. We ended up falling back to sleep and then we woke up late. Far too late for breakfast and a little bit too late for lunch, but we got dressed and went out for lunch anyway.

Ashton took me to a lovely little bistro where we had a Sunday roast with all of the trimmings and then we went back to his place and watched a movie together. He wanted me to stay over again and I wanted to more than anything, but I knew if I did, we would be up half of the night and we both have work the next day.

One thing I'm determined to make happen: to make sure having a relationship with Ashton won't affect my work. If I was working for someone else, I would have insisted on going home on Sunday evening, getting an early night and get ready for the day ahead of me. So that's what I did. It was hard walking away from the thought of another night of sex, but I did it. Ashton tried to convince me it would be okay, that I could come in late if I wanted to, but I explained to him that I wasn't going to let us being together affect my performance at work.

There are two reasons for this. Firstly, it's a matter of pride. I like to go home at the end of the working day, knowing I've done a good job and given my best. And secondly, I don't want to give anyone in the office ammunition to say I'm getting any sort of preferential treatment. I know the story of Ashton and me going on a date last week flew around the office, and I'm pretty sure it'll still be the talk of the office today. And certain people, like Beatrice for example, will be watching me, just waiting for an excuse to call me out over the relationship.

Eventually, I made Ashton understand where I was coming from, and he dropped me off at home. It took a lot of willpower to get out of that car alone, especially when he pulled me in for a kiss after he parked outside of my house. It brought back instant memories of our first date, how he had worked me in the car until I came in his hands. And I remembered how much I regretted not inviting him in that night. Now we're together and I know we'll be together again, so in that sense, the holding back a little and the waiting will only make it more delicious.

I'd like to say I've stuck to my guns completely and kept it professional in the office, and in some ways, most ways, I have. I'm getting my work done on time and correctly, and Ashton is pleased with my work. So I know I haven't left myself open for anyone else to think my work ethic has gone downhill. I still can't quite keep my hands off Ashton though.

Every time one of us goes to the other person's office, we sneak a kiss. And when we're not alone, we're constantly glancing at each other and looking away quickly with a smile. To say it's making the working day a little bit more interesting is an understatement to say the least.

We're on our way to a meeting with a client now, and as we walk down the corridor side by side, I feel like I'm walking on air. There are people everywhere and we have to keep our hands to ourselves, but I can't help but imagine what I would do right now if I thought we were alone in the building. I would grab Ashton and kiss him, push him up against the glass wall of his office. I would open his fly and he would lift me up. I would wrap my legs around his waist and fuck his brains out right there.

I am wet just thinking about it, but I force myself to think about something else instead. Like the client we're going in to meet. It's not going to be a long meeting. The client has already been talking with Ashton via telephone calls and emails for quite some time now, so we already know what he wants. The meeting is a formality really, a chance for the client to sign the paperwork. But I need to be alert, because I'll be taking notes on the meeting, notes the client will sign off on, and I have to make sure I get what he wants exactly right or we could lose his business altogether.

We reach the conference room. It's in one of the small ones, one that isn't made of glass, thank God. If there was one thing I would change about this place, it's the goldfish bowl effect. And not just because it means Ashton and I are often on display when we get a moment alone together. I just find it distracting. We might as well have one large room with no offices at all.

The client is already in the conference room.

Sandra already informed us of his arrival and had brought him refreshments.

Ashton looks at me and smiles. "Ready?"

I feel my pussy clench. I ignore the feeling and nod.

"This has to go well," he states. "Or the last few weeks of correspondence have all been a waste of time."

"It will go well," I say quickly. "We already know he wants to sign on with us. Let's do it."

Ashton nods and opens the conference room door.

The client stands up as we enter. Ashton gives him a wide smile and shakes his hand over the table. "Mr. Purvis, it's nice to finally meet you in person."

"Call me Bill. And yes, it is," Bill says. He focuses his attention on me for a moment as I shake his hand and introduce myself.

We sit down and the meeting gets underway. I note down everything the client tells us he wants. It takes about fifteen minutes to note it all down and for Ashton to explain a couple of the finer points. He even manages to convince Bill to take on a slightly higher package than the one he was thinking of.

When they finish discussing the details, Ashton turns to me with a smile. "If you can just confirm everything we've discussed here today and have Bill sign the notes, then I can get the paperwork drawn up and brought in,"

I smile back at Ashton, then at Bill as I proceed to read out the list of services Bill has requested.

When I get to the end, Bill nods his head and smiles. "That about covers it."

I hand him the sheet of paper and a pen.

He scrawls his signature on the bottom and hands them back to me with a flourish.

Ashton taps his pockets and grimaces. "I'm so sorry Bill, I seem to have left my phone in my office. I'll just dash along to Sandra's desk and have her get the paperwork together."

Bill nods at him.

Ashton excuses himself and steps out of the room.

"I'm sorry about this," I say, just to break the silence in the room.

"Don't worry," Bill says, waving away my apology. "The whole world has gone mobile phone mad. To be honest, it's a welcome relief to be in a meeting with someone where their damned phone isn't beeping every couple of seconds."

"People do that in meetings?" I say, genuinely surprised. "Phones have an off button for a reason."

"Ah, you're old school like me I see." Bill smiles. "You know, just between you and me, I kind of miss the days where if I wasn't in the office, I wasn't reachable."

"And the days where you went out with friends and you all actually talked to each other," I add. "Instead of all looking at your phones talking to other people and spying on their lives."

"Yes, that." Bill laughs.

Chapter Thirty-five

Elena

Ashton comes back into the room and apologizes again as he sits down.

"No need to apologize," Bill says. "I was just saying to Elena how it annoys me sometimes how dependent we all are on the damned things."

Ashton and Bill keep talking about how technology is changing and debating the merits of it versus the downsides. I throw in the odd comment, but mostly, I am focused on Ashton. He's so damned hot and I am feeling a little brave. Maybe it's the luxury of being in a room that's not all glass. Maybe it's the fact that I haven't been alone with Ashton all day.

Whatever it is, I want him. I slip one of my shoes off beneath the table, confident that Bill can't see me. I stretch my leg out and lightly run my toes up Ashton's shin. He keeps talking, but he glances at me, his face unreadable.

I move my toes higher, running them over his inner thighs. He shifts slightly in the chair. He keeps up his end of the conversation, but I can see I am affecting him. He pulls at his shirt collar slightly as he talks. I bite my lip to keep myself from smiling and then I move my foot higher, running it over Ashton's cock. I can feel he's hard, ready for me. This time, I have to bite my tongue to stop myself from telling Bill to leave.

Ashton gasps slightly as I apply a bit more pressure to his cock, moving my foot up and down over it.

"Are you all right?" Bill asks with a frown.

"Sure," Ashton says with a smile, back under control. "I just remembered something that's all."

"Do you need to be somewhere? I'm sure Elena and I can finish up here," Bill says.

"Oh no, not at all. Right here is exactly where I need to be," he says.

I look down at the table and grin slightly. Right here is where he needs to be for sure. I keep working him and he keeps up his end of the conversation with Bill remarkably well. He shifts in his seat a few times, but other than that, no one would know anything strange was happening.

A knock sounds on the door and I move my foot away from Ashton. I give him an innocent looking smile as I slip my shoe back on.

Ashton calls come in.

Sandra comes in with the paperwork. "I'm sorry about the delay. The printer was acting up."

She leaves again, and Bill signs the paperwork. He stands up and Ashton does too.

I have a moment where I panic. Bill is going to see Ashton is hard. Ashton has fastened his jacket though and it hides the evidence. I stand up and shake Bill's hand too. "I'll walk you to the elevator." I smile.

"Thank you," Bill says. "It's a pleasure to be doing business with you Ashton."

Ashton nods as he gives Bill a handshake. As we step out of the room, Ashton calls after me, asking me to return to the conference room after I see Bill out.

I smile to myself, my stomach rolling in anticipation. I have to make a conscious effort not to let my excitement show as I walk Bill to the elevator and press the call button for him. It arrives after what feels like an age as Bill and I exchange a few more pleasantries and then he's finally gone.

I hurry back to the conference room, my pussy dripping wet at the thought of what's going to happen in there. I push the door back open and go inside, closing it behind me. "That went well," I say, pretending like I have no idea why Ashton asked me to return.

He looks at me, his eyes dark and intense with lust. He doesn't speak, he just comes towards me, already unbuttoning his trousers. He reaches me and hoists my skirt up over my hips and then he picks me up. I wrap my legs around his waist and he slams me against the inside of the door, a good way to stop anyone from walking in on us. It's like he read my mind earlier when I fantasized about what I'd like to do to him.

He pushes my panties roughly to one side and then he enters me in one long, hard thrust and I bite my lip to keep from moaning as he fills me. He kisses me hard as he starts to pound into me.

Aware that we have to be quick, we don't hold back. We were both already turned on, already on the edge of this, and within minutes, I am orgasming hard. I throw my head back, pressing it against the door as pleasure assaults me. Ashton doesn't slow down for even a second, keeping the waves of pleasure coming.

He nuzzles his face against my neck, kissing me and nipping on my skin between his teeth. I feel his cock pulsing inside of me and he comes hard, spurting into me. He holds me in place for a moment as we both coast down from our orgasms and then he sets me down on the ground. I grin at him as I pull my skirt down and put my panties right.

He fastens his pants. "Well, that's not usually how these meetings end!" He laughs.

"I damned well hope not!" I laugh back.

Ashton pulls me close again and kisses me, a tender kiss. "That was really fucking hot," he whispers. "And it was only a warm up for tonight." He picks the contracts up and exits the conference room.

This leaves me wanting more. I've just come and already I'm tingling again, ready for more. I don't know what Ashton has planned for tonight, but I know how it's going to end.

I leave the conference room with my notes and walk back towards my office. I can barely keep the dreamy smile off my face. I duck into the bathroom beside the conference room, take a wet and dry towel to clean myself up. I then check in the mirror to see if my hair is all over the place. It's not too bad and running my fingers through it easily tames a few wispy strands. There's not much I can do with my pink, swollen lips, so I just have to hope no one notices them. They probably won't. Things always seem more noticeable to yourself. At least that's what I tell myself.

I start to think I've gotten it wrong. Maybe my pink and slightly swollen lips are way more noticeable than I thought as I walk down the glass corridor towards my office. It seems everyone in every office I pass looks at me as I pass by. A few grin, a few shake their heads. No one meets my eye, not even when I wave to them. I get a few half-hearted waves in return and nothing more.

What the fuck? Even if my lips are noticeably swollen, I think this reaction is a little bit over the top. Oh God, my skirt is tucked into my panties at the back isn't it? I subtly run my hands over my skirt and find that it's not. I am relieved about that, but I'm still confused about all of the looks.

I reach the secretary's cubicles. They're all gathered around one computer, looking at the screen. They're giggling and pointing at the screen. Karen clicks her mouse and they all gasp.

"Afternoon ladies. What are you all looking at?" I ask.

The conversation and the giggling dies instantly. They all scurry back to their seats, their expressions like rabbits caught in headlights.

All except Beatrice who gives me a sickly smile. "Just something someone sent to us," she says.

It's clear from their reaction to my appearance that it's something they shouldn't be looking at while at work. Although I want to be let in on the joke, it's obvious they don't want to show me whatever it is, and I don't ask again. I don't want them to think I'm trying to get information out of them to feed back to Ashton and get them into trouble.

"Ok, well catch you all later," I say awkwardly.

Chapter Thirty-six

Elena

As I walk away, I can hear them getting back up again. Whatever had their attention very much still has it. I shrug it off. Let them have their private joke. I don't need them. I have Ashton and what we do in private is much more entertaining than some meme or cat video or something else they shouldn't be looking at while working.

I reach my office and go inside. I close the door, although it does nothing to hide me. I grab my handbag and pull a mirror out. My lips are barely pink anymore and any hint of swelling has gone down. There's no way everyone was looking at them. I'm being paranoid. They were just focused on their work, that's why they weren't looking at me as I passed their offices.

I shrug it off and pull my phone out, switching it back on. Instantly, it beeps. I think about ignoring it, but I see Ashton's name flashing up with an email. The time stamp is from when he was out of the meeting. I guess I wasn't the only one thinking hot thoughts. He's sent me something, an email, expecting me to pick it up there and then. He must have ducked back to his office after talking to Sandra.

I turn to my computer. The email has come to my work email address and it'll be quicker to just read it on the computer. I smile as I open it. The smile fades when I see the first line of the email.

Elena Woods. Slut.

What? That's not sexy. How can Ashton think I would find that sexy? I tell myself not to be so uptight. Some women like stuff like that, but I honestly thought Ashton would know I'm not into being degraded.

I scroll down and I see the first picture I sent him. Its caption reads dirty whore. I should just close the thing and talk to him later, telling him I'm not into that shit, but I don't. I keep scrolling. It's like a car crash site. I don't want to look at it, but I just can't look away.

The rest of the pictures I sent him are all in the email, each with another degrading caption. The email ends with a little paragraph about how sending unsolicited nudes is never going to work, and will only end up in me embarrassing myself.

I shake my head. This is so far from the sexy mark that I'm actually starting to question how well I really know this new Ashton. Clearly, he doesn't know me very well. I go to close out the email and I freeze, my hand hovering in the air.

The CC box has two words in it. Two words that make my blood run cold and bile rise in my throat. Copy all.

The words Ashton uses to send out memos to the full fucking office. It all makes sense now. Why no one would look me in the eye. Why they all looked uncomfortable. The smirks and the head shaking. And the secretaries. They weren't looking at cat videos. They were looking at me. Fucking hell, no wonder Beatrice looked so damned smug.

I am shaking and waves of nausea roll over me. Ashton hasn't changed one bit. This has all been a game to him. And this time, he's broken me in style. He made me fall in love with him, with an idea of him, and then he did — this. The whole office has seen my most intimate pictures. They all know exactly what he thinks of me.

I want to get up and run from the office, but I'm not sure my legs will hold me right now. What do I do? Do I call HR? Do I call the police? What would be the point? It wouldn't change the way I feel. I feel used, dirty. But most of all, I feel heartbroken. How can anyone be so fucking cruel? It's not even so much the pictures, it's the words. Words that are always directed at women when someone wants to belittle them. Words that hurt me deep inside. And the way Ashton did it hurts like hell. I can't believe I thought he had changed. I can't believe I fell for him.

My eyes settle on the opening line of the email again. Elena Woods. Slut. It should read *Elena Woods. Fucking idiot.* I shake my head, trying to shake the image away. I close my eyes, but that makes the room spin, and I open them again. I see the words again and I feel a sharp pain in my stomach as it cramps and I retch. I scoot backwards and reach down, grabbing my bin just in time as my lunch comes back up.

Hot bile sears my throat and tears fill my eyes. I retch again as my body tries to purge itself of what I have just seen. It's no use. Nothing can change this. Nothing can make me unsee this. I keep retching and throwing up until my stomach is empty, and still, it cramps, making me emptily retch over the bin.

"Elena? Are you all right?"

It's Ashton. He's fucking here, standing in my office door, full of fake concern. Does he think I haven't seen it? Does he think I'll laugh at his joke? Or is he just here for the final humiliation?

I don't want to say anything to him. I don't want to react to his sick mind games and let him know that once again, he has hurt me, broken me inside. I look up, keeping my face blank, ready to tell him I'm just fine. I see him looking at me. His sexy eyes, his sensual lips, lips that have explored every inch of my body. I am seething with anger and hatred and I know I'm not going to be able to hold myself back.

"Elena?" Ashton says again, stepping into my office and closing the door behind him.

"How could you?" I hiss at him.

"How could I what?" he asks.

Great. He's playing dumb. He wants to hear me say it? Then fine, I'll say it. "How could you betray me like this? What the fuck did I ever do to you that was so bad? Are you really so fucked up in the head that you think this shit is okay?" I point towards my computer as I spit out the words.

Ashton looks so totally confused, that for a moment, I want to believe he has no idea what I'm talking about. But of course he does. He's the only person who had those pictures, and the email came from his personal email address.

He steps closer and looks at my screen. "What the fuck?" he exclaims as he peers at the screen and its horrible message. He leans over me to scroll down.

I scoot backwards again, getting to my feet and stepping around him, going to the other side of the desk. I can't bear to be so close to him, not after this.

"Elena you don't honestly think I sent this, do you?" He looks up at me, his eyes begging me to believe him.

But I don't. He's taken me for a fool one time too many already and I'm not about to fall into this trap again. "Who else would do it Ashton? Who else had those pictures? And who else has access to your email account?"

He just stares at me.

I feel some of the humiliation turning to anger. How does he think he can pull this stunt and get away with it? "Answer me!" I scream.

"No one," he says finally. "No one else has the photos and no one else has my email password. But Elena, look at the time stamp. I was in the meeting with you and Bill when this went out. And I didn't have my phone with me remember?"

"Right. You forgot your phone," I say, putting air quotes around the word forgot. "That was a nice little display. Pretending not to have your phone with you, stepping out of the room and sending this shit. And then playing innocent. How fucking stupid do you think I am Ashton?"

"I wasn't pretending, Elena. I just stepped into my office and found my phone on my desk," Ashton explains.

"Yeah right!" I retort.

"Look I get that you're upset..." Ashton starts.

"Upset doesn't even begin to cover it," I interrupt him. "I think livid might be closer to how I'm feeling right now."

"Right. Yes. I get that. And trust me, I'm livid myself. But I didn't send this email. And I will get to the bottom of exactly who did," he says.

"Save it Ashton. Save your bullshit for the next sucker who is stupid enough to let you in okay? Because I'm done. You haven't changed a bit have you? This was your plan all along. Trick me into thinking you were different and then *bam*. Ruin my life." I can feel the anger draining away now, leaving behind a horrible, empty sadness. I feel tears forming in the corners of my eyes. I don't even bother trying to wipe them away. "Why would you do this, Ashton? Is this still about school? Because you thought I didn't notice you? We were kids then," I say, my voice breaking.

"It's not like that Elena, I swear. You have it all wrong. Just give me some time to figure it all out okay?" He starts towards me.

I shake my head. "Don't you dare even think about coming any closer to me right now," I snap.

He stops advancing on me and raises his palms, trying to placate me. "Okay. I won't come any closer. But you have to believe that I didn't do this. Why would I? I know you don't believe my feelings for you are real, but even aside from that, why would I send something like this from my own company email address? Do you have any idea how unprofessional that would be?"

"And that's why you did it. Because anyone who doesn't know what you're really like would believe that wouldn't they? They would believe you didn't send it. Well, I see you, Ashton. I see you for exactly who you are."

Ashton sits down hard in my chair. He shakes his head. He looks like a little boy who is totally lost.

I have to hand it to him. His performance is fucking world class. He should get an Oscar for this shit.

Chapter Thirty-seven

Elena

"I can't believe you think so little of me that you would actually believe I sent this," he says quietly.

I laugh then. A manic, humorless laugh, but a laugh all the same.

Ashton looks at me in surprise.

I shake my head. "And I can't believe you're turning this around and playing the victim. Yeah fucking boo-hoo Ashton."

Ashton leaps up suddenly and storms towards me.

I shrink back, sure he's going to lash out at me. The hurt look on his face stops me short.

He shakes his head. "You're still afraid of me aren't you?"

"I wasn't until I saw this, but now I have no idea what you're capable of anymore," I admit.

"I'm going back to my office. That's all I was trying to do. I'm going to get to the bottom of this and prove I wasn't the one who sent this, Elena," he says.

"You know what? Don't bother," I say, shaking my head. "I'm sure you can concoct some story that sounds believable, but I'm done falling for your lies, so tell them to someone else okay. I don't want to talk to you, I don't want to hear from you, and I don't even want to look at you. We're done Ashton and I quit." I pick up my hand bag and drop my phone into it. I get my jacket and put it on.

"Please calm down, Elena," Ashton urges.

I ignore him. I'm not getting into this again. I've said everything that needed to be said, and I'm not going to stand here and try to defend myself while Ashton makes it sound like I'm being hysterical.

"Go home, relax, do whatever you need to do. And when you're ready, we'll talk," he says.

"Never. But you win, Ashton. You did what you never quite managed as a kid. You broke me. Bravo. Go crack open your champagne and revel in your glory, because sooner or later, everyone in your life will see through the act and you'll be left all alone."

I leave the office before he can say or do anything to try and stop me. I walk down the corridor with my head held high, making a point of holding onto whatever tiny scraps of dignity I have left. I can feel myself shriveling up inside as I pass the secretaries, but I don't let it show. That's one thing I learned at school; break on the inside, but put your game face on. I feel their eyes on me. I debate ignoring them, but I decide against it. Instead, I turn my head towards them and smile. "Night ladies," I say, real nice.

"Ummm, night Elena," Sandra manages.

I keep walking, not looking back. I'm glad I spoke to them, because keeping quiet out of shame wouldn't have pro-tected me, it would have protected them. I wanted to remind them that the girl they've been whispering about and laughing at is the same girl who was starting to become friends with them. I want them to feel ashamed of themselves.

"It's pretty fucking shitty what he did to her if you ask me," I hear Karen say just before I'm out of ear shot.

I smile to myself. It's a tiny victory, but it's mine.

As I approach the lobby, I hear voices and I slow down, sure they're talking about me.

"There'll be hell about those pictures you know. She'll sue for sexual harassment or whatever," a male voice says.

"So she should," a female voice replies.

I don't recognize their voices, and I know I should show myself, but apparently, I haven't suffered quite enough humiliation for one day and I want to hear what they have to say about me.

"It's double standards though isn't it?" the male voice goes on. "I mean if a guy sends an unsolicited dick pic and the woman he sends it to plasters it over the internet, everyone applauds her. But a woman sends those pics and a guy exposes her as a sex pest, and somehow, she's still the victim. It's not right."

This is getting worse by the second. The insults in the email were bad enough, but that last paragraph really sealed my fate. Even the ones who are sympathetic to me are going to view me as some desperate loser who threw herself at her boss and got rejected.

I have to get out of here. I can feel tears forming and I know I won't be able to hold them in much longer. I step out into the lobby.

The man who was speaking blushes when he sees me.

I smile at him, although it hurts me to do it. "You know something? I could show you a string of texts that prove that nothing I sent Ashton was unsolicited. But I won't. Because unlike some people, I actually respect people's privacy. Have a good evening."

I don't wait to see his reaction. I just go to the elevator.

The receptionist picks up the phone and starts talking. It didn't ring and she didn't dial any number. She just doesn't want to have to deal with me.

It suits me. I don't want to have to deal with her either.

The elevator comes and I get in. Thankfully, I'm alone, because the tears start to pour down my face. I wipe them away angrily, but they keep coming. I give up trying to wipe them away and instead, I just stand ramrod straight, starting at the doors until I reach the ground floor and they ping open. I step into the lobby and practically run across it. Half blinded by tears, I collide with someone in the doorway.

"Sorry," I mumble, stepping to one side.

"Elena?" I look up and see Jess. She's looking at me in concern. "Let's walk."

She turns and walks out of the building with me. I don't want to have to try and explain any of this to her, but I am glad to have someone walking beside me as I rush to my car, not looking up from the pavement.

Jess walks right to my car with me, and when I unlock it, she gets into the passenger seat uninvited.

I sigh and get in. "I just want to go home Jess," I say.

"I saw the email," she says, ignoring my statement. "I was just on my way up to your office to talk to you and make sure you were okay."

"Do I look ok?" I snap.

She shakes her head.

I sigh again. "I'm sorry. It's not your fault and I shouldn't have snapped at you. Especially, considering you're the only person who has actually spoken directly to me since the email went out. Well except Ashton, but I'm barely thinking of him as a person right now."

"Elena, you don't honestly think Ashton did this do you?" Jess asks.

"Well, yeah!" I exclaim. "Who else can it have been? The photos only went to him and the email came from his account, which he admitted no one else has access to."

"Someone could have gotten their hands on his phone or used his computer," she suggests. "And you know you can schedule an email to go out at a later time right? So it wouldn't necessarily matter whether Ashton was at his computer at the time of the email going out or not."

"Ok, I didn't think of that," I admit. "But at the end of the day, I only sent those pictures to him. Even if he didn't send the email, he passed those pictures on to someone else. God, I'm so fucking stupid."

"You're far from stupid," Jess says. "And anyone with eyes knows there was nothing unsolicited about this. Ashton is crazy about you, and everyone can see it."

"He's just a good actor, Jess," I say.

"No one is that good an actor," Jess insists. "Look, I get how this looks, but Ashton isn't the type of guy who would do this. I don't know who has done it, but I do intend to get to the bottom of it."

"And when that path leads you to Ashton? Which it will," I say with a raised eyebrow.

"If it does, and that's a big if, then I'll hold my hands up, and I'll be the second in the queue to punch him." Jess smiles. "After you."

"You can be first," I say with a sad smile. "I never want to set eyes on him again. Not even to punch him."

"Then I'll do it twice." Jess grins.

"Deal," I say, surprised to find myself grinning back at her.

"And if it wasn't him?" Jess says quietly.

"Then we'll both be in the queue to punch whoever it was," I say.

"Good enough for me," Jess says. She reaches for the door handle. "I'd better get back to work. I've just been out to see a client who wants a whole new program and he wants it like yesterday."

"Don't they all." I smile as Jess gets out of the car.

She smiles back in at me. "Call me anytime, Elena," she says and then she closes the door and walks away.

I sit in the car park for a few minutes, getting my head straight. What started out as such a good day has become one of the worst days of my life. And the worst part? Despite everything, I already miss Ashton.

Chapter Thirty-eight

Ashton

I go into work on Tuesday with a heavy heart. I left the office last night pretty much as soon as Elena did. I told her I was going to find out the truth of who did this, but I have no idea where to start, and last night, I was too furious to think straight. I knew I wouldn't be able to do anything productive at the office, so I left.

I drove over to Elena's place, but she refused to open up the door if she was even home. I didn't push it too hard. I saw the way she flinched away from me yesterday, and the last thing I want to do is scare her. But how can I prove that I love her and I would never do anything to hurt her if she won't even speak to me? There's only one way. I have to find out who sent that fucking email and send her the proof that I had nothing to do with it.

In some ways, this is my own stupid fault. I should have deleted the pictures she sent, but I just couldn't bring myself to do it. She looked so fucking sexy in them, deleting them would have felt like a crime. I wish I had now though, and none of this would have happened. She would still be mine.

I try calling Elena again, as I sit down at my desk. The call rings and goes to her voicemail like I knew it would. Like the other thirty four calls I made last night and this morning have. I don't bother leaving a message. If the other twelve don't convince her to call me back, then this one won't either. I still can't resist sending her another text though.

No matter what happens Elena, I want you to know how much I love you. And that I didn't send that email. A x

No answer, just like I expected. I sigh again and run my hands over my face. How the fuck do I go about proving my innocence in this? Before I can even begin to formulate an answer to that question, there's a knock at my door. I look up and see David Malone from HR. Great. Just what I need. I wave him in and he comes in looking awkward.

"I'm assuming you know what this is about?" he says as he sits down opposite me.

"I'd be willing to make a good guess," I say. "Look, I get that it's your job to follow up on stuff like this, but I want it on the record right now, that I didn't send that email and—"

David holds up his hand, cutting me off midsentence.

I am so surprised by the forwardness of his gesture that I stop talking and let him interrupt me.

"No one in the HR department thinks you're stupid enough to have sent an email like that from your own account. But we have to treat this seriously and as such, we need to freeze your account while we investigate it."

"That won't be possible," I say.

He goes to interrupt me again, but this time, I don't let him. "Believe me, I appreciate the seriousness of this David. I've already lost Elena because of it. I refuse to lose my business over it. And if clients can't reach me, then that's a very real possibility. I have no issue with you investigating the matter. I intend to launch an investigation of my own too, and I am willing to tell you whatever you need to know to get to the bottom of this, but I need my emails."

"But—"

"Look," I cut him off. "I know this is your job, but ultimately, you work for me, and I'm telling you not to block that account. Other than that, you have free reign to do whatever you need to do. I have nothing to hide and you can poke around in the account all you want as long as it doesn't affect clients."

"Then may I suggest a compromise?" David offers.

I nod for him to go on.

"The email luckily didn't go to clients. It was sent as an internal memo. May we freeze the account's ability to send and receive internal communications, but still allow it to send and receive external emails, so clients aren't affected?"

It's still not ideal. It means I'll spend half of my day on the phone to staff members, but it's a fair compromise, and if I refuse this, I'm only making myself look guilty. "That's fine," I say. "I assume you'll want to interview me too?"

"Yes, but we'll need to do that later on after we've made our initial investigation." He stands up. "Thank you for your cooperation on this."

"I want to get to the bottom of it as much as you do. Maybe more so," I tell him.

He nods and leaves my office.

My phone beeps beside me and I grab for it, my stomach fluttering. Can it possibly be her? Is she willing to at least talk to me? My heart sinks when I read the text message. It's not from Elena. It's from the florist. I sent Elena a huge bouquet of flowers this morning, and the text is the florist informing me that delivery wasn't possible as the recipient refused to take them.

Perfect.

I look up from my phone again as another knock comes on my door. I need to get on with this investigation but I can't just ignore the staff. It's Jess, and she left me a message last night informing me that one of our big clients has tasked her with building him a whole new platform and if she has something she needs for that, then I have to grant it. Whatever it is. I wave at her and she comes in.

She sits down in the chair David has just vacated. She sits in a casual slump, and there is nothing awkward about her. She doesn't beat around the bush. "I know you didn't send that email," she says.

"Well I'm glad for that Jess," I say. "Now what can I do for you?"

"You can start by switching seats with me," she says with a grin.

I raise an eyebrow.

"I want to take a deep dive into that email," she explains. "On the surface, it came from your phone's IP address. But there's a possibility that someone cloned your email account. To anyone looking at its source, it would show as coming from your phone, but there would be some tiny, subtle differences in the blueprint of the thing, and to find them, I need to get into the master account..."

A lot of what she's saying is going over my head, but I know enough to know she has a much better chance of proving my innocence than I do and I'm already out of my seat before she's even finished her sentence.

She sits down and I take the seat she's just vacated. She clicks, studies, clicks, studies.

"Why are you doing this?" I ask, unable to hold my curiosity back any longer.

"Well, like I said, any subtle differences will only be visible on the master account or—"

"No," I say. "Not that. Why are you helping me?"

She's still clicking around. She shrugs one shoulder as she keeps clicking. "I want a pay raise."

"You find the culprit and it's yours," I say without hesitation.

"I was joking." Jess laughs. "You've always been sound with me and I don't believe you're *that* guy. Plus, Elena is my friend and I want to catch the bastard that's done this to her. My guess is it's the same person who was sabotaging her when she first started working here, only now they've seen that's not working, so they've upped their game."

"You're still getting a pay rise if you suss this thing out." I smile.

She smiles at me and keeps clicking. After a couple of minutes, she slams her fist down on the desk hard.

I jump slightly.

"Dammit," she says. "The account wasn't cloned. Who else has access to your phone?"

Chapter Thirty-nine

Elena

I think for a moment. "No one. I mean I guess Elena could have gotten it over the weekend, but there's no way in hell she did this. Oh, wait... I went into a meeting yesterday afternoon and left my phone in my office."

"So literally anyone who works here, or who was visiting could have taken it for a while and snuck it back without you knowing?" Jess asks.

I nod.

"I'm going to say something now," Jess starts. "... and it's on the condition I don't get fired or punished in any way, and you ask no questions about how I came by this knowledge."

I nod for her to go on. It's something big for her to include a disclaimer like that.

"I know about the internal cameras," she says. "Are there any in here?"

I nod. Of course. The cameras. How could I forget such a big thing? I don't even care how Jess knows about them. She's one of the employees I trust the most and I know she would have kept it quiet. My excitement at being reminded about the cameras fades and I shake my head slowly.

"What?" Jess says. "Don't tell me there are no cameras in here."

"There are," I tell her. "But the condition of having internal cameras that no employees know about is that I don't have access to the footage. The only way the footage sees the light of day is with a warrant from a cop or an acting judge. And that could take months."

"What security company do we use?" she asks.

I think for a moment then get up and go to my filing cabinet. I pull my keys out and unlock the bottom drawer until I find the paperwork. "This one," I say, handing her the file. "But it's no use. They won't break their confidentiality agreement."

"Let me ask you a few things," Jess says. "How important is Elena to you?"

"More important than anything," I answer without hesitation. "I've loved her for as long as I can remember."

"Right. So if it came to it and you had to find a new security company, you would do that for her?"

I nod. "Of course."

"I'll be right back." Jess darts out of my office, ignoring me calling after her.

I sit in stupefied silence for a moment. I have no idea where she's gone or what she's doing, but I know the company won't talk, no matter what story she feeds them.

She comes back after a couple of minutes holding what I think is an external hard drive. "What I'm about to do stays between us," she says. "I need to know I can trust you on this."

"You can. But it doesn't matter what you tell the company, they won't budge."

"I'm not planning on asking for their permission to see the footage." Jess grins. She plugs the hard drive into my computer tower and types out a few things on the keyboard. "I'm hacking into their system. That device allows me to access things I shouldn't. And it covers my tracks. They will never be able to prove we were the ones who hacked them, even if they discover the breach. But it won't take a rocket scientist to work it out when all that's touched is our footage and I have no intention of spending time in their systems looking at other people's private things to create a ruse. That's why I said you might need to change companies. There's a good chance they won't even notice I've been in, but just be aware of it."

"Go for it," I say. "There are plenty of other companies I can use for surveillance and alarm systems."

"If I find anything, it won't hold up in court," she explains. "So you can never, ever show it to the police or anyone in authority. I want to help you, but I have no intention of doing time for you."

"Fucking hell Jess, do you really think I'd throw you under the bus like that?"

"Not intentionally or I wouldn't be doing this. I do know how tempting it will be to get justice against the person who did this though."

"As long as I can show Elena the footage and prove to her I didn't do this, that's all I care about. And I might just have to have a little chat with the culprit, see if I can get them to trip themselves up." I grin.

"Bingo," Jess says. "We're in. Now, it was yesterday you left your phone in the office right? What time?"

"The meeting was at three thirty. And I was probably out of the office for about an hour, all told."

Jess taps at the keyboard for a moment and then she beckons me around to her side of the desk. She plays the footage at a fast speed until someone appears on the screen and then she slows it down. The camera sits behind my desk, in a place that gives a view of the whole office, including the door.

I watch as Lincoln, one of the junior IT technicians, peers through my door. He's holding a piece of paper. He looks this way and that, seemingly debating whether or not he should come in. He decides to do it. I knew that already, because that piece of paper he was holding was an important contract which was waiting on my desk when I came back from the meeting.

Lincoln steps into my office and puts the paper on my desk. He looks around for a moment, and I think his eyes are on my phone, but then he reaches for the post it notes beside the phone and writes the message I read, informing me he needs my signature on this. He sticks the note on the paper and leaves my office.

"Dammit," Jess comments. "I thought for sure we had him there when he was looking at your phone. Except he wasn't. God, how can someone be that nervous all the time, so they look terrified at the idea of using someone else's post it notes?" She speeds the footage back up.

Now, I'm starting to lose hope. I look away from the screen and sign the contract Lincoln brought me while it's fresh in my mind.

Jess nudges me. "Look," she says.

Beatrice has appeared on the screen. Unlike Lincoln, she doesn't hesitate. She walks in, her head held high and goes to my desk. She picks up my phone and drops it into her jacket pocket and then she leaves the office.

Jess and I look at each other with open mouths.

Jess keeps scanning forward, and sure enough, not ten minutes later, Beatrice returns and puts the phone back on my desk. She looks awfully pleased with herself. She slips back out of the office.

"Son of a bitch," I say quietly. I go back around the desk and sit down. I am so shocked. I mean I know Beatrice acted a little weird about the whole me and Elena thing, but this? This is a step further than I ever thought she would go.

"Fucking hell," Jess says. "I don't know who or what I was expecting, but not... well, maybe. She acts so odd at times."

I nod.

"And at the risk of sounding totally sexist, I guess I expected it to be a man. I didn't think a woman would do that to another woman, not even one she doesn't like. What's Elena done to her to deserve that?"

"This isn't about Elena. I've suspected for a while that Beatrice has a thing for me. I mean I didn't think it would go this far. But I think she took the phone probably with the intention of sending Elena a mean text from me and trying to cause trouble between us. And then she saw the photos and went a hell of a lot bigger."

"There's only one problem with all of this," Jess says as she roots through my drawers for a flash drive. She finds one and holds it up. "Can I put the footage on here?"

I nod.

She inserts it into the computer and goes back to her original point, "Beatrice taking your phone within the right time frame for her to have put the email together and sent it is pretty damning in our minds. But technically, it's only circumstantial. All it proves is that she had your phone."

"I think it'll be enough to convince Elena I'm innocent in this. She already knows Beatrice doesn't like her. I tried to convince her she was being paranoid, but she obviously wasn't. And besides, I think it's enough for me to bluff a confession out of Beatrice."

Jess bends down and pulls the flash drive and her hard drive out of the computer tower. "All done," she says, handing me the flash drive. "And remember, my name doesn't come into this."

"Thanks Jess. You're a fucking legend. I'll get the paperwork for your pay raise sorted by the end of the week."

"I feel like I should protest that a little, but I'm not going to because you're right. I am a fucking legend." She smirks at me and then leaves my office.

I go back around to my side of my desk and I think for a moment. When I have a plan in place, I open my top drawer slightly and hit record on my phone then slip it into the drawer. It's something else that will never stand up in court, but it's not for court. It's for Elena. So there can be no doubt in her mind that Beatrice did this.

Chapter Forty

Elena

I pick up my desk phone and call through to the secretary's pool.

Karen picks up.

"Hi Karen. Can you ask Beatrice to come to my office please?" I ask.

She says she will and ends the call.

I don't have long to wait until Beatrice appears at my door.

I take a deep breath and swallow down my anger. It's going to be hard to do this without giving myself away, but I have to. "Sit down." I smile.

Beatrice does as I say. She looks a little nervous, but she is holding herself together surprisingly well.

I decide to get straight to the point, "Beatrice I know you stole my phone yesterday and sent that email," I say. She opens her mouth to speak but I go on, "You were seen taking my phone, so don't try to deny it."

"I did take your phone, but it was an accident. I picked some papers up and it must have been in amongst them. I brought it back as soon as I noticed," she says.

"I'm going to pretend you didn't just insult my intelligence with that story," I say with a smile. "Look I'm not mad okay, I get it. And I want to help you. But I need you to be honest with me all right?"

She doesn't say anything.

It's not the confession I had hoped for, but at least she's no longer outright denying everything. I'm going to have to execute my full plan, nudge her along until she snaps. "I understand that unrequited love can be hard, and I know that the only reason you did what you did was because you were acting on your emotions. You wanted to break up Elena and me, so you had a chance with her. I can imagine how much harder this is for you when you're living a lie, pretending to be straight when you're clearly into Elena. And to learn she doesn't like women in that way. I can see how that would push you over the edge."

"You think I'm in love with Elena?" Beatrice asks while looking stunned.

I'm pretty sure the shock on her face is genuine. I nod and smile kindly at her.

She shakes her head quickly. "I'm not in love with her. I fucking hate her." She almost spits the word 'her' out like it's a swear word.

"Now come on Beatrice, we're all adults here," I try to soothe her. "You can tell me the truth. I know you have a thing for her. Why else would you have tried to break us up? I've seen the way you look at her. The way you go out of your way to come to my office for things you could tell me over the phone, just so you can glance in at her." Come on Beatrice, bite, I think to myself. I can see her starting to get angry and I'm confident this will work if I can just keep it going a little bit longer. "I can see why you're so taken with her. She's a very attractive woman, but—"

"I'm not fucking in love with Elena, you fool!" Beatrice snaps. "I'm in love with you. I've loved you since the moment I saw you, but you never saw me as anything other than dependable old Beatrice. And then that bitch came along and stole you right out from underneath my nose. And I had to make you see that she's not right for you. When the email went out, did she give you the benefit of the doubt? Did she even let you explain?" She pauses.

I don't say anything. She kind of has a point though. Elena was pretty quick to vilify me. I get why though.

My face must give my thoughts away because Beatrice smiles at me."She didn't, did she? She just assumed you were the sort of guy who would do that. And that's why she's no good for you. I would have listened to you. I would have believed you and stood by you when no one else would. Don't you see it, Ashton? We're meant to be together. I know you're probably a little angry, but you'll calm down and then you'll see I only sent that email to show you the truth. One day, we'll laugh about this. You'll see."

"Beatrice, you're fired. Get the hell out of my office. I don't ever want to see your face again. Think yourself lucky I'm not having you fucking arrested for what you've done!" I shout.

"You can't fire me!" she shouts. "We're going to be a couple. You don't fire your girlfriend."

Fucking hell. Her delusions go deeper than I thought. I stand up and point to the door. "You are not my girlfriend.

Nor will you ever be. I would rather die than be with you. Now get the hell out of here before I call security and have you escorted out!" I shout.

Beatrice jumps to her feet and looks me in the eye. Gone is the excitable girl who thought this was our moment to kiss and make up. In her place is a cold, calculating woman. "Fine. I'll leave. But tell Elena to watch her back, because if I can't have you, she certainly fucking can't."

Her words chill me to the bone. It's not so much what she said, as the cold way she said it and the way her mouth curled up into an evil smile.

Chapter Forty-one

Elena

My phone beeps beside me. I know who it is without having to look at the screen. Ashton. I've lost count of the calls, the voicemails, the text messages. He even tried to send me flowers earlier on this morning. As if flowers were going to fix this. I want to turn my phone off, so I don't have to have this constant reminder of what I've lost, but I can't. I quit my job yesterday and put myself right back into the mess that I took the job at Ashton's firm to get out of and I've spent the morning sending out resumes. It's hardly going to win me any prizes if anyone calls me for an interview and my phone is switched off.

I try to ignore my phone now, but the notification light flashes insistently at me, taunting me. I turn the phone over, but I still know I have an unread text message, and as much as I hate Ashton for what he's done to me, I can't help but want to know what he's saying.

I snatch my phone up angrily and open the text message. I read it and shake my head.

I know you're mad at me, but this is important. You're in danger Elena. Lock your doors and stay inside. Don't open

them to anyone but me. I'm on my way over. I'll explain every-
thing. A x.

This is a new low, even for him. He's not content with
ruining my reputation and breaking my heart. Now he's trying to scare me into becoming some sort of fucking recluse.
Well fuck him. That's not going to happen.

I stand up, leaving my phone behind. If anyone calls
about a job, they can leave me a message and I'll call them
back later. I'm not going to sit here like an idiot, so Ashton
can come over and laugh at me for being stupid enough to
take his threat seriously.

I pull my jacket on, grab my keys and step outside. I slam
the door, lock it and start down my path. I already feel better for ignoring Ashton's taunting and going out. I wonder
what he'll do when he gets here and see I've gone out. Hopefully, he'll take the hint and stop contacting me, because as
angry and humiliated as I am, I can't just turn my feelings for
him off. Every time he contacts me another little piece of my
heart breaks.

I shake off the feeling of loss, telling myself I'm not missing Ashton at all. It's a lie and I know it, but I have to get
through this, and if lying to myself is the way to do it, then
I'll go there.

I pull the gate open and turn right. I have no idea where
I'm going, so I just pick a direction at random and start
walking. I have barely stepped out of my gate when I hear a
noise behind me. I start to turn around, but a hand comes
over my shoulder and clamps down on my nose and mouth.
The hand pushes a piece of cloth over my face. A stringent,
bitter smell like raw alcohol penetrates my nostrils and I

taste something sweet on my lips. I try to push the hand away, but my arm is too heavy to lift. My energy is draining out of me.

Panic tries to grip me, but even that takes too much energy and I feel myself sagging, my consciousness slipping away as my eyes close and the world goes black.

I START TO WAKE UP although I keep my eyes closed. My eyelids feel too heavy to open yet. My mind feels groggy, and my thoughts are fuzzy like my head is filled with cotton wool. My throat is dry and scratchy while the insides of my nostrils are stinging ever so slightly. I am sitting up right. I must have dozed off in front of the TV or something.

My memory comes back in one blinding flash and my eyes fly open. I didn't fall asleep anywhere. I was on my way out, trying to get away from Ashton, and the realization is sudden that some fucker chloroformed me. Ashton was telling the truth. I was in danger. I should have listened to him. But I didn't and here I am. I need to try and work out what's going on rather than thinking *what if*.

I am alone in a semi dark building that looks like a warehouse. It has high ceilings with rows and rows of shelves. The shelves are all empty. Great. An abandoned warehouse. I'm probably going to be murdered, and it's not even in an original place. My death is going to be a cliché.

I rein my thoughts back in and take a further look at my surroundings. There's nothing here except empty shelving. Even if the place were full of loaded guns, they'd be no use to me. My wrists are tied up behind me, my ankles and waist are bound to a wooden, straight backed chair. I'm not gagged, but I don't bother to call for help. Whoever did this knows what they're doing. If there were a chance of anyone hearing me scream, I'd be gagged.

I don't know who has me, why they took me, what they want from me, or where they are, but I do know that if I start yelling and they're close by, they're going to know I'm awake. Something tells me that won't end well for me. I pull at my wrists, trying to drag them apart, but it's no use. I'm bound too tightly. I pull them closer to the chair and try to saw through the ropes on the chair back, but it's totally smooth and I can't get the right angle to build up any friction at all.

There's a large roller shutter ahead of me, and next to it is a fire door. I have to try and get over there and just hope to hell that the fire door works. I push down against the seat of the chair and then spring up into the air. The chair jumps an inch forward and I smile. This is going to take a long time, but it might just work.

"Well, well, well, look who woke up."

The voice from behind me dampens any hopes I had of escaping. It's a male voice, deep and with a hint of the local accent. I don't recognize it. A large man steps around in front of me and grins down at me. I have no idea who he is or what he could possibly want with me. If it wasn't for the warning I got from Ashton, I would assume I was just in the wrong place at the wrong time, but this has to be more personal than that.

"What do you want?" I say.

The man reaches out and caresses my cheek.

I resist the urge to retch as I shrink away from his touch.

He laughs, a humorless sound. "I want to mess up that pretty little face of yours." He grins.

My insides shrivel up. This man is a fucking tank. He could kill me with his bare hands without even breaking into a sweat.

"Soon," a female voice says.

The man smiles at me again and then he leans over me, grabs the back of the chair and spins me around. He steps aside.

Now, I see a woman sitting on a similar chair to mine, although she's not bound to hers.

"Beatrice?" I say, shocked at seeing her.

"What? You don't believe stupid little Beatrice who's only good for fetching coffee is clever enough to pull this off?" she demands.

"Well actually, I didn't believe you were psycho enough to do something like this," I say.

She frowns and the thug closes in on me. Beatrice waves him away. "All in good time Henry. I'm not going to let the wonderful fucking Elena get under my skin anymore."

Somehow, Henry isn't the right name for this guy. He should have been called something like Spider or Satan, some nickname that sounds a bit edgy. Henry is the name of a posh school boy.

"You must be wondering why you're here Elena," Beatrice says.

"I am a little curious," I admit. My outward nonchalance is the polar opposite to how I feel inside. Inside, I am a wreck, terrified of what's going to happen to me. But I guess

I have Ashton to thank for my outward calm appearance. I learned early on that if I showed fear, Ashton's torment grew. If I maintained a causal indifferent attitude, like I was mildly amused by him, he would get bored quicker and move on. I don't think Beatrice is just going to get bored and let me go, but maybe I can buy myself some time to come up with some sort of plan. God knows what that might be though. I have no weapon, no phone, and I'm tied up. It's looking pretty hopeless to say the least.

"Well Ashton and I had a little chat this morning that resulted in me being fired," she says.

I raise an eyebrow. I did not see that one coming.

Beatrice smiles at me. "That must make you happy, huh?"

"No. Why would I be happy about that?" I ask.

"Because it keeps me away from Ashton. And while I'm not around him, I can't make him see that he should be with me," she explains. She says it as though she's explaining something to a child. She really is totally insane.

That doesn't bode well for me.

"Ashton was going to be mine long before you came along. And then you came swanning into the office with your pretty little eyes and your shiny fucking hair and the rest of us didn't stand a chance. But I wasn't going to give up that easily. Oh no. You see, you might be used to getting your own way princess, but I don't play by those rules."

It seems like she doesn't play by any rules, not even the actual fucking law, but I don't bother pointing that out to her. She would probably think it was a compliment.

"I figured you were this shiny new thing and I could understand why Ashton was interested, but I knew he would get bored of you and come for me. The thing is, I'm not a patient person Elena, and you were getting in my way, so I decided to get rid of you. I switched out a report and you gave the shareholders the wrong information, but instead of firing you, Ashton took your side. He knew precious little Elena could never fuck up like that. I did a few other things, things that made you look like an incompetent fool and yet, Ashton still couldn't see past those long eyelashes and those pert little tits of yours."

I don't know what to say to any of this, and I keep quiet, just taking in Beatrice's level of crazy while trying and failing to think of some way out of this mess. I am glad to hear that I was right about her being off with me though. I wasn't paranoid. She was sabotaging me. Bitch.

"It was the final straw when you two started dating. You'd look at each other all starry eyed and Ashton might as well have gotten 'Beatrice who?' tattooed on his fucking forehead. But I knew it wasn't his fault. I knew it was all you. That you were tempting him, seducing him. I knew if I could only make him see what a bitch you were, I could take him for myself. I went into his office and took his phone. My plan was to send you a couple of nasty text messages. You'd get pissed off and he'd see you never trusted him in the first place. That's what you would have done right?" She pauses.

I then realize she's waiting for an answer. I nod. It's exactly what I would have done, and there's very little point in denying it. She wouldn't believe me anyway.

"See? Isn't it nice when we're honest with each other Elena?" Beatrice beams.

No, I think. It's fucking terrifying. It's like a glimpse into the who's who of the lunatic world. I nod again.

Satisfied, Beatrice goes on, "As I was thinking of what I could write in this text message, I had a quick look through your old texts, wanting to see how Ashton worded things. I didn't want it to be obvious he hadn't sent the messages after all. And I found a real gem. The photos. It was obvious what I had to do."

"You sent the email," I say.

"Yup!" Beatrice nods while beaming. "It was genius, although even I have to admit it was a stroke of good luck rather than planning on my part. And you reacted exactly as I had predicted. You accused Ashton of betraying you and you wouldn't even hear him out. It never even occurred to you that he might not have done it. Proving what we both know you don't deserve him."

I look down into my lap, feeling ashamed. She's right. That's exactly what I did. Maybe I don't deserve a guy like Ashton. A guy who was still trying to get me to talk to him even after I accused him of something terrible. Who still warned me I was in danger, despite me not even giving him a chance to explain himself to me.

"Yeah. You should look ashamed of yourself," Beatrice says, pulling my attention back to her. "You're a bitch Elena and you don't deserve anyone, let alone someone like Ashton. I figured he'd see it now that you'd shown your true colors, but he didn't. Like a fucking love sick puppy, he ran after you, trying to get you to come around. And then he had the nerve to fire me."

"Did you really think he wouldn't fire you? You made him out to be someone who sexually harasses his employees," I point out.

"Yeah, so my plan wasn't perfect." Beatrice shrugs. "I figured he'd get over that part when he realized how romantic it was that I'd fought so hard for him. He didn't for the record. He's still into you after everything. Which leads me nicely into why you're here. I'm not letting Ashton go and I need him to see that. So I'm going to have Henry here mess up your pretty little face and then kill you. Ashton will see then that he can't be with anyone else, because he'll see what happens to them when he tries. That will show him how serious I am about him."

"No, it'll show him how deranged you really are," I say without thinking.

Beatrice stands up and smiles. "Either way, I win and you lose." She comes closer to me and stands over me, looking down on me for a moment, and then she slaps me hard across the face.

My head slams to the side with the force of her blow, my cheek smarting from it. Tears of pain fill my eyes. I blink them back quickly, but not before Beatrice sees them.

"Oh honey, you are not going to enjoy the next half an hour if that made you cry." She looks up at Henry. "She's all yours." She walks away.

Henry steps in front of me, that malicious smile back on his face. "We're going to have a lot of fun together, you and me Elena." He grins.

Chapter Forty-one

Ashton

Beatrice flounces out of my office, leaving me standing there open mouthed with shock. There is no doubt in my mind that she's serious about her threat to Elena. The cold way she said it, the malicious gleam in her eyes as she talked, and her obsession with us being together all come together to paint the picture of someone who's beyond deranged.

I think for a moment. What should I do? I can't go to the police. They won't just take my word for it that Beatrice is nuts and go arrest her. And I can't use the recording on my phone to prove it. She didn't elaborate on her threat in the conversation, so it would be inadmissible as evidence. Dammit, when I get something solid on her, something I can use, I'm not letting her get away with it on a technicality like this.

Before I work out how I'm going to take Beatrice down and get her locked away somewhere she can't hurt anyone, I have to warn Elena about what's coming. I go to my desk and pull my phone out. I stop the recording and save it – it might not be admissible in court, but it will prove my innocence to

Elena and it might help to convince her just how dangerous Beatrice really is.

I open up my text messages and think for a moment. What can I say that might convince Elena this isn't just me trying to force her to talk to me? I can't think of anything, and so I decide to just go with the truth and hope she sees the truth of it.

I type out the text and read back over it. I hit send. It'll have to do. I'm no Shakespeare and I don't have time to try to be. I'm just going to go over there and explain, and if she won't let me in, I'll put my phone to her door and tell her to listen to the recording.

I grab my jacket and my keys. I put my jacket on as I leave the office and slip my phone and my keys into the pocket. I don't wait for the elevator. I take the stairs, running down them two at a time. I'm not convinced it was really quicker when I reach the bottom, gasping for breath, but it felt like progress where standing waiting for the car would have felt like time being wasted. I run to my car, ignoring the burning feeling in my lungs. I really need to up my cardio game.

I drive directly to Elena's place. Her car is outside of her house which makes me feel good. She must have listened to me. I run up her path and bang on her door. No answer. I try again. Still nothing.

I crouch down and shout through her letter box, "Elena, it's me. I know you don't want to talk to me, and if you don't want to hear my explanation about the email then fine, but you have to let me in. You're in danger. Real danger!"

No answer. Dammit. I slam the letter box closed and go to her lounge window. I don't like doing this – I don't want to scare her – but I'm a lot less scary than Beatrice. I press my hands against the glass, cupping my face and peering inside. It doesn't look like Elena is home. There's no sign of any movement inside of the house, and there are no tell-tale sounds of anyone moving around.

Fuck. She's ignored my text in more ways than one. She didn't reply, which is to be expected right now, but she ignored the warning too. She's fucking gone out, most likely to make some sort of point to me that I can't tell her what to do or whatever.

I pull my phone out and try calling her, even though I'm certain she won't pick up. I end the call and slam my phone away in anger when I hear her phone ringing through the glass. She's not only gone out she hasn't even taken her phone with her. If anything does happen, she can't even call for help.

Maybe it's not the end of the world though. If she's not home, then Beatrice won't know where to find her. Hell, I know Elena way better than Beatrice does and I wouldn't even know where to start looking for her, so there's no chance Beatrice will know.

Or maybe this is even better than I could have hoped for. Maybe Elena was already out when I texted her, and she left her phone behind because she's sick of dodging my calls and texts. If that's the case, then she's definitely safe.

I decide to go back to my car to sit and wait for Elena to come home. She has to come back eventually, and I can talk to her then. Even if I have to follow her up her garden path and shout at her in the street, I'll make her aware of the danger she's in.

As I move back to my car, something white catches my eye on the ground. It looks like a sleeve off a shirt or something. I pick it up, curious about why a sleeve would be in Elena's garden. God, I hope I'm not too late. What if it's her sleeve and there was a fight, one Elena didn't win?

I unfold it. It's not a sleeve. It's a piece of cloth, probably someone's old duster that got thrown away and caught in a breeze somewhere along the way. It feels damp though and I realize it has a chemically smell. It hits me what it is and I drop it quickly.

It's fucking chloroform.

My heart is racing, I jump into my car. Fuck, where would Beatrice have taken Elena if she had chloroformed her? Somewhere deserted where she could do whatever she wanted to her. But where specifically?

I think for a moment and then I pull my phone out and make a call. "Jess, it's Ashton," I say as she picks up. "Listen to me. Can you trace a company mobile phone? Like its location?"

"Yes. Whose is it?"

"Beatrice's," I say.

I can hear her clicking away on her keyboard. "It's just tracing the signal now. What happened?"

I quickly fill her in on Beatrice's threat, me firing her, and the chloroform soaked rag at Elena's place.

"Shit," she says. "For once, it was a lucky break that a disgruntled employee kept their company phone. I've got it. I can't get an exact location, but she was in the King's Close area for a good ten minutes. Stationary. Could that be Elena's place?"

"Yes. Where did she go after that?"

"She's stationary again. She's somewhere around Bancroft Road."

I plug the street name into my sat nav and take off. I switch my phone onto bluetooth and throw it on the passenger seat. "Any idea what's around there?" I ask.

"I'm looking on Google Earth now," Jess says. "It's an industrial area. Shit, Ashton, there's an abandoned looking building right at the back. I don't know for certain that's where she is, but if I chloroformed someone and took them somewhere, that's where I'd go."

"Me too," I agree. "I'm heading over there now. Jess, call the police and get them out there now."

"On it," Jess says.

The call cuts off and I turn my full attention to the road. I am breaking the speed limit, but I don't care. If I get pulled over, I'll just keep driving and lead the police right to them. In typical fashion, I don't see a sign of a single cop car on my drive. If I was running late for a meeting and driving like this, I could guarantee I'd have gotten pulled over.

I reach Bancroft Road and I see Jess was right. It's an industrial area. It looks pretty quiet. There are plenty of cars parked up around the place, but not much foot traffic. That's normal for a place like this though. The units are workshops and storage units, not the sort of place customers generally visit, making it the ideal place for someone who wants to do something shady in private.

I follow the main road through the place, heading for the back of the buildings. Jess said there's an abandoned place up at the back and that's the building I'm heading for. I spot it.

It looks run down, weeds growing up the sides and no sign of life anywhere. I know I'm in the right place though. Beatrice's car is parked beside the unit. I park and jump out of my car.

I can hear sirens coming closer and I send up a silent thank you. Jess came through and got the police out here fast. I'm not going to wait around for them though. If I can hear the sirens, Beatrice can hear them too and it might push her into doing something worse than she planned. Or if she had planned for the worst, then it could make her act much quicker. I just hope I'm not already too late. Her car gives me hope that I'm not. If she'd already killed Elena, she wouldn't be hanging around here afterwards.

Even the thought of it sends a cold shiver through me and I break into a run. I run to a small side door beside the huge roller shutter. I push the door and get a lucky break. It opens. I take in the scene quickly.

Beatrice is sitting on a chair watching some fucking goon who is towering over someone tied to a chair. I don't have to see the woman's face to know it's Elena in the chair.

"What the fuck," the man says, looking up.

"Ashton?" Beatrice exclaims.

I ignore Beatrice focusing on the man. I run towards him and shove him away from Elena. He swings for me, but I duck and his punch goes wide. I throw a punch of my own, catching him in the mouth. His bottom lip splits and blood runs down his face. I punch him square on his wide jaw and he staggers backwards.

The door bursts open and two police officers run in.

"Stop. Police," one of them shouts.

I back away from the goon with my hands up. I finally relax.

Elena has a red mark on her cheek, a hand print by the looks of it, but she's otherwise okay and that's all that matters.

Chapter Forty-two

Ashton

The police release Elena then take Beatrice and the thug away into custody. I sigh my relief. It's been a long day. Even after I knew Elena was safe, it was far from over. We have spent hours telling it all, down at the police station, giving statements and being questioned. It was after six when they finally let us go. They did offer to take Elena to the hospital to be checked over before taking her down to the station, but she refused. I offered the same thing when they released us, and again, Elena refused. I've driven her home and this is our first real moment alone.

"Will you come in?" Elena says. "We need to talk and I don't like talking in the street."

"Of course," I say.

We get out of the car and go into Elena's house. We go inside and she says she needs a shower before we do anything. I tell her I'm going to cook dinner while she showers and she tells me to order Chinese instead.

After what feels like forever, Elena comes down the stairs. She's wearing pink pajamas and her hair is still wet. She smiles at me as she comes and sits down beside me.

"First, I want to thank you Ashton... you know, for saving my life and all that."

"Ah, it's all in a day's work." I smile.

She turns serious and she looks at me for a moment.

"I also wanted to say I'm very sorry. Beatrice told me everything. I hate myself for how I reacted, Ashton. I never should have doubted you when you told me you didn't send that email."

I wave away her apology. "It was an email sent from my account containing photos only I had. I can understand why you thought it was me."

"I still should have heard you out. And I should have trusted you enough to believe you wouldn't do that. Again, I'm sorry. I can make no excuses really. I shouldn't have..." A tear rolls down her face. "Please forgive me?'"

"How about we leave the past in the past and concentrate on the future," I suggest as I reach across and swipe the tear away. "I thought you might be gone forever, so I don't care about the rest. Because I meant what I said Elena... I love you and I want to be with you, always."

She smiles at me and nods her head. "I like that plan. And Ashton, as much as I've tried to fight it, I love you too," she says.

My heart soars at her words. I don't think it's possible that I could be happier than I am in this moment.

Elena proves that theory wrong when she comes closer to me and plonks herself down in my lap. Her lips find mine and I feel ready to explode with happiness. It's taken me over a decade, but I've finally got the girl of my dreams right here in my arms.

Epilogue

Ashton
Two Months Later

SO MUCH HAS CHANGED over the last two months. Beatrice and her goon went to court. Both pleaded guilty to all the charges against them. Beatrice has been sent to a secure facility where she will get the help she needs for her mental health issues. The goon, Henry something or other, was given a seven year prison sentence for his part in this.

Elena has moved in with me, and she's got a job working at a large retail company as the personal assistant to the CEO. She didn't feel comfortable coming back to work for me while knowing everyone had seen that email. So I called a long term client who I knew was looking for a personal assistant. I explained the situation and he hired Elena on the spot on the strength of my recommendation. She loves it there, and I think we're both doing better in our careers when we're not distracted by each other all day long. And knowing I'm coming home to Elena makes me a lot less likely to work late too.

I've just texted Elena and asked her to meet me at the duck pond in the park. I pace nervously, waiting for her to show up.

She arrives quickly and smiles at me. "You left in such a hurry this morning," she says. "And now this. What's going on?"

"Well, there was something I had to pick up." I shrug my shoulders.

"What? Why do you look so nervous?"

"This," I reply. I pull the ring box out of my pocket and get down on one knee.

Elena's jaw drops as her gaze flows my descent to the grass.

"Elena Woods, I have loved you since I was just a boy. And I don't want to wait a moment longer to ask you this. Will you do me the honor of agreeing to be my wife?"

"Yes. Oh, my God, yes!" she says, laughing even though tears roll down her face.

I push the ring onto her finger and then I stand and kiss her. I pull back and smile down at her. "Right now?"

"What?" Elena asks while looking dazed.

I grin at her and take her hand. I lead her to the band-stand.

It's wrapped up in swirls of white voile decorated with pink and white roses. Chairs dressed in white and pink line the area in front of it. A band is placed behind the chairs and the whole area is decked out with fairy lights.

"Oh, my God!" Elena exclaims.

"So what do you think? If you agree, there's a marquee set up behind those trees with hair and makeup people waiting, and a bunch of dresses for you to choose from."

"Let's do it," Elena says, half laughing and half crying.

I kiss her again and then I pull a walkie-talkie out of my pocket, "We're on," I say into it. I smile at Elena. "Go. Our friends and family are going to be here in ten minutes."

Her jaw drops and she hurries away.

I WATCH MY BEAUTIFUL bride walking down the makeshift grassy aisle with Jess beside her as her maid of honor. Elena looks beautiful. She's chosen an off the shoulder gown that hugs her body and flows out into a fairy tale wedding skirt of lace. Her hair is in ringlets and she looks stunning. Her face is flushed with excitement and her eyes twinkle.

She looks as happy as I feel.

Elena reaches me and it takes everything I have not to kiss her right now, before the officiant gives his permission. We exchange our vows and finally, the time comes for me to kiss the bride. I kiss her with everything I have, letting my kiss tell her how much this moment means to me.

We walk back down the aisle as a married couple. I whisk Elena away for photographs and when we come back, a team has been in and removed the chairs, replacing them with picnic benches that are now laden down with food and drinks. A dance floor has been erected in the center of it all, and even though it's far from dark, the fairy lights have been switched on.

The band sees us approaching and the singer speaks into the microphone, "Ladies and gentlemen, for the first time, please welcome Mr. and Mrs. Miller to the dance floor."

Our guests clap and cheer as I take Elena's hand and lead her out into the middle of the floor. I pull her into my arms and she laughs as the first notes of Lady in Red ring out over the park.

I feel like I've died and gone to heaven as I swirl her around the dance floor, holding her right where she should always be – nestled tightly in my arms, against my heart – a heart that always belonged to her.

The End.

Coming Soon...

Chapter One

G *rady*

"Where's your secretary?" Allen, my Chief Financing Officer, and my best friend for as long as I can remember, asks from my door.

I lift my head from the training development report I'm reviewing and look at him as he nonchalantly takes his seat at my table, and with furrowed brows, I move my gaze to the door. "Has she not arrived yet?"

"Nope."

Irritation begins to simmer in the pit of my stomach.

"Wow," he says. "You look murderous. Have you ever given her this look before?"

I release a heavy sigh. My annoyance at my secretary's absence is beginning to boil over into anger. I put the report aside. My concentration is already shot to hell anyhow. "I need a new secretary."

"We'll get to that, but what I need you to do right now is to express your excitement at the Inc 500 ranking. We're at number twenty-three. Twenty fucking three! Can you believe it? Just a few years ago we were at zero and pitching our business to anyone who would listen."

"The list's not officially out yet," I say. "How did you find out?"

"Got a call from Scott, Inc's editor-in chief." He seems mighty pleased with himself. "He told me he was going to give you a call too."

My gaze darkens once again as it returns to the door to my office. "He probably tried to, but *she* wasn't at her desk."

"Yikes," Allen replies. "You really do need a new secretary, but you can't fire her. She was my dad's secretary."

"If that's the only fucking reason she's still here, I'm screwed."

"All right fire her then," he says. "There must be lots of more qualified candidates in the company. My dad will understand. We've just received our billion dollar evaluation. It's almost laughable that one of your problems is finding a proper secretary."

"She's not completely horrendous," I reply, thinking of the stern man who had been my greatest mentor. It felt wrong to criticize any of his decisions.

He flashes a blinding grin at me and holds his arms apart. "You'll actually be doing her a favor."

I frown. "How so?"

"The only thing that'll make her happy is finally getting a good acting role somewhere. She's dying to do it, but she doesn't have the guts. Pushing her off the ledge would be a blessing."

"Hmmm..."

Just then, there's a knock at the door. It is pushed open without the courtesy of waiting for my permission come in, and that clearly indicates who it is.

Mariam Stean walks in, my actress-in-waiting secretary.

I have to do a double take at her appearance. On her cheeks are patches of red with bold whiskers painted over them.

"I apologize, Sir," she says with a smile. "My acting class had a production last night, and the paint has refused to come off. Most of it will be gone by the end of the day. Also, I apologize for coming in late. That IT security lady just dropped this off for you. She says you are expecting it?"

"You're having wild nights, Mariam," Allen teases.

She flashes a coy smile at him.

I, on the other hand, have no words for her. Thank God, I have no business meetings or clients coming in today. I accept the folder she hands to me and immediately pull it open and start looking down the row of sales figures. "Have you scheduled the outing with the Bloom executives for tomorrow?" I ask.

"I'll get right on it, Sir," she replies.

My head shoots upwards.

Before I can chastise her once again, for dragging her feet on such an incredibly important task, she turns around and hurries away.

"She sure knows how to escape, I'll give her that." Allen says.

I rub the back of my neck. "How's it going with the baby?"

"Don't ask," he laments. "My entire last week was spent literally hands deep in shit, changing Alexa's diapers, and trying my best to survive with the stack of disgusting almond flour waffles my wife left for us before she went on her trip."

I smile as I resume my perusal of the training development report.

"I mean I'm not complaining," he continues quickly. "I love my wife and daughter very much, but good Lord that kid can shit for England—"

"What does England have to do with it?" I ask amused. "Well, her maternal grandmother is English."

"You need to get out more, man."

He looks dreamily out of the window. "Yeah, somewhere, where there's alcohol."

"Do you want to come along to the meeting with Baron?""

"Nah," he says mournfully. "Alexa's still recovering from her illness stunt last week so I'm on toddler duty while Meredith goes to Tampa for another business trip over the weekend."

"You can't call her illness a stunt."

"That was exactly what it was. She threw tantrums no less than a dozen times, and during one of those she fell to the floor in tears. I just left her there. I got a beer, and turned the volume up on the TV to catch up on my game."

My mouth falls open. "You're joking.'

"I swear it. I'm not bringing up an entitled snowflake."

I grin. "Yeah, right. How long did your nonchalance last?"

"Three minutes. The wife called to find out how we were doing and I couldn't let her hear the wailing child over the phone. Plus, my conscience was beginning to eat at me. So I calmed her down and called her back. After lying to her that we were doing great, she asked for another kid."

I drop my document and burst out laughing. "So more dirty diapers then?"

He laughs heartily too and ends our little detour with his domestic tales.

"Will you go on your own for the meeting?" he asks.

"Yup."

"I see why my dad was never worried about the company for even a second. We're already this big and you're still in the trenches. You love that grind, don't you? As the CEO you're meant to manage and leave all the grunt work to the lower guys, but here you are, still recruiting clients on your own."

"The chase is thrilling."

With a tap on my desk, he rises to his feet. "Maybe, but I can tell you of a much more thrilling pursuit."

I don't even bother asking. I return my attention to my document.

Of course, he speaks anyway, "A woman. That's the greatest pursuit that man has been called to."

"You're an absurd human being," I say, just as my phone begins to ring.

"I mean it," he says.

"Hello," I put the phone to my ear.

A few seconds go by as I listen to the man complain to me.

"I'll call you back," I say and end the call.

Allen is still watching me, especially at the deep frown on my face. "Mariam still hasn't set it up, has she?"

"She really knows how to piss me off," I hiss, and storm over to the door. I jerk the door open and walk out to the reception to find her on the phone.

She is cackling out loud with her feet on the table, and her forefinger twirling the curls in her hair. She immediately sits up when she sees us walk out. "Brenda, I'll call you back," she says, and clears her throat at my approach.

"You haven't set the meeting up?" I ask quietly.

Her expression turns sheepish for a moment. "I'll do it now. Sorry, I had to take a call."

I lose my temper. "You're fired. Pack your things and leave. Right now."

The shock strikes her face like a hand slap. "W-what?"

Without answering her I turn around to leave.

"You can't fire me," she blurts out.

I stop for a moment to process her response, and then turn back to her. "Excuse me?"

"Mr. Canter owns a part of the company. He guaranteed that I'd always have a place here."

I cock my head at her. "Which Mr. Canter are you referring to? The one behind me right now, or the one who passed away some time ago?"

Her lips parts dramatically in distress. She really is a much better actress than she is a secretary.

"Mariam you can't say that to him," Allen states. "My father only passed fifteen percent on to me. He owns the rest."

Her eyes fill with tears. "B-but, he promised I'd always have a place here."

I walk back to her, the heat of my anger scorching the pit of my stomach. "Is that the reason why you've taken the liberty to be absolutely useless around here? We have a thousand employees to manage and you think this is a joke?"

"I gave this company ten years of my life. All I'm trying to do now is to—"

"Leave," I growl. "Right now. Out of respect for Robert, I've given you more than enough chances and you've screwed up over and over again. I'm not going to take it anymore."

Tears flow down her cheeks.

I turn away to return to my office.

After a few puffs of grief, she calls after me, "Fine, I'll leave! I don't need you. I don't need this company. I have an audition tomorrow and I'll make sure to ace it and everything else that comes my way. I'm going to be big, do you hear me? I'm going to be really big!"

"Good. Go do what you love and stop wasting your time here." I slam the door to my office shut, and return to my desk.

A few seconds later, it reopens, and Allen stands at the entrance. "I guess now, you really need a new secretary, but don't worry I'll handle it personally," he says. "Do you have anything in particular you need?"

"An ability to work hard. This is the last time I'll ever keep a useless employee on out of sentiment."

"Roger that." He grins evilly. "I think I have the perfect candidate for you." With that, he turns around, and takes his leave.

For a second. I wonder about that grin, then I lose myself in the report.

Chapter Two

B *lair*

"When are you going to find out?" I ask. "If the baby's a boy or a girl?"

"In about two weeks," Layne replies. "We have a visit scheduled for the 28th."

"We? Matthew's going to be around?"

"He will. He'll be back from the oil field by then."

"Nice," I say and once again press my ear to her protruding belly. Suddenly, there's is a slight movement against her skin and I scream.

"'Blair!" Layne looks startled.

"'They just moved. I mean he—or she."

"Yeah," my sister laughs. "They, or he or she moves from time to time.

"Oh, my God," I squeal again.

She shakes her head and moves my hands away from her stomach. "I'm not having twins," she says.

"I know." I laugh. "I just lost it for a moment there. Oh, my God. I can't wait to be an aunt." My heart is racing in my chest.

"Well, I'm scared out of my mind," she says as she heads over to the refrigerator to retrieve a carton of milk.

"Don't be." My voice softens at the worry in her tone. "You're going be fine. Everything is going to be fine."

She sighs as she opens the carton, her face away from me. "Yeah, but I'm scared of handling it alone."

I return to my seat on one of the stools in the corner. "What do you mean alone? You have Matthew and you have me."

"I have Mathew but Matthew's not always here. And neither are you. You're just in to visit for the weekend."

My lips part to speak but I have nothing to say, so I give it all some thought. "Well, I could move. It's not like I have anything holding me back in Texas. I just graduated, so all I'm doing now is looking for a job. And to be honest, I'd rather search for one here where I can be close to you than somewhere else random."

She turns to me her, eyes sparkling at my words even though she tries not to show it. "Are you serious? Would you have any prospects here in Denver?"

"Layne, I have a degree in computer science. I think I'll have a pretty good chance wherever I go."

She thinks on the idea for a moment and then turns away. She pours herself some of the milk, and then downs it all at a go. "No," she says as she wipes the corners of her mouth.

I'm not surprised at her response. I know exactly why she's refusing my idea, and it warms my heart.

"This is the best time of your life," she says. "I'm not going to let you squander it on me. Go out into the world and apply to wherever you want. You've always said that you wanted to try New York or somewhere in Europe? Do that."

I sigh. "Layne, I'm not squandering anything on you. There are great opportunities here in Denver and rather than reside in some strange place where I won't known anyone or have anyone, I'd rather be here with you. I'd be happier. That's what you want, isn't it? For me to be happy?"

She spins around to face me. "Of course it is."

"Exactly. So, I'm going to increase my focus in applying to positions here in Denver. An exciting offer can come from anywhere but I'll prioritize here."

"No, prioritize your interest. I'll be fine."

My phone begins to ring so I roll my eyes at her and head over to where my purse was abandoned on her sofa. "We'll be fine Layne, and I'll be here for you. Stop overthinking everything." I glance down at my phone, and am slightly taken aback that there is no caller ID.

I consider ignoring it, but then it occurs to me that it might be regarding one of the countless positions I have applied to. So I lift the phone to my ear. "Hello?"

"Hello," a man's voice comes through the receiver, smooth and strong. "Is this Blair Tatum?"

"Yes, this is Blair. Who am I speaking to?"

"Allen Canter. We met a couple of weeks ago at the job fair in the University of Texas,"

My heart fell into my stomach. "Allen Canter? The CFO of FireEye?"

"Yes, that is me. How are you doing?"

My airway constricts. "Um, I'm doing great ... Sir." I'm not sure but I think I can feel his smile through the phone.

When I met him a few weeks ago at the event, he had been open and friendly, so it is probably the same countenance that I'm projecting onto him now.

"I'm calling regarding a position that might be a fit for you. I remember the last time we met you spoke about your interest in cyber security and your experience during your internship at Zimperium."

"Yes sir," I reply, and turn around to glance at Layne.

She has her attention on me, surprised at my sudden formal tone.

Even I'm rattled, not exactly sure if this is some sort of courtesy call, or if I am now in an interview for a potential position. It's 7pm on a Friday night, and if the latter is the case, I'm not at all prepared for this.

"I have an opening that I think you might be able to fill considerably well," he continues. "Would you like to come in, so we can talk about it further?"

I become too nervous to remain still, so I begin to pace the living room, one hand underneath my elbow to support the weakened hand holding my phone. Most definitely sir."

"Alright," he says. "How soon can you make it to Denver?"

I clear my throat. "I'm already here, Sir. I'm visiting family."

"That's fantastic," he replies. "How about we set up a meeting for Monday then? Sound good?

"Sounds great... sir."

"Alright. You'll be able to find your way to FireEye right? It's downtown."

"Most definitely sir."

"Okay. I'll slot you in for an appointment at 9am. Have a great weekend."

"Sure. Thank you ... sir," I respond. The call comes to an end and I pull the phone away from my ear as though in a trance.

"Who was that?" Layne asks.

I turn to her. "I just got an interview. Here in Denver."

"Oh, my God!" Her hand covers her mouth. "We were just talking about this. Where? I mean what company."

"FireEye."

"FireEye? I've never heard of it what do they do?"

"It's a cyber security awareness company. It's massive."

"Wow, that's great. You applied for it? What position are they interviewing you for?"

I head back to the stool to take my seat. "That's the thing. I didn't apply. I just met the CFO about two months ago at a job fair in school. I was still interning at Zimperium then, so I gave him my card."

"And he kept it? You must have made quite the impression."

"Absolutely not," I replied. "I was a babbling idiot. I kept asking stupid questions and making the most awkward jokes, which now that I think about it, he did actually find quite funny. What is going on?"

Her smile is angelic. "The stars are aligning in our favor." She rubs her stomach.

I couldn't hold back my delight either. "Oh my God if I get a position there, I'm going to collapse. That's a freaking unicorn company!"

"A what? Unicorn? I thought you said they're in cyber-security."

I laughed at her naivety. "I don't mean an actual unicorn. I mean they're really successful-fairly new and privately owned and valued at a billion dollars. Companies like that are called unicorns because it's so rare to be that successful within a short frame of time."

Her eyes nearly bulge out of her sockets. "A billion dollars? Wow, that does sound massive."

"Exactly. Wow... I'm shaking. It would be such a privilege to work there."

"It does sounds like a great opportunity," she agrees. "What position is he calling you in for?"

"He didn't say. All he did was set up a meeting for Monday. And oh my God, he's the CFO... and he called me himself. His father founded the company along with the current CEO, and he called me himself. Not through personnel but directly."

"Okay, calm down." Layne laughs. "You're hyperventilating."

"I know but this is unreal," I say, close to jumping out of my skin. Overwhelmed with emotion, I do realize I need to calm myself down, so I take deep breaths, and focus on reducing my excitement and subsequent nervousness.

"Okay we need to celebrate," Layne says. "Tomorrow night. I've had a tiring day and this to be momma needs to crash."

I laugh. "What do you mean? There's nothing to celebrate. This was just to set up the interview."

"Well, we're going to celebrate you even getting the call. Then we're going to toast to your acing the interview and getting some fantastic position there."

"Well, I'm not going to say no to that, but are you going to be able to come out?" My eyes lower to her bulging belly.

"Honey, this night out is more for me than it is for you. I need to get out of this house." She does a little swirl with her hips. "I can't wait."

I laugh again."Neither can I," I reply. "Neither can I."

"Ask Jodie if she wants to come along with us. The more the merrier."

I lift my phone to pull up my best friend's number. "I doubt it. I think she has to work at the restaurant tomorrow."

"On a Saturday night? I doubt Jodie would ever give up her Saturdays to work. I think you have the day mixed with Friday or Sunday even."

I dialed her number and lifted the phone to my ear.

Chapter Three

G*rady*

Both men, the Senior Vice President Mark Cuomo and the recluse, Jack Clay share a look with each other before placing their document on the table.

The marble surface is filled with two bottles of aged malt whiskey and platters of stingray fins and squid tempura. Allen's secretary had secured the private room for us at the downtown club and just the perfect ambience for the conversation I intend to have with them.

It is set against the back drop of a dim and rowdy dance floor below, lit with colorful lights, and the deafening music hitting the panels of our glass encased lounge. It is just enough to remind us of where we are, but yet allow us the detachment that I paid heavily for.

"Grady," Mark begins. "What you're proposing we can do internally."

Both men share a look with each other once again, so I pick up my tumbler of whiskey and take a swig of it.

I pull out two more folders and hand them over. Both men receive their copy and quickly start reading through it, as I continue to sip calmly from my glass.

I watch their eyes widen in shock.

"Where did you get this?" Mark asks, his voice now cold.

"Through our analysis. Even your team hasn't picked up on this security issue. So you see, even your waiting room feature is flawed and if I can discover this, someone else out there will sooner or later. I'm disclosing this vulnerability to you as a courtesy. Fix it and give me a call. Now let's push all this aside and get back to the second reason we're here."

Mark leans back into the sofa with a laugh. "Oh. I thought this was the end of the road."

"What do you mean?" I ask innocently.

"Thus far, you've hosted us in a lounge and then brought us here. We've been waiting for this shoe to drop. Now that it has and you've hassled us into doing business with you, I expected that you'd call it a night and be on your way."

"I don't hassle, Mark," I correct. "That's for people that don't know what they're doing. What I've done is given you a chance to save your house before its engulfed in flames, and it's up to you to take or reject it. But it wasn't my sole intention in bringing you here either, otherwise we could have handled this discussion in either of our offices."

"So what is this second reason then?"

I rise to my feet. "To dance, of course."

Mark laughs again. "I can do that."

"You're joking," Jack says, his face frigid with horror. "I don't dance."

Their reaction amuses me. "That's alright, Jack. I'm joking. Neither do I. I'm sure we'll come up with better ways to have a good time. In the meantime, have a look at these." I hand them my proposals.

Then I excuse myself from the room and head to the restroom. After handling my business, I'm about to return to them when I decide against it. It is better to give them some more time alone to look over the data that I have presented. So I instead head towards the bar.

It has been quite a few months since I have come to a club like this. My insane schedule and unending responsibilities have kept me away from most social pastimes like this unless is business related, but since my goal for the evening is somewhat complete, I allow myself to bask in the simple pleasure of herd excitement for a few minutes. I weave through the throngs of gyrating bodies in the humidity, and soon arrive at the bar.

I want a cocktail, something I haven't had the liberty of enjoying of late. So the moment the bartender comes up to me I make my order. "Sidecar?"

He nods in understanding. "Coming up."

Soon he delivers it and I flick away the orange peel attached to the glass.

To my surprise however, a slender set of fingers catch it before it can roll off the counter to the floor. I follow the fair limbs all the way up her glistening alabaster skin, to the dark red strap across her delicate shoulders.

The face on those shoulders is even more exquisite, and as my gaze connects with the deep green eyes of the shiny blonde woman before me, I feel my breathing hitch.

For a few seconds, I don't say a word or rather nothing comes to mind, so I look way to try to recollect my thoughts. It occurs to me then, what just happened. The sight of her—literally fried my brain. The hand holding my glass freezes midway to my mouth. I glance at her once again.

She has turned her face away from me and makes her order, "Cranberry with ice,"

I listen to her velvety voice. She is speaking louder than usual as we all are so that we can be heard over the racket, but I can still make out the creamy flow to her tone. "You don't drink alcohol?" I find myself asking.

She hears me and turns with a smile on her face.

I empty my drink without realizing it and set the empty tumbler down on the counter.

"I do," she replies. "This is for my sister...she's pregnant."

I hear every word of what she says mainly because my gaze is so focused on her lips, and the forms that they are shaping into so she can communicate with me. Her lips are covered in lipstick the same exact red shade of her dress. They are plump and curved in a way to seemingly solely entice me. I want to kiss her badly... to sink my teeth gently into that warm and tender flesh...feel her heat and scent swirl around me.

I take a step closer to her, almost needing to inhale her scent more than I need my next breath and it makes me wonder what is so severely attracting me to her. Is it the way the color compliments her skin, or is it her almost doe-eyed gaze?" I can't remember the last time I'd ever been this immediately drawn to a woman. "Let me pay for the drink," I say.

Her smile widens. "No need, I can handle it."

I am even more intrigued. "Why?" I ask.

She blinks. "Why what?"

"Why are you refusing me?"

"I'm not refusing you." She laughs. "I just... want to pay for my own drink. "

"Fair enough. So what would you have me do for you then?"

This time around, she boldly holds my gaze, and tells me exactly what she wants, but I can't possibly have heard it right. How could I have when I heard her say...

Fuck me. Brutally, until I lose my mind. Against a surface, in the air... everywhere.

Preorder Craving The CEO Here:
getbook.at/CravingtheCEO[1]

CPSIA information can be obtained
at www.ICGtesting.com
Printed in the USA
BVHW030947271220
596467BV00008B/184